TRANSGRESSIONS

Edited by Ed McBain

HOSTAGES
Anne Perry

THE CORN MAIDEN:
A LOVE STORY
Joyce Carol Oates

THE RESURRECTION MAN
Sharyn McCrumb

FORGE®

A TOM DOHERTY ASSOCIATES BOOK
NEW YORK

The novellas collected in this volume and the three companion volumes
of *Transgressions* were previously published in 2005 as a single-volume
hardcover edition under the title *Transgressions*.

A Forge Book
Published by Tom Doherty Associates, LLC
175 Fifth Avenue
New York, NY 10010

www.tor.com

Forge® is a registered trademark of Tom Doherty Associates, LLC.

ISBN-13: 978-0-765-35419-8
ISBN-10: 0-765-35419-5

First mass market edition: November 2006

Printed in the United States of America

0 9 8 7 6 5 4 3 2 1

Contents

Introduction

When I was writing novellas for the pulp magazines back in the 1950s, we still called them "novelettes," and all I knew about the form was that it was long and it paid half a cent a word. This meant that if I wrote 10,000 words, the average length of a novelette back then, I would sooner or later get a check for five hundred dollars. This was not bad pay for a struggling young writer.

A novella today can run anywhere from 10,000 to 40,000 words. Longer than a short story (5,000 words) but much shorter than a novel (at least 60,000 words) it combines the immediacy of the former with the depth of the latter, and it ain't easy to write. In fact, given the difficulty of the form, and the scarcity of markets for novellas, it is surprising that any writers today are writing them at all.

But here was the brilliant idea.

Round up the best writers of mystery, crime, and suspense novels, and ask them to write a brand-new novella for a collection of similarly superb novellas to be published anywhere in the world for the very first time. Does that sound keen, or what? In a perfect world, *yes*, it *is* a wonderful idea, and here is your novella, sir, thank you very much for asking me to contribute.

But many of the bestselling novelists I approached had never written a novella in their lives. (Some of them had never even written a short story!) Up went the hands in mock horror. "What! A novella? I wouldn't even know how to *begin* one." Others thought that writing a novella ("*How* long did you say it had to be?") would constitute a wonderful challenge, but bestselling novelists are busy people with publishing contracts to fulfill and deadlines to meet, and however intriguing the invitation may have seemed at first, stark reality reared its ugly head, and so . . .

"Gee, thanks for thinking of me, but I'm already three months behind deadline," or . . .

"My publisher would *kill* me if I even

dreamed of writing something for another house," or . . .

"Try me again a year from now," or . . .

"Have you asked X? Or Y? Or Z?"

What it got down to in the end was a matter of timing and luck. In some cases, a writer I desperately wanted was happily between novels and just happened to have some free time on his/her hands. In other cases, a writer had an idea that was too short for a novel but too long for a short story, so yes, what a wonderful opportunity! In yet other cases, a writer wanted to introduce a new character he or she had been thinking about for some time. In each and every case, the formidable task of writing fiction that fell somewhere between 10,000 and 40,000 words seemed an exciting challenge, and the response was enthusiastic.

Except for length and a loose adherence to crime, mystery, or suspense, I placed no restrictions upon the writers who agreed to contribute. The results are as astonishing as they are brilliant. The three novellas that follow are as varied as the women who concocted them, but they all exhibit the same devoted passion and the same extraordinary writing. More than that, there is an underlying sense here that the writer is attempting something new and unexpected, and willing to share her own surprises with us. Just as their names are in alphabetical order on the book cover so do their stories follow in reverse alphabetical order: I have no favorites among them. I love them all equally.

Enjoy!

ED MCBAIN
Weston, Connecticut
August 2004

ANNE PERRY

Anne Perry is the bestselling author of two Victorian detective series that are practically mandatory reading for any aficionado of the historical mystery. Her Thomas Pitt series and the William and Hester Monk series, although both set in the same nineteenth-century London, take very different looks at English society. She is also writing another acclaimed historical series set during the French Revolution, and consisting of the books *A Dish Taken Cold* and *The One Thing More*. She has also started another series set during World War I, which launched with the acclaimed novel *No Graves As Yet*. Besides this, she has also written a fantasy duology, *Tathea* and *Come Armageddon*. But no matter what genre she writes in, her deft, detailed research, multifaceted characters, and twisting plots have garnered her fans around the world. In her spare time she lectures on writing in such places as the cruise ship the *Queen Elizabeth II*. Recent books include *Angels in Gloom* and *Dark Assassin*.

HOSTAGES

Anne Perry

Bridget folded the last pair of trousers and put them into the case. She was looking forward to the holiday so much there was a little flutter of excitement in her stomach. It would not be the west coast she loved with its clean wind off the Atlantic and the great waves pounding in, because that would mean crossing the border into Eire, and they could not do that. But the north coast held its own beauty, and it would be away from Belfast, from Connor's responsibilities to the church, and most of all to the political party. There was always something he had to do, a quarrel to arbitrate, someone's bereavement to ease, a weakness to strengthen, a decision to make, and then argue and persuade.

It had been like that as long as she had known him, as it had been for his father. But then the Irish Troubles were over three hundred years old, in one form or another. The courage with which you fought for your beliefs defined who you were.

There was room for more in the suitcase. She looked around to see what else to put in just as Liam came to the door. He was sixteen, tall and lean like Connor, not yet filled out with muscle, and very conscious of it.

"Are you packed yet?" she asked.

"You don't need that much, Mum," he said dismissively. "We're only going for a week, and you can wash things, you know! Why are we going anyway? There's nothing to do!"

"That's exactly what I want to go for," she answered with a smile. "Your father needs to do nothing."

"He'll hate it!" Liam responded. "He'll be fretting all the time in case he's missing something, and when he comes home he'll only have to work twice as hard to put right whatever they've fouled up."

"Has it ever occurred to you," she said patiently, "that nothing will go wrong, and we'll have a good time? Don't you think perhaps it would be nice to be together, with no one else to think about, no one demanding anything, just for a few days?"

Liam rolled his eyes. "No," he said candidly. "It'll bore me out of my mind, and Dad too. He'll end up half the time on the phone anyway."

"There's no phone there," she told him. "It's a beach house."

"The mobile!" he said impatiently, his voice touched with contempt. "I'm going to see Michael."

"We're leaving in a couple of hours!" she called after him as he disappeared, and she heard his footsteps light and rapid along the passage, and then the back door slammed.

Connor came into the room. "What are you taking?" he asked, looking at the case. "What have you got all those trousers for? Haven't you packed any skirts? You can't wear those all the time."

She could, and she intended to. No one would see them. For once appearance would not matter. There would be no one there to criticize or consider it was not the right example for the wife of a minister and leader of the Protestant cause. Anyway, what she wore had nothing to do with the freedom of faith he had fought for since he was Liam's age, costing him the lightheartedness and the all too brief irresponsibility of his youth.

But was it worth arguing now, on the

brink of this rare time together? It would sour it from the outset, make him feel thwarted, as if she were deliberately challenging him. It always did. And she wanted this week for them to have time away from anxiety and the constant pressure and threat that he faced every day at home, or in London.

Wordlessly she took the trousers out, all but one pair, and replaced them with skirts.

He did not say anything, but she saw the satisfaction in his face. He looked tired. There was a denser network of fine lines around his eyes and he was greyer at the temples than she had realized. A tiny muscle ticked intermittently in his jaw. Although he had complained about it, denied it, he needed this holiday even more than she did. He needed days without duty, without decisions, nights of sleep without interruption from the telephone, a chance to talk without weighing every word in case it were misjudged, or misquoted. She felt the little flutter of pleasure again, and smiled at him.

He did not notice. He left, closing the door behind him.

She was crushed, even as she knew it was stupid. He had far too much else on his mind to bother with emotional trivialities. He had every right to expect that she should take such things for granted. In the twenty-four years of their marriage he had never let her down. He never let anyone down! No matter what it cost, he always kept his word. The whole of Northern Ireland knew that, Catholic and Protestant. The promise of Connor O'Malley could be trusted, it was rock solid, as immutable as the promise of God—and as hard.

She heard the words in her mind with horror. How could she even think such a thing, let alone allow it to come into her head. He was engaged in a war of the spirit, there was no room for half measures, for yielding to the seduction of compromise. And he used the right words, she could feel her own temptation to water down the chastenings, in order to achieve a little peace, to yield on truth just for respite from the constant battle. She was heart and soul weary of it. She hungered for laughter, friendship, the ordinary things of daily life, without the pressure of outward righteousness and inner anger all the time.

And he would see that as weakness, even betrayal. Right cannot ever compromise with wrong. It is the price of leadership that there can be no self-indulgence. How often had he said that, and lived up to it?

She looked at the trousers she had taken

out of the case. They were comfortable, and she could wear flat, easy shoes with them. This was supposed to be a holiday. She put two pairs of them back in again, at the bottom. She would do the unpacking anyway, and he would never know.

It was not difficult to pack for him: pyjamas, underwear, socks, plenty of shirts so he would always have a clean one, sweaters, lighter coloured casual trousers, toiletries. He would bring his own books and papers; that was an area she was not expected to touch.

Three middle-sized cases and Connor's briefcase would fit into the trunk of the car easily. The bodyguards, Billy and Ian, would come separately, following in another car, and they were not her responsibility. In fact she would try to imagine they were not there. They were necessary, of course, as they always were. Connor was a target for the I.R.A., although as far as she knew they had never physically attacked him. It would be a politically stupid thing to do; it would be the one thing that would unite all the disparate Protestant factions in one solid outrage.

And for the verbal attacks, he gave as good as he received, or better. He had the gift of words, the knowledge, and above all the passion so that his sermons, and his political speeches, almost interchangeable, erupted like lava to scorch those who were against his vision of Protestant survival and freedom. Sometimes it was directed just as fiercely at those on his own side who wavered, or in his view committed the greatest sin of all, betrayal. He despised a coward even more than he hated an open enemy.

The doorbell rang, and then, before anyone had had time to answer it, she heard the door open, and then Roisin's voice call out. "Hello, Mum! Where are you?"

"Bedroom!" Bridget answered. "Just finishing the packing. Like a cup of tea?"

"I'll make it," Roisin answered, arriving in the doorway. She was twenty-three, slim, with soft, brown hair like Bridget's, only darker, no honey fair streaks. She had been married just over a year and still had that glow of surprise and happiness about her. "You all ready?" she asked.

Bridget heard a slight edge to her voice, a tension she was trying to conceal. Please heaven it was not a difference with Eamonn. They were sufficiently in love it would all iron out, but Bridget did not want to go away for a week leaving Roisin emotionally raw. She was too vulnerable, and Eamonn was like Connor, passionate about his beliefs, committed to them, and expecting the same kind of commitment from those he loved, unaware of how little of himself he gave to his family, forgetting to put into word or touch what he expected them to know. "What is it?" she said aloud.

"I've got to speak to Dad," Roisin answered. "That's what I came for, really."

Bridget opened her eyes wide.

Roisin took a quick breath. "Sorry, Mum," she apologized. "I came to wish you a good holiday too. Heaven knows, you need it. But I could have done that over the phone."

Bridget looked at her more closely. She was a little flushed and her hands were stiff at her sides. "Are you alright?" she said with a pinch of anxiety. She almost asked her if she were pregnant, there was something about her which suggested it, but it would be intrusive. If it were so, Roisin would tell her when she was ready.

"Yes, of course I am!" Roisin said quickly. "Where's Dad?"

"Is it political?" It was a conclusion more than a question. She saw the shadow deepen in Roisin's eyes, and her right hand clench. "Couldn't it wait until we get back? Please!"

Roisin's face was indefinably tighter, more closed. "Eamonn asked me to come over," she answered. "Some things don't wait, Mum. I'll put the kettle on. He's not out, is he?"

"No . . ." Before she could add anything else, Roisin twisted around and was gone. Bridget looked around, checking the room for the last time. She always forgot something, but it was usually a trivial thing she could do without. And it was not as if they were going abroad. The house on the shore was lonely, that was its greatest charm, but the nearest village was a couple of miles away, and they would have the car. Even though they took bread and potatoes and a few tins, they would still need to go for food every so often.

She went through to the kitchen and found Roisin making the tea, and Connor standing staring out of the window into the back garden. Bridget would like to have escaped the conflict, but she knew there was no point. She would hear what had been said sooner or later. If they agreed it would be a cause for celebration, and she would join in. If they didn't, it would be between them like a coldness in the house, a block of ice sitting in the kitchen to be walked around.

Roisin turned with the teapot in her hand. "Dad?"

He remained where he was, his back to the room.

She poured three cups. "Dad, Eamonn's been talking with some of the moderates about a new initiative in education . . ." She stopped as she saw his shoulders stiffen. "At least listen to them!" Her voice was tight and urgent, a kind of desperation lifting it a pitch higher. "Don't refuse without hearing what it is!"

He swung around at last. His face was bleak, almost grey in the hard light. He sounded weary and bitter. "I've heard all I need to about Catholic schools and their methods, Rosie. Wasn't it the Jesuits who said 'Give me a child until he's seven, and I'll give you the man'? It's Popish superstition founded on fear. You'll never get rid of it out of the mind. It's a poison for life."

She swallowed. "They think the same about us!" she argued. "They aren't going to give in on teaching their children as they want, they can't afford to, or they won't carry their own people!"

"Neither am I," he replied, nothing in his face yielding, his jaw set, his blue eyes cold.

Bridget ached to interrupt, but she knew better. He found her ideas woolly and unrealistic, a recipe for evasion, an inch by inch surrender without the open honesty of battle. He had said so often enough. She had never stood her ground, never found the words or the courage to argue back. Somebody had to compromise or there would never be peace. She was tired of the cost of anger, not only the destruction of lives, the injury and the bereavement, but the loss of daily sanity, laughter and the chance to build with the hope of something lasting, the freedom from having to judge and condemn.

Roisin was still trying. "But Dad, if we gave a little on the things that don't matter, then we could stick on the things that do, and at least we would have started! We would look reasonable, maybe win over some of the middle parties."

"To what?" he asked.

"To join us, of course!" She spoke as if the answer were obvious.

"For how long?" There was challenge in his voice, and something close to anger.

She looked puzzled.

"Rosie, we're different parties because we have different principles," he said wearily. "The door has always been open for them to join us, if they will. I am not adulterating my beliefs to please the crowd or to win favours of anyone. I won't do it because it's wrong, but it's also foolish. As soon as they've got one concession, they'll want another, and another, until there's nothing left of what we've fought for, and died for all these years. Each time we give in, it'll be harder to stand the next time, until we've lost all credibility, and our own can't trust us any more. You're one or another. There's no half way. If Eamonn doesn't know that now, he'll learn it bitterly."

She would not retreat. She was beaten on logic, but not on will. "But Dad, if no one ever moves on anything, we'll go on fighting each other forever. My children will live and die for exactly the same things your parents did, and we're doing now! We've got to live together someday. Why not now?"

Connor's face softened. He had more patience with her than he did with Bridget. He picked up his cup in both hands, as if he were cold and warming himself on it. "Rosie, I can't afford to," he said quietly. "I've made promises I have to keep. If I don't, I have no right to ask for their trust. It's my job to bind them together, give them courage and hope, but I can only lead where they are willing to follow. Too far in front, and I'll lose them. Then I'll have accomplished nothing. They'll feel betrayed and choose a new leader, more extreme, and less likely to yield to anything than I am."

"But Dad, we've got to yield over something!" she persisted, her voice strained, her body awkward as she leaned across the table. "If you can't in education, then what about industry, or taxes, or censorship? There's got to be somewhere we can meet, or everything's just pointless, and we're all playing a charade that's going to go on and on forever, all our lives! All of us caught in a madman's parade, as if we hadn't the brains or the guts to see it and get out. It isn't even honest! We pretend we want peace, but we don't! We just want our own way!"

Bridget heard the hysteria in her voice, and at that moment she was sure Roisin was pregnant. She had a desperation to protect the future that was primal, higher and deeper than reason. Perhaps it was the one real hope? She stepped forward, intervening in her own instinct to shield.

"They're just people with a different faith and political aim," she said to Connor. "There must be a point where we can meet. They've moderated a lot in the last twenty years. They don't insist on Papal censorship of books any more . . ."

Connor looked at her in amazement, his eyebrows rising sharply. "Oh! And you call that moderation, do you? We should be grateful to be allowed to choose for ourselves what we can read, which works of philosophy and literature we can buy and which we can't, instead of being dictated to by the Pope of Rome?"

"Oh, come on, Dad!" Roisin waved her hand sharply. "It's not like it used to be . . ."

"We are not living under Roman Catholic laws, Roisin, not on marriage and divorce, not on birth control or abortion, not on what we can and cannot think!" His voice was grating hard, and he too leaned forward as if some physical force impelled him. "We are part of the United Kingdom of Great Britain and Northern Ireland, and that is the guarantee of our freedom to have laws that are the will of the people, not of the Roman Catholic Church. And I will die before I will give away one single right to that." His fist was clenched on the table top. "I don't move from here!"

Roisin looked pale and tired, her eyes stunned with defeat. When she spoke it was quietly. "Dad, not everyone in the party is behind you, you know. There are many who want at least to listen to the other side and make a show of being reasonable, even if at the end we don't change anything that matters." She half reached towards him, hesitated, then her hand fell away. "It's dangerous to appear as if we won't move at all." She was not looking at him, as if she dared not, in case she did not complete what she felt compelled to say. "People get impatient. We're tired of killing and dying, of seeing it going on and on without getting any better. If we're ever to heal it, we've got to begin somewhere."

There was sadness in Connor's face, Bridget could see it and pity wrenched inside her, because she knew what he was going to say. Maybe once there had been a choice, but it had gone long ago.

"We don't begin by surrendering our sovereignty, Roisin," he said. "I've tried all my life to deal with them. If we give an inch they'll take the next, and the next, until we have nothing left. They don't want accommodation, they want victory." He let his breath out in a sigh. "Sometimes I'm not even sure they want peace. Who do they hate, if not us? And who can they blame every time something goes wrong? No." He shook his head. "This is where we stand. Don't try to push me again, and tell Eamonn to do his own errands, not send you." He reached across as if to touch her hair, but she backed away, and Bridget saw the tears in her eyes.

"I'm frightened for you," Roisin said softly.

He straightened up, away from her. Her movement had hurt, and that surprised him.

"If you stand for your beliefs, there'll always be people who fight you," he answered, his lips tight, his eyes bitter. "Some of them violently."

Bridget knew he was thinking of the bombing nearly ten years ago in which his mentor had lost both his legs, and his four grandchildren with him had been killed. Something in Connor had changed then, the pain of it had withered compassion in him.

"Would you rather I were a coward?" he demanded, looking at Roisin. "There are different kinds of deaths," he went on. "I'll face mine forwards, trusting in God that He will protect me as long as I am in His service." Emotion twisted his face, startlingly naked for an instant. "Do you admire a man who bends with the wind because it might cost him to stand straight, Rosie? Is that what I've taught you?"

She shook her head, the tears spilling over. She leaned forward very quickly and brushed his cheek with her lips, but was gone past him before he could reach out his arm to hold her, and respond. She looked at Bridget for an instant, trying to smile. Her voice trembled too much to say more than a word of good-bye, and she hurried out. They heard her feet down the hall, and the front door slammed.

"It's Eamonn," Connor said grimly, avoiding meeting her eyes.

"I know," she agreed. She wanted to excuse Roisin and make him understand the fear she felt, the fierce driving need to protect the child Bridget was more than ever sure she was carrying. And she wanted to ease the hurt in Connor because he was being questioned and doubted by the daughter he loved, even if she had no idea how much, and he did not know how to tell her, or why she needed to know.

"He wants to impress her," she tried to explain. "You're the leader of Protestantism in Ireland, and he's in love with your daughter. He needs her to see him as another strong man, like you, a leader not a follower. He admires you intensely, but he can't afford to stand in your shadow—not with her."

Connor blinked and rubbed his hand wearily across his face, but at last he looked at her, surprise and a fleeting gratitude in his eyes.

Bridget smiled. "It's happened as long as young men have courted great men's daughters, and I expect it always will. It's hard to fall in love with a man who's in your own father's mould, just younger and weaker. He has to succeed for himself. Can't you see that?" She had felt that about Connor twenty-five years ago. She had seen the strength inside him, the fire to succeed. His unbreakable will had been the most exciting thing she could imagine. She had dreamed of working beside him, of sharing defeat and victory, proud just to be part of what he did. She could understand Roisin so well it was as if it were herself all over again.

Bridget had been lovely then, as Roisin was now. She had had the passion and the grace, and perhaps a little more laughter? But the cause had grown grimmer and more violent since then, and hope a little greyer. Or perhaps she had only seen more of the price of it, been to more funerals, and sat silently with more widows.

Connor stiffened. The moment was past. He looked at his watch. "It's nearly time we were going. Be ready in twenty minutes. Where's Liam?" He expected her to know, even though she had been here in the kitchen with him. The requirement for an answer was in his voice.

"He's gone to see Michael. He knows when to be back," she answered. She did not want an argument just as they were leaving, and they would have to sit together in the car all the way to the coast, verbally tiptoeing around each other. Liam would side with his father, hungry for his approval whatever the cost. She had seen his unconscious imitating of Connor, then catching himself, and deliberately doing differently, not even realizing it when he began to copy again. He was always watching, weighing, caught between admiration and judgment. He wanted to be unique and independent, and he needed to be accepted.

Connor walked past her to the door. "He'd better be here in ten minutes," he warned.

The journey to the coast was better than she had feared. The bodyguards followed behind so discreetly that most of the time she was not even aware of them. Usually she did not even know their names, only if she looked at them carefully did she notice the tension, the careful eyes, and perhaps the slight bulge of a weapon beneath their clothes if they turned a particular way, or the wind whipped a jacket hard against the outline of a body. She wondered sometimes what kind of men they were, idealists or mercenaries? Did they have wives at home, and children, mortgages, a dog? Or was this who they were all the time? They drove in the car behind, a faintly comforting presence in the rearview mirror.

She still wished they were all going west to

the wildness of the Atlantic coast with its dark hills, heather-purpled in places, bog-deep, wind-scoured. It was a vast, clean land, always man's master, never his servant. But even this gentler coast would be good. They would have time together to be at ease, to talk of things that mattered only to them, and rediscover the small sanities of ordinary life. Perhaps they would even recapture some of the laughter and the tenderness they had had before. Surely neither of them had changed too much for that?

She spoke little, content to listen to Liam and Connor talk about football, what they thought would happen in the new season, or the possibilities of getting any really good fishing in the week, where the best streams were, the best walks, the views that were worth the climb, and the secret places only the skilled and familiar could find.

She smiled at the thought of the two of them together doing things at which they were equally skilled, no leader, no follower. She was prepared to stand back and let that happen, without thinking of herself, or allowing herself to miss Connor because he gave his time, and his pleasure in it, to someone else. She was glad he had the chance to let go of the responsibility, not have to speak to anyone from the Party, and above all not to have to listen to their bickering and anger. She would be happy to walk alone along the beach and listen to the sound of the water, and let its timelessness wrap itself around her and heal the little scratches of misunderstanding that bled and ached at home.

They reached the village a little after five. The sun was still above the hills and only beginning to soften the air with gold. They stopped to buy fresh milk, eggs, an apple pie and a barbecued chicken to add to what they had brought, then drove on around the curve of the bay to the farther headland. Even Connor seemed to be excited when they pulled up at the cottage standing alone in a sheltered curve, almost on the edge of the sand. He looked around at the hills where they could climb, then across at the windows of the village where the first lights were beginning to flicker on, the dark line of the jetty cutting the golden water and the tender arch of the fading sky above. He said nothing, but Bridget saw his body relax and some of the tension iron out of his face, and she found herself smiling.

They unpacked the car, the guards, Billy and Ian, helping, Billy slender and energetic, his dark hair growing in a cowlick over his forehead, Ian fair-haired with freckles and strong, clever hands. It was he who got the gas boiler going, and unjammed the second bedroom window.

When everything was put away they excused themselves. "We'll go up the rise a little," Billy said, gesturing roughly behind him. "Set up our tent. It's camouflaged pretty well, and in the heather up there it'll be all but invisible."

"But don't worry, sir," Ian added. "One of us will be awake and with our eyes on you all the time." He gave a slight laugh. "Not that I don't feel a fraud, taking money to sit here in the sun for a week. Have a nice holiday, Mr. O'Malley. If ever a man deserved it, you do." He glanced at Bridget, smiling a little shyly. "And you, ma'am."

She thanked them and watched the two of them get back into their car and drive away up the hill until they disappeared into what seemed to be a hollow where the track ended, and she turned back and went inside. The air was growing cool and she realized how happy she was.

They ate cold chicken and salad, and apple pie. Liam went to his room with a book.

Bridget looked across at Connor. It was twilight now and the lamp on the table cast his face into shadows, emphasising the hollows under his cheeks and the lines around his mouth.

"Would you like to go for a walk along the beach?" she invited.

He looked up as if the question had intruded on his thoughts.

"Please?" she added.

"I'm tired, Bridget," he said, his voice flat. "I don't feel like talking, especially if you're going to try explaining Roisin to me. You don't need to. I understand perfectly well that she's young, thinking of having children, and she wants peace. Just leave it alone."

"I wasn't going to talk!" she said angrily. "About Roisin, or anything else. I just wanted to be outside." She added in her own mind that there used to be a time when they could have talked about anything, just for the pleasure of sharing ideas, feelings, or being together, but it sounded sentimental, and it exposed her hurt too clearly. And companionship was of no value once you had had to ask for it.

She went out of the door onto the hard earth, and then a dozen yards across it, past the washing line and through the sea grass to where the sand was softer, cool and slithering away under her feet. The evening was calm, the wave edge barely turning over, pale under the starlight. She walked without thinking, and trying to do it without even dreaming. By the time she came back her face and hands were cold, but there was a warmth inside her.

In the morning Connor seemed to be more relaxed. He was even enthusiastic about going fishing with Liam, and hummed to himself as he sorted out and chose his tackle, instructing Liam what he should take. Liam looked over his shoulder at Bridget and raised his eyebrows, but he accepted the advice goodnaturedly, secretly pleased. They took sandwiches, cold pie and bottles of water, and she watched them climb up the slope side by side, talking companionably, until they disappeared over the crest.

It was a long day without them, but she was happy knowing how much it would please Liam. Connor had sacrificed much for the cause, and perhaps one of the most costly was time with his son. He had never spoken of it, but she had seen the regret in his face, the tightening of his muscles when he had to explain why he could not be at a school prize-giving, or a football match, or why he could not simply talk, instead of working. At times it had seemed that everyone else mattered more to him than his own family, even though she knew it was not true.

At midday Ian came down to make sure everything was still working in the house, and she did not need anything. Billy had followed Connor and Liam, at a discreet distance, of course.

"It's fine, thank you," she told Ian.

He leaned against the door in the sun, and she realized with surprise that he was probably no more than thirty-two or -three.

"Would you like lunch?" she offered impulsively. "There's still some apple pie— enough for one, and I don't want it."

He smiled. "I'd love it, Mrs. O'Malley, but I can't come inside for more than a moment or two. Can't see the road."

"Then I'll put the pie on a plate, and you take it," she said, going inside to fetch it before he could refuse.

He accepted it with evident pleasure, thanking her and striding away up the hill again, waving for a moment before he disappeared.

Connor and Liam came back, faces flushed, delighted with their success. For the first time in months Bridget heard him laugh.

"We've caught more than enough for us," he said triumphantly. "Do you want to go and ask Ian and Billy if they'd like a couple?" He turned to Bridget. "You'll cook them, won't you?"

"Of course," she agreed, liking the thought, and beginning immediately as Liam went out of the back door. She had them ready for the pan when he came back again, walking straight past her to the sitting room. "Dad, I can't find them!"

"Go back and look properly!" Connor said with impatience. "And hurry up! Ours'll be ready to eat in a few minutes."

"I have looked," Liam insisted. "And I called out."

"Then look again," Connor ordered. "They can't be far. At least one of them is on duty. The other one could have taken the car for something. Maybe gone to the pub to fetch a crate of Guinness."

"The car's there," Liam told him.

Connor put his newspaper down. Bridget heard the rustle of it. "Do I have to go and look myself?" he demanded.

"I'll go!" Liam was defensive, the friendship and the equality of the afternoon were gone. He marched past Bridget without looking at her, angry that she should have seen it shatter, and went outside into the darkness.

She took the frying pan off the heat.

It was another ten minutes before Liam came back alone. "They're not there," he said again, this time his voice was sharp, edged with fear.

Connor slammed the newspaper down and came out of the sitting room, his face tight and hard, the muscle jumping in his jaw. He walked past both of them and went outside. They heard him shouting, the wind carrying his voice, fading as he went up the hill.

Liam said nothing. He stood awkwardly in the kitchen, looking suddenly vulnerable, and acutely aware of it. He was waiting for Connor to return, successful where he had failed. He dreaded looking stupid in his father's eyes, far more than anything Bridget might think of him.

But when Connor came in quarter of an hour later his face was white and his body rigid, shoulders stiff. "They're not there," he said angrily. "Damn it, they must have walked over to the pub in the village." His mouth closed in a thin line and there was an icy rage in his eyes.

For the first time Bridget was touched with real fear, not of his temper but of something new, and far uglier. "They won't be far," she said aloud, and the moment the words were out of her mouth she realized how pointless they were.

He spun round on her. "They're out of earshot!" he said between his teeth. "If you screamed now, who'd hear you? For God's sake, Bridget, use your brains! They're supposed to be bodyguards! We may not be in Belfast, but we're still in Ireland! I'll have them dismissed for this."

Bridget felt the heat burn up her face, for Ian and Billy who had taken trouble to help, and even more for herself. She knew her words had been foolish, but he had had no need to belittle her in front of Liam. His lack of regard for her hurt more than she wanted to face. It was probably part of growing up, separating the man from the boy. But she was losing him, and each new widening of the gap twisted inside her.

"Don't worry, Dad," Liam said awkwardly. "No one else knows we're here. We'll be okay. We can always fry them up tomorrow."

Connor hesitated, his anger easing out of him. "Of course we will," he agreed. "It's a matter of discipline, and loyalty." He turned to Bridget, no warmth in his eyes. "You'd better put the extra fish in the fridge, and do ours. It's late."

She did as she was told, and they ate in silence. It was a long evening. Connor and Liam talked a little, but not to her. She did not intrude, she knew she would gain nothing by it, and only invite them to make her exclusion more obvious. She saw Liam glance at her once or twice, anxious and a little embarrassed, but he did not know what to say.

She went to bed early. She was still awake an hour later, and heard Connor come in, but she made no movement, and he did not attempt to waken her, as if it had not even occurred to him.

She woke to hear a steady banging, and it was several minutes before she understood what it was. There was someone at the door. It must be Billy and Ian back, probably full of remorse. They were wrong to have gone, but she wanted to protect them from Connor's anger. In theory it could have cost him his life, but actually no harm had come of it. They wouldn't have been gone any more than that brief half hour of suppertime. And no one had ever attempted to harm him physically. It was all just threat.

She swung her feet out of bed, slipped her coat over her nightgown, and went to answer before Connor heard them. She closed the bedroom door softly and tiptoed across the hall to the front door. She opened it.

It was not Billy and Ian there, but three men she had never seen before. The first was tall and lean with fair brown hair and a slightly crooked face that looked as if he laughed easily. The one to the left of him was darker, his features more regular, but there was a seriousness in him that was heavy, almost brooding. The third man was thin with bright blue eyes and hair with a strong tinge of auburn in it.

"Good morning, Mrs. O'Malley," the first one said with a smile. "It's a beautiful day, is it not?" But he did not look at the sweep of the bay, glittering in the sun, or the dark headland behind them.

It was a moment before the chill struck her that he knew her name. Then it came with a cold, tight knot.

He must have seen it in her eyes, but his expression altered only fractionally. "My name's Paddy." He gestured to the dark man. "This is Dermot." He motioned the other way. "And this is Sean. We've brought some fresh eggs with us from the farm over the way, and perhaps you'd be good enough to cook them for us, and we'll all have breakfast together—you and Mr. O'Malley, and us—and the boy, of course." He was polite, still smiling, but there was no question in his voice, no room for refusal.

She backed away from him. It occurred to her for an instant to close the door on him, but she knew he could force his way in if he wanted. "Come back in half an hour, when we're up," she said quite sure even as she spoke that he would refuse.

"We'll wait in the sitting room." He took a step towards her, holding out the open box of eggs, smooth and brown, faintly speckled. There were at least a dozen of them. "We'll have them fried, if that's alright with you? Sean here has a fresh loaf of bread, and a pound of butter as well. Here, Sean, give it to Mrs. O'Malley."

Sean held them out and Bridget took them from him. She needed time to think. She was angry at the intrusion, but she dared not show it. As she led the way to the sitting room and watched them go in easily, as if they had a right to be there, she thought how often she was angry, and suppressed it because she was afraid of making it worse, and losing what she already had. She had done it for so long it was habit.

Connor was sitting up when she returned to the bedroom.

"Where have you been?" he said irritably. "Did you go out to warn Billy and Ian? I know you!" He swung his feet out of bed and stood up. "You've no idea of the gravity of it. I don't tell you of the threats I get, there's no need for you to know, but going off as they've done is a betrayal of me—and the cause."

"No, I didn't!" she said curtly. She was frightened and angry, and the accusation was true in spirit. She would have, had they been there. "There are three men in the sitting room to speak to you . . ."

For an instant he was motionless, frozen in time and place. Then slowly he turned to stare at her. "What men?" His mouth was so dry his voice was husky. "What men, Bridget?"

She swallowed. "I don't know. But they won't go until you speak to them. They're waiting in the sitting room. They told me to get them breakfast."

He was incredulous. "They what?"

"I don't mind!" she protested, wanting to stop him from quarrelling with them needlessly. She was used to men with that hard, underlying anger in them, and the threat of violence close under the surface. Religious politics always seemed to be like that. She wanted it over as soon as possible. Let the wind and the sea wash them clean from the taste of it. She started to dress.

"Where the hell are Billy and Ian?" She heard the first cutting edge of fear in his

voice, higher and sharper than the anger. It
startled her. She swung around to look at
him, but it was gone from his face, only fury
remaining.

"Don't you dare make their breakfast!" he
ordered. "Tell them to come back when I'm
shaved and dressed . . . and I've eaten."

"I already did, and they won't do it," she
replied, fastening her skirt. "Connor . . ."
she gulped. She felt separate from him and
she needed intensely to have the safety, the
courage of being together. "Connor . . .
they aren't going to go until they want to.
Just listen to them . . . please?"

"What are they going to say? Who are
they?" He demanded it as if he believed she
already knew.

It was ridiculous, but her throat tightened
as if she was going to cry. "I don't know."
This time she went out, leaving him alone to
shave and dress. In the kitchen she started
making breakfast for five. Liam was still
asleep, and perhaps he would stay that way
until after the men had gone.

By the time Connor appeared she had
laid the table and made tea and toast and
was ready to serve the eggs and bacon.

"Very civil of you, Mrs. O'Malley," Paddy
said appreciatively, taking the seat at the
head of the table. The other two sat at the

sides, leaving spaces for Connor and Bridget between them.

A flicker of annoyance crossed Connor's face, but he accepted and sat also, and started to eat. It was a race against time until either Billy or Ian should appear, or better still, both of them. They were armed and would get rid of Paddy and his friends in moments. Then Connor would crucify them for not having prevented it in the first place. She dreaded that. They were lax, but years of physical safety had left them unprepared for the reality of such intrusion. They would be horribly ashamed, and she would have given them a second chance.

"Now, Mr. O'Malley," Paddy said, putting his knife and fork together on his empty plate. "To business."

"I have no business with you," Connor replied, his eyes level, his voice flat.

"Well that's a shame now." Paddy did not lose his slight smile. "But I'm not easily put off. You see, I'm after peace, not all of a hurry, because it's not a simple thing, but just a beginning."

"So am I," Connor answered. "But only on my terms, and I doubt they're yours, but put them, if you want."

"I doubt that we can agree, Mr. O'Malley. I know right enough what your terms are.

It's not as if you were backward about it, or had ever shifted your ground."

"Then where have you shifted?" Connor asked. "And who do you represent, anyway?"

Paddy leaned back in his chair, but the other two remained exactly as they were, vigilant. "Well I haven't shifted a great deal either," Paddy said. "And that's the trouble. We need to have a change, don't you think?" He did not stop long enough for Connor to answer. "This is getting nowhere, and sure enough, I don't see how it can. I'm a moderate man, Mr. O'-Malley, reasonable, open to argument. And you're not."

A shred of a smile touched Connor's lips, but Bridget could see half under the table where his fists were clenched and his feet were flat on the floor to balance if he moved suddenly.

"That's the change I propose," Paddy went on.

"You've already said that you know I won't change," Connor pointed out, a very slight sneer on his face.

"Perhaps I haven't made myself plain." Paddy said it as a very slight apology. "I'm suggesting that you step down as leader, and allow a more amenable man into your place." He stopped as Connor stiffened.

"Someone who's not tied by past promises," Paddy went on again. "A fresh start."

"You mean I should abandon my people?" Connor's eyebrows rose. "Walk away from them and leave the leadership open to someone of your choosing, that you can manipulate! You're a fool, Paddy—whoever you are, and you're wasting my time, and yours. You've had your breakfast, now take your friends and get out. Leave my family alone. You're . . ." He stopped.

Bridget was certain that he had been going to say that they were lucky the bodyguards had not come in and thrown them out, then he had realized that they had been here half an hour already, in fact thirty-five minutes by the kitchen clock, and neither Billy nor Ian had come. Why not? Where were they? The flicker of fear was stronger inside her and more like a bird's wing than a moth's. Was that why he had stopped, because he had felt that as well?

Paddy made no move at all, he did not even straighten in his chair. "Give it a bit of thought now, Mr. O'Malley," he persisted. "I'm sure you don't want all this trouble to go on. If there's ever going to be peace, there's got to be compromise. Just a little here and there."

"Get out," Connor repeated.

There was a slight movement in the hall doorway and as one man they all looked at Liam, in his pyjama trousers, blinking at them, his face half asleep, confused.

"And you'll be Liam," Paddy remarked. "Wanting your breakfast, no doubt. Come on in, then. Your mother'll lay a place for you. There's plenty of food left—eggs and bacon, fresh from the farm, they are."

Liam blushed. "Who are you? Where are Billy and Ian?"

"My name's Paddy, and these are my friends, Dermot and Sean. We just dropped by to have a word with your father. Have a cup of tea." He gestured to Sean. "Get up now, and let the boy have your place."

Wordlessly Sean obeyed, taking his used dishes to the sink.

Bridget stood up. "Sit," she told Liam. "I'll fry you some eggs."

Connor's face was white. "You'll do no such thing!" he said furiously. "Liam, go and get dressed! You don't come to the table like that, and you know it."

Liam turned to go.

Sean moved to the door to block his way.

Liam stopped.

Connor swivelled around in his chair.

"Come back to the table, Liam," Paddy said levelly. "It's a fine morning. You'll not be cold. Get him his breakfast, Mrs. O'Malley. Feed the boy."

Connor drew in his breath sharply, his face now twisted with anger. Bridget dreaded what punishment Ian and Billy would get when they finally showed up. It would finish their careers, perhaps even finish them ever getting work in Belfast. Connor would never forgive them for allowing him to be humiliated like this in his own house.

Then like having swallowed ice water she realized that Billy and Ian were prisoners somewhere else, just as they were here. They had not come because they could not. She turned to face Paddy and he looked across at her. She tried to mask the knowledge in her eyes, but it was too late. He had already seen it. He said nothing, but the understanding was like a rod of iron between them.

Liam sat down, looking at his father, then away again, embarrassed.

Bridget relit the gas and moved the frying pan over onto the heat.

"Are you sure you won't think again, Mr. O'Malley?" Paddy asked gently. "There are men just a little more to the centre than you are, who could afford to yield a point or two, and still hold to the rest. You've had your day at the top. It's not as if you'd not made it . . ."

"You arrogant fool!" Connor exploded. "Do you think that's what it's about—being leader?" His voice burned with contempt. He half rose in his seat, leaning across the table towards Paddy who still lounged in his chair. "It's about principle, it's about fighting for the freedom to make our own laws according to the will of the people, not the Church of Rome! I don't care that much," he snapped his fingers, "who's leader, as long as they do it with honour and the courage to yield nothing of our rights, whoever threatens them or promises money or power in exchange for the surrender of our birthright."

Liam straightened up in his chair, squaring his bare shoulders.

Bridget put bacon into the frying pan, and two eggs. She had known that was what Connor would say, and there was a kind of pride in her for his courage, but larger than that, overtaking it, was pity and anger, and sick fear.

"That's right, Mr. O'Malley," Paddy said calmly. "You're hostage to all the fine speeches you've made one time or another. I understand that you can't go back on them. You've left yourself no room. That's why I'm thinking it'd be a fine idea for you to step down now, and allow someone new to take over—someone who has a little space to move."

"Never!" Connor forced the word between his teeth. "I've never yielded to threats in my life, and I'm not beginning now. Get out of my house." He straightened up, standing tall, almost to attention. "Now!"

Paddy smiled very slightly. "Don't be hasty, Mr. O'Malley. Give it some thought before you answer."

Bridget had the frying pan in her hand, full of hot fat, the eggs and bacon sizzling.

"I wouldn't do that, Mrs. O'Malley," Paddy said warningly.

Connor swivelled around, his jaw slack for an instant, then he realized what Paddy meant. He leaned across the table and picked up the teapot and flung it not at Paddy, but at Sean standing in the doorway. It hit him in the chest, knocking him off balance and he staggered backwards.

Suddenly Dermot was on his feet, a gun in his hand. He pointed it at Liam.

"Sit down, Mr. O'Malley," Paddy said quietly, but there was no gentleness in his voice any more. "I'm sorry you won't be reasonable about this. It puts us all in an unpleasant situation. Perhaps you should consider it a little longer, don't you think? When you've finished the boy's breakfast, how about another cup of tea, Mrs. O'Malley." It was an order.

Connor sank to his chair. It seemed he had only just grasped the reality that they were prisoners. He was shaking with anger, his hands trembled and the muscle in his jaw flicked furiously.

Bridget picked up the spatula and served the eggs and bacon, using two hands because she was shaking as well, and she thought of the mess she would make on the floor if she dropped the plate.

Liam seemed about to refuse it, then met Paddy's eyes, and changed his mind.

Bridget returned the teapot to the stove, and cleaned up the spilled leaves and water on the floor. She boiled the kettle again and made more. Paddy thanked her. The minutes ticked by. No one spoke.

Liam finished his meal. "Can I go and get dressed?" he asked Paddy.

Connor's temper flared, but he did not speak.

"Sure you can," Paddy answered. "Sean'll go with you, just to make sure you don't forget to come back."

When they were gone he turned to Connor. "We've got all week, Mr. O'Malley, but it'll be nicer for everyone if you make the right decision sooner rather than later. Then you can have a nice holiday here with your family, and enjoy it just as you intended to."

"I'll see you in hell first," Connor replied.

"Now that's a shame," Paddy answered. "Hell's surely a terrible place, so I hear the preachers say. But then you're a preacher aren't you, so you'll know that already."

"You'll know it yourself, soon enough!" Connor returned.

Dermot rose to his feet. "That's your last answer, is it?"

"It is."

He shrugged. "Sean!" he called out.

Sean reappeared, Liam behind him, fully dressed now.

"Mr. O'Malley's not for changing his mind," Dermot said. "Leave the boy here. You and I have a job to do."

Sean pushed Liam, nudging him forward into the kitchen.

"What?" Connor demanded.

"You're staying here," Dermot told him. He signalled to Sean and the two of them went outside. Paddy stood up, revealing the gun in his hand also. He lounged against the door post, but it would have taken less than a second for him to straighten up and raise the barrel if one of them threatened him.

There were several moments' silence, then a shout from outside. Paddy looked up sharply, but it was Connor's name that was called. He lowered the gun and Connor walked to the outside door and opened it.

Bridget followed a step behind him.

On the tussock grass just beyond the gate Ian and Billy stood facing Dermot; their hands were tied behind their backs. Dermot jerked the gun up, gesturing with his other arm.

Billy knelt down.

Dermot put the gun to Billy's head and a shot rang out, sharp and thin in the morning air, sounding surprisingly far away. Billy fell forward. Ian swayed.

Dermot pointed again. Ian knelt. A second shot cracked. Ian fell forward.

Connor gave a strangled cry in his throat and staggered over to the sink as if he could be sick. He dry-retched and gulped air.

Bridget felt the room reel around her, her legs turn to jelly. She clasped onto the door jamb until the nausea passed, then turned to look at Liam, ashen-faced by the table, and Paddy by the stove, the gun still in his hand.

A terrible sadness overwhelmed her. It was a moment that divided forever the past from the present. Billy and Ian were dead. They had helped her, casually, smiling, not knowing what was ahead of them. They had never deserted their posts, and they were lying out there with bullets through their heads, butchered almost without thought.

Liam was ashen. Connor looked as if he might be sick.

Bridget ached to be able to help someone, help herself, undo the moment and see Billy and Ian alive again. And it was all impossible, and far too late.

She made a move towards Liam, and he jerked away from her, too hurt to be touched, blaming her in some way, as if she could have prevented it. School friends had been caught in bomb blasts. He had seen plenty of injury and bereavement, but this was the first murder he had seen. Connor went to him, holding out his hand, wordlessly. Liam took it.

Time stretched on. Bridget washed the dishes and put them away. Sean and Dermot returned. She noticed that their boots had earth on them, and there were marks of sweat on their shirts, as if they had been involved in some heavy physical exertion.

Connor stood up.

"Sit down," Dermot said pleasantly, but he stood still, waiting to be obeyed.

"I'm going to the bathroom!" Connor snapped.

"Not yet," Dermot answered. "My hands are dirty. Sean's too. We'll go and wash, then you can. And don't lock yourself in. We'll only have to break the door down, then Mrs. O'Malley'll have no privacy, and you don't want that, do you?"

"For God's sake, you can't . . ." Connor began, then he knew that they could—they would.

The morning passed slowly, all of them in the kitchen except when someone needed to use the bathroom. Bridget made them tea, and then started to peel potatoes for lunch.

"We haven't enough food for five," she pointed out. "Not beyond this evening, anyway."

"They'll be gone before then!" Connor snapped at her.

"If you've made the right decision," Paddy agreed. He turned to Bridget. "Don't worry, we've got plenty, and it's no trouble to get more. Just make what you've got, Mrs. O'Malley."

"You don't tell her what to do!" Connor turned on him.

Dermot smiled. "Sure he does, Mr. O'-Malley. She knows that, don't you, Bridget?"

Connor was helpless, it was naked in his face, as if something were stripped from him.

Bridget longed to protect him, but he had made it impossible. Everything that came to her mind to say would only have made it worse, shown up the fact that she was used to being ordered around, and he was not. She realized it with a shock. Usually it was Connor, for different reasons, and now it was two strangers, but the feeling of being unable to retaliate was just the same.

"We've got to eat," she said reasonably. "I'd rather cook it myself than have one of them do it, even if I had the choice."

Connor said nothing.

Liam groaned and turned away, then slowly looked up at his father, anxiety in his face, and fear, not for himself.

Bridget dug her nails into the palms of her hands. Was Liam more afraid that Connor would be hurt, or that he would make a fool of himself, fail at what he needed to do, to be?

"You'll pay for this," Connor said at last. "No matter what you do to me, or my family, you won't change the core of the people. Is this your best argument—the gun? To hold women and children hostage?" His voice descended into sarcasm, and he did not notice Liam's sudden flush of anger and shame. "Very poor persuasion! That's really the high moral ground!"

Dermot took a step toward him, his hand clenched.

"Not yet!" Paddy said warningly. "Let him be."

Dermot glared at him, but he dropped his hand.

Bridget found herself shaking so badly she was afraid to pick up anything in case it slipped through her fingers. "I'm going to the bathroom," she said abruptly, and pushed past Sean and out of the door. No one followed her.

She closed the bathroom door and locked it, then stood by the basin, her stomach churning, nausea coming over her in waves. They were prisoners. Billy and Ian were dead. Connor was frightened and angry, but he was not going to yield, he couldn't. He had spent all his life preaching the cause, absolutism, loyalty to principles whatever the cost. Too many other men had died, and women and children, he had left himself no room to give anything away now. He might have, even yesterday, when it was only Roisin who asked him, but today it would be seen as yielding to force, and he could never do that.

They were prisoners until someone rescued them, or Dermot and Sean killed them all. Would Connor let that happen? If he gave in to save them, he would hate them for it. She knew without hesitation that he would resent them forever for being the cause of his weakness, the abandoning of his honour, even his betrayal of all his life stood for.

How blindingly, ineffably stupid! For a sickening moment rage overtook her for the whole idiotic religious divide, which was outwardly in the name of Christianity!

But of course it wasn't. It was human arrogance, misunderstanding, rivalry, one wrong building on another, and the inability to forgive the terrible, aching losses on both sides. Religion was the excuse they clothed it in, to justify it. They created God in their own image: vengeful, partisan, too small of mind to love everyone, incapable of accepting differences. You might fear a god like that, you could not love him.

She dashed cold water over her face and dried it on the rough towel. She hung it up and saw that they were going to run out of toilet paper with six of them in the house. And laundry powder. She would have to tell Paddy that, as well as getting food.

"I'll remember," he said with a smile when

she told him early in the afternoon. The others were still in the sitting room and she was in the kitchen going through the store cupboard to see what there was.

"And washing-up liquid," she added.

"Of course. Anything else?"

She straightened up and looked at him. He was still smiling, his slightly lopsided face softened by humour.

"How long are you going to stay here?" she asked.

There was a shadow around his eyes. It was the first uncertainty she had seen in him. She did not find it comforting. Suddenly she was aware, with a sharp pain of fear, how volatile the situation was. He did not know the answer. Perhaps he really had expected Connor to step down, and now that he knew he would not, he did not know how to proceed. She felt cold inside.

"That's all," she said without waiting for him to answer. "Except some bread, I suppose. And tea, if you want it." She moved past him, brushing his arm as she went back to the sitting room.

Connor was standing looking out of the window, his shoulders stiff. She could imagine the expression on his face by seeing his back. Liam was huddled in the armchair, watching his father. His unhappiness was written in every line of his body. Sean was lounging against the door. Dermot was nowhere to be seen.

The afternoon wore on in miserable silence, sporadic anger, and then silence again. Dermot returned at last. He looked at his watch. "Half past five," he observed. "I think we'll eat at seven, Mrs. O'Malley." His eyes flickered to Connor and saw the dull flash of anger in his face. A tiny smile touched his mouth. "And you can go to bed at nine, after you've done the dishes."

The muscle in Connor's jaw twitched. He was breathing slowly, trying to control himself. Liam stared at him, fear and embarrassment struggling in his eyes. He was mortified to see his father humiliated, and yet he was also deeply afraid that if he showed any courage at all he would be hurt, and then humiliated even more. Bridget found his confusion painful to watch, but she had no idea how to help. Exactly the same fear twisted inside her stomach, making her swallow to keep from being sick.

"How about a cup of tea?" Dermot went on. She moved to obey, and saw his satisfaction.

"Get your own tea!" Connor said curtly. "Bridget! Don't wait on them!"

"I don't mind," she told him. "I've nothing else to do."

"Then do nothing!" He swung around to face her. "I told you not to wait on them. For God's sake, they're not so stupid they can't boil water!"

She saw Paddy's expression, and realized with surprise that Connor had spoken to her in exactly the same tone of voice that Dermot had used. Was that deliberate— Dermot mimicking Connor? And she was so accustomed to obeying that she was going to do it automatically.

Now she was totally undecided. If she obeyed Dermot she would further reduce Connor, and if she did not she might provoke the violence she feared, or at best make him exert his control in some other way.

They were all watching her, waiting, particularly Liam.

"Actually I'm going to do the laundry," she said. "Just because we're prisoners here doesn't mean we shouldn't have clean underwear. If any of you can be bothered to follow me you can, but it's pretty stupid. You know I'm not going to leave. You've got my family here." And without looking at Paddy or Dermot, she walked out and went to the bedrooms to collect whatever she could find to wash. No one came after her.

The evening passed slowly, with tension in the air so brittle every time anyone moved suddenly, or made a sound with knife on china, or Liam dropped his fork, they all stiffened, and Sean in the doorway lifted the barrel of his gun.

Bridget washed the dishes and Liam dried them. They went to bed at nine o'clock, as ordered.

As soon as the bedroom door was closed Connor turned on Bridget.

"Why are you obeying them?" he said furiously, his face mottled dark with rage. "How can I make a stand against them if you defy me all the time?"

"You can't make a stand against them," she replied wearily. "They've got guns." She started to undress, hanging her skirt and blouse up in the wardrobe.

"Don't turn your back on me when I'm talking to you!" His voice shook.

She turned around. It was only one full day, not even a night, and already he was losing his mastery of himself, because nothing was in his control. She looked at him steadily, unblinking.

"We have no choice, Connor. I'm not defying you, I'm just not making them angry when there's no point. Besides, I'm used to doing what someone else tells me to."

"What do you mean by that?"

She turned back to the wardrobe. "Go to bed."

"You don't care, do you!" he accused. "You think I should give in to them, let them have whatever they want, buy our freedom now by surrendering everything we've fought for all our lives!"

"I know you can't do that." She went on undressing, looking out for a clean nightgown because she had washed the other one, for something to do. "You haven't left yourself room. I don't suppose they have either. That's the trouble with all of us, we're hostage to the past we've created. Go to bed. Staying up all night isn't going to help."

"You're a coward, Bridget. I didn't think I'd ever be ashamed of my own wife."

"I don't suppose you thought about it at all," she replied. "Not really, not about me, I mean." She walked past him, putting the nightgown on and climbed into her side of the bed.

He was silent for several minutes. She heard him taking off his clothes, hanging them up as well, then she felt the bed move a little as he got in.

"I'll excuse that, because you're afraid," he said at last.

She did not answer. She was not helping him, and she felt guilty, but it was his intransigence that had made dealing with him impossible. It was a matter of principle, and she knew he could not help it, not now, anyway. He had ordered her around for years, just the way Dermot was ordering him. And it was her fault too, for obeying. She had wanted peace, wanted him happy, not always for his sake but for hers, because he was kinder then, closer to the man she wanted him to be, the man who made her laugh sometimes, who enjoyed the small things, as well as the great, and who loved her. She should have been honest years ago.

Now she could not even protect Liam from the disillusion that was already beginning to frighten him more deeply than the threat of violence from Dermot or Sean. There was nothing she could do. She slid down a little further, and pretended to be asleep.

The next day was worse. Tempers were tighter, edges more raw. There was nothing to do, and they were all cramped inside the cottage. Sean, Paddy, and Dermot took turns watching and sleeping. They had nailed the windows closed, so the air was stuffy, and there was no escape except through one of the two doors.

"What the hell are they waiting for?" Connor demanded when he and Bridget were alone in the bedroom, Sean just beyond the door.

"I don't know," she replied. "I don't know what can happen. You aren't going to change, and neither are they." What was really in her mind was Billy and Ian murdered in front of them and buried somewhere up the hillside, only she did not want to acknowledge it in words. Then she would have to face the consequences of what it meant, and the possibilities it closed off.

"Then what are they waiting for?" he repeated. "Have they asked somebody for money? Or are they going to keep me here until someone else has taken power?"

She had not thought of that. It was a relief, because it made sense. "Yes," she said aloud. "That could be it." Then doubt came to her again. She had become aware that Dermot was waiting, just small signs, a turning when there was a sound, a half listening attitude, a certain tension in him that was not in Paddy. Sean she saw far less of—in fact she had not watched him at all.

"You sound pleased," Connor said.

She looked at him. His face was deeply lined, his eyes pink-rimmed as if he had not slept at all. The muscle in his jaw jumped erratically. "I'm not pleased," she said gently. "I'm just glad you thought of something that makes sense. It's easier to deal with."

"Deal with?"

"Live with," she corrected. "I'm going back out, before they come for us." She left him alone because she did not know what more to say.

It was the third day when she was standing in the back garden, picking a handful of mint for the potatoes, and staring across the stretch of tussock grass towards the sea, when she was aware of someone behind her.

"I'm coming," she said a little tartly. Dermot was irritating her. She had watched him deliberately baiting Connor, ordering him in small, unnecessary things. She swung around, to find Paddy a yard away.

"No hurry," he answered, looking beyond her to the water, barely restless in the slight wind, the waves no more than rustling as they turned over on the sand.

She followed his glance. It had beauty, but she ached for the wilder Atlantic shore with its vast width, the skies that stretched for ever, the wind so hard and clean it blew mares' tails of spume off the incoming rollers so that when they crashed on the sand the streamers of foam trailed behind them.

"I miss the west," she said impulsively.

"And of course you can't go there any more." His voice was quiet, almost gentle. "It's a high price we pay, isn't it?"

She drew in her breath to challenge him for including himself, then she realized that perhaps he too was bound by choices he had made long ago, things other people expected of him, as Connor had always expected of her.

"Yes," she agreed. "Penny by penny, over the years."

He said nothing for a little while, just watching the water, as she did.

"Do you come from the west?" she asked.

"Yes." There was regret in his voice.

She wanted to ask him how he had come to be here, holding Connor at gunpoint, what had happened in his life to change a crusade for his beliefs into this kind of violence, but she did not want to anger him with what was undoubtedly intrusive. Perhaps like her, he had started by wanting to please someone he loved, to live up to their ideas of courage and loyalty, and ended clinging onto the shreds of love, because that was all there was left, hoping for something that honesty would have told him did not exist. She had not wanted to face that. It invalidated too much she had paid for with years of trying, swinging from hope to defeat, and then creating hope again.

He started to speak, and stopped.

"What were you going to say?" she asked.

"I was going to ask you something it's none of my business to know," he replied. "And maybe I'd rather not, anyway. I know what you'd say, because you'd be loyal, and perhaps I'd believe you, perhaps not. So maybe it's better we just stand and look at the water. The tides will come and go, the seabirds will call exactly the same, whatever we do."

"He won't change," she said.

"I know. He's a hard man. His time is past, Bridget. We've got to have change. Everyone's got to yield something."

"I know. But we can't take the hard liners with us. They'll call him a traitor, and he couldn't bear that."

"Captain going down with the ship?" He had a slight, wry humour in his voice, but a knowledge of tragedy as well.

"I suppose so," she agreed.

A gull wheeled above them, and soared up in the wind. They both watched it.

She thought of asking him what they were waiting for, but she was not certain that Paddy was waiting, not as Dermot was. Should she warn him, say that Dermot was different, darker? Perhaps he already knew, and it would be disloyal to Connor if she were to say anything to Paddy that could be of help to him. Perhaps she shouldn't be speaking to him at all, more than was necessary.

"I must go in," she said aloud, turning towards the kitchen door.

He smiled at her, not moving from her path, so she passed almost close enough to brush him. She smelled a faint odour of aftershave, clean cotton from the shirt she had laundered. She forced the thoughts out of her mind and went inside.

The evening was tedious and miserable. Connor paced back and forth until Dermot lost his temper and told him to stop. Connor glared at him, and kept pacing. Dermot walked over to Liam and lifted the gun, held by the barrel.

"You don't need to do that!" Paddy said angrily. "Mr. O'Malley's going to do as he's told. He doesn't have the control of his nerves that Bridget has. He doesn't take easily to not being master of his fate."

The dull red colour rose up Connor's face, but he did not take his eyes off Dermot, the gun still within striking distance of Liam's head.

Liam sat motionless, white with misery, not fear for himself, but embarrassment for his father, and helpless anger that Bridget had been singled out for strange and double-edged praise. His loyalties were torn apart. The world which had been difficult enough had become impossible.

"I'm going to bed!" Connor said in a voice so hard it rasped on the ear.

"Good," Paddy agreed.

Dermot relaxed.

Liam stumbled to his feet. "So am I! Dad! Wait for me!"

Bridget was left alone with Paddy and Dermot. She did not want to stay, but she knew better than to follow Connor yet. He needed time on his own, to compose himself, and to pretend to be asleep when she came. There was nothing she could say to comfort him. He did not want her understanding, he would only take it for pity. He wanted respect, not companionship, honour, loyalty and obedience, not the vulnerability of love.

She would stay here for at least another

hour, saying nothing, making tea for them if they wanted it, fetching and carrying, doing as she was told.

The morning began the same, but at quarter to ten suddenly Dermot stiffened, and the moment after, Bridget also heard the whine of an engine. Then it cut out. Sean went to the door. Everyone else waited.

The silence was so heavy the wind in the eaves was audible, and the far cry of seabirds. Then the footsteps came, light and quick on the path. The door opened and Roisin came in. She looked at Bridget, at her father, then at Paddy.

Paddy beckoned her to follow him, and they went into Liam's bedroom.

Dermot started to fidget, playing with the gun in his hand, his eyes moving from Connor to the door, and back again.

Connor stared at Bridget.

"I don't know," she whispered. "Some kind of a message?"

"Maybe it's money . . ." he mouthed the words.

"Where would she get money?"

"The party," Liam was close beside them. "They'd pay for you, Dad. Everybody'd give."

Bridget looked at him, he was thin, very young. In the sunlight from the window she could see the down on his cheek. He shaved, but he didn't really need to. He was desperate to believe that his father was loved, that the party respected him and valued him enough to find whatever money was demanded. She was afraid they would be politically astute enough to see the value of a martyr—three martyrs—four if Roisin were included. Please God she wasn't! Why had Eamonn sent her, instead of coming himself?

The door opened and Roisin came out, Paddy on her heels.

Dermot stared at him, the question in his eyes.

Connor was so stiff he seemed in danger of losing his balance.

Paddy faced him. "There's been a slight change, Mr. O'Malley," he said softly, his voice a trifle husky. "One of your lieutenants, Michael Adair, has gone over to the moderate camp."

"Liar," Connor said immediately. "Adair would never desert. I know him."

Bridget felt her stomach clench inside her. Connor spoke as if to change one's mind were a personal affront to him. She had felt Adair's doubt for several months, but Connor never listened to him, he always assumed he knew what he was going to say, and behaved as if he had said it. Almost as he did with her!

"It's not desertion, Dad," Roisin said awkwardly. "It's what he believes."

Connor's eyebrows rose. "Are you saying it's true? He's betrayed us?" His contempt was like a live thing in the air.

"He has either to betray you or himself," Roisin told him.

"Rubbish! You don't know what you're talking about, Rosie. I've known Adair for twenty years. He believes as I do. If he's turned his coat it's for money, or power, or because he's afraid."

Roisin seemed about to say something, then she turned away.

"Traitor!" Liam said, his pent-up fury breaking out at last. "You're best without him, Dad. Someone like that's worth nothing to them, or to us."

Connor touched his hand to Liam's shoulder in the briefest gesture, then he turned to Paddy. "It makes no difference. If you thought it would, then you're a fool!"

"Adair carries weight," Paddy answered. "He represents many. He could still carry most of your party, if you gave him your backing."

"My backing?" Connor was incredulous. "A traitor to the cause? A man who would use my imprisonment by you to seize the leadership? He's a greedy, disloyal coward, and you'd deal with him? You're an idiot! Give him a chance and he'll turn on you too."

"He's doing what he believes," Roisin repeated, but without looking at her father.

"Of course he is!" Connor spat. "He believes in opportunism, power at any price, even betrayal. That's so plain only a fool couldn't see it."

Paddy glanced at Bridget, but she knew the denial was in his eyes, and she looked away. Roisin was right. Connor had expected, bullied, ignored argument and difference, until Adair had been silenced. Now in Connor's absence, and perhaps hearing that he was hostage, he had found the courage to follow his own convictions. But she did not want Paddy even to guess that she knew that. It seemed like one more betrayal.

Paddy smiled, a funny, lopsided gesture with self-mocking in it as well as humour, and a touch of defiance. "Well, Mr. O'Malley, aren't there enough fools? But for the sake of argument, what if you were to give Adair your support, written in your own hand, for Roisin here to take back, would that not be the best choice open to you now? All things considered, as it were?"

"Ally myself with traitors?" Connor said witheringly. "Endorse what has happened, as if I'd lost my own morality? Never."

"Then maybe you could just retire, on grounds of health?" Paddy suggested. He was leaning against the kitchen bench, his long legs crossed at the ankle, the light from the window shining on his hair. The lines on his face marked his tiredness. He had seemed younger at the beginning, now it was clear he was over forty. "Give it some thought."

"There's nothing wrong with my health!" Connor said between his teeth.

Dermot twisted his gun around. "We could always do something about that," he said with a curl to the corners of his mouth that lacked even the suggestion of humour.

"And explain it as what?" Paddy rounded on him. "A hunting accident? Don't be stupid." He turned back to Connor before he saw the moment of bleak, unadulterated hatred pass over Dermot's face, making it dead, like a mask. Then he controlled it again, and was merely flat, watchful. It touched Bridget with a quite different, new fear, not just for herself but for Paddy.

"You're wasting your time," Connor answered, exactly as Bridget had known he would. He was not even considering it, not acknowledging change, he never had. Now he did not even know how to. He had made his own prison long before Paddy and his men came here with guns.

"Are you sure about that?" Paddy said softly.

"Of course he is!" Dermot cut across him. "He was never going to agree to anything. I could have told you that the day you set out." He jerked his head towards Sean, standing at the far door and the way out to the beach. Sean straightened up, holding his gun steady in front of him.

Paddy was still staring at Connor, as if he believed that he might yet change his mind. He did not see Dermot move behind him, raise his arm and bring it across sharply on the side of his jaw. Paddy crumpled to his knees, and then forward onto the floor.

"Don't!" Sean warned as Connor gasped, and Roisin made a sharp move towards Paddy. "He'll be alright."

Dermot was taking the gun out of Paddy's waistband. He stood up again, watching Bridget rather than Connor or Liam. "Just don't do anything heroic, and you'll be alright."

"Alright?" Connor was stupefied. "What

the hell's the matter with you? He's your own man!"

Roisin ignored him and bent to Paddy who was already stirring. She held out her arms and helped him to climb up, slowly, his head obviously paining him. He looked confused and dizzy. He was gentle with Roisin, but did not speak to her. Awkwardly he turned to Dermot, who was careful to keep far enough away from him he was beyond Paddy's arm's length. He held the gun high and steady.

Sean was watching the rest of them. "The first one to move gets shot," he said in a high-pitched voice, rasping with tension. "None of you'd want that, now would you?"

"Dermot?" Paddy said icily.

"Don't be losing your temper, now," Dermot answered. "We did it your way, and it didn't work. Not that I thought it would, mind. O'Malley wasn't even going to change. He can't. Hasn't left himself room. But you wouldn't be told that, you and your kind. Now we'll do it our way, and you'll take the orders."

"You fool!" Paddy's voice was bitter and dangerous. "You'll make a hero out of him! Twice as many will follow him now!"

"Not the way we'll do it," Dermot answered him. "And stop giving me orders,

Paddy. You're the one that'll do as you're told now."

"I'm not with you. This is the wrong way. We already decided . . ."

"You did! Now I'm in charge . . ."

"Not of me. I told you, I'm not with you," Paddy repeated.

Dermot's smile was thin as arctic sunshine. "Yes, you are, Paddy, my boy. You can't leave us. For that matter, you never could—at least not since we shot those two lads up the hill, and buried them. Markers are left, just so we could direct anyone to find them, if it were ever in our interest." He raised his black eyebrows in question.

The blood drained out of Paddy's skin, leaving him oddly grey. He was not old, yet Bridget, looking at him, could see the image of when he would be.

"That's why you killed them . . ." he said with understanding at last.

"We killed them, Paddy," Dermot corrected. "You were part of it, just like us. Law makes no difference who pulls the trigger. Isn't that right, Mr. O'Malley?" He glanced at Connor, who was still standing motionless. Then the ease in Dermot's face vanished and his voice was savage. "Yes of course that's why we did it! You're one of us, whether you like it or not. No way out, boy, none at all. Now are you going to take your gun and behave properly? Help us to keep all these people good and obedient, until we decide exactly what's to be done with them. Now we've got the pretty Roisin as well, perhaps Mr. O'Malley will be a bit more amenable, not to mention her husband. Though to tell the truth, maybe we'd be better not to mention him for yet a while, don't you think?"

Paddy hesitated. Again there was silence in the kitchen, except for the wind and the sound of the gulls along the shore.

Liam stared at his father, waiting.

At last Paddy held out his hand.

"For the gun?" Dermot enquired. "In a little while, when I'm satisfied you've really grasped your situation. Now, Mrs. O'Malley." He turned to Bridget. "We've one extra to feed. You'd best take a good look at your rations, because there'll be no more for a while. I'm not entirely for trusting Paddy here, you see. Not enough to send him off into the village, that is. So be sparing, eh? No seconds for anyone, in fact you'd best be cutting down a bit on firsts as well. D'you understand me?"

"Of course I understand you," she replied. "We've got a whole sack of potatoes. We'll live on those if we have to. We haven't much to season them with, but I suppose that doesn't matter a lot. Connor, you'd better move in with Liam, and Roisin can come in with me. I'll wash the sheets. It's a good day for drying."

"That's a good girl, now," Dermot approved. "Always do what you're told, don't you! I'd like a woman like you for myself, one day. Or maybe with a bit more fire. You can't be much fun. But then I don't suppose Mr. O'Malley is much of a man for fun, is he? Got a face like he bit on a lemon, that one. What do you see in him, eh?"

She stopped at the doorway into the hall and looked directly at him. "Courage to fight for what he believes, without violence," she answered. "Honour to keep his word, whatever it cost him. He never betrayed anyone in his life." And without waiting to see his reaction, or Connor's, she went out across the hall and into first Liam's bedroom, taking the sheets off the bed, then her own. They could watch her launder them if they wanted to. She wouldn't have gone anywhere before, but with Roisin here as well, she was even more of a prisoner.

There was a separate laundry room with a big tub, a washboard, plenty of soap, a mangle to squeeze out the surplus water, and a laundry basket to carry them out to the line where the sea wind would blow them dry long before tonight.

She began to work, because it was so much easier than simply standing or sitting, as Connor and Liam were obliged to do.

She had filled the tub with water and was scrubbing the sheets rhythmically against the board, feeling the ridges through the cotton, when she heard the footsteps behind her. She knew it was Roisin.

"Can I help, Mum?" she asked.

"It doesn't take two of us," Bridget replied. "But stay if you want to."

"I can put them through the mangle," Roisin offered.

They worked without speaking for several minutes. Bridget didn't want to think about why Roisin was here, who had sent her with the message, but the thoughts crowded into her mind like a bad dream returning, even when her eyes were open. She was the only one they had told where they were going, not even Adair knew. Roisin had tried so hard to persuade Connor to moderate his position on education before they left. Bridget had never seen her argue with such emotion before. When he had refused, she had looked defeated, not just on a point of principle, but as if it hurt her profoundly, emotionally. The loss was somehow permanent.

"You're pregnant, aren't you?" she said aloud.

Roisin stopped, her hands holding the rinsed sheets above the mangle. The silence was heavy in the room. "Yes," she said at last. "I was going to tell you, but it's only a few weeks. It's too soon."

"No, it isn't," Bridget said quietly. "You know, that's all that matters." She wanted to be happy for her, congratulate her on the joy to come, but the words stuck in her throat. It was why Roisin had betrayed her father to the moderates, and for Eamonn. She not only wanted peace, she needed it, for her child. Everything in her now was bent on protecting it. It was part of her, tiny and vulnerable, needing her strength, her passion to feed it, keep it warm, safe, loved, defended from the violence of men who cared for ideas, not people. Perhaps Bridget would have done the same. She remembered Roisin when she was newborn. Yes, she would have done whatever was necessary to protect her, or Liam, or any child.

Roisin started the mangle again, keeping her face turned away; she did not yet realize that Bridget knew. She would have done it for Eamonn as well. He was another idealist, like Connor. Roisin was vulnerable herself. It was her first child. She might be ill with it.

She would certainly be heavy, awkward, needing his love and his protection, his emotional
support. She might even be afraid. Childbirth was lonely and painful, full of doubts
that the baby would be well, that she would
be able to look after it properly, do all the
things she should to see nothing went wrong,
that the tiny, demanding, infinitely precious
life was cherished. She would be desperately
tired at times. She would need Eamonn. Perhaps she had no choice either.

"Your father doesn't know," she said
aloud.

Roisin pulled the wrung sheet out from
between the rollers and put it into the basket, ready for the line. "I'll tell him in a couple of months."

"Not about the child." Bridget passed her
the next sheet. "He doesn't know that you
told the I.R.A., or whoever Paddy is, where
we are."

Roisin froze, hands in the air. There was
no sound but the dripping water.

"I know why you did it," Bridget went on. "I
might have done the same, to protect you, before you were born. But don't expect him to
understand. I don't think he will. Or Liam."

Roisin's face pinched, looking bruised as
if some deep internal injury were finally
showing. Roisin realized she had always ex-

pected her father to reject her, but she had not thought about Liam before. It was a new pain, and the reality of it might be far worse than the idea, even now.

"I thought when he realized how many of us want peace, he might change, even a little," she said. "Someone has to! We can't go on like this, year after year, hating and mourning, then starting all over again. I won't!" She bit her lips. "I want something better."

"We all do," Bridget said quietly. "The difference is in how much we are prepared to pay for it."

Roisin turned away, blinking, and bent her attention to the sheets.

When they were finished Bridget took them out and hung them on the line, propping up the middle of it with the long pole, notched at the end to hold the rope taut so the sheets did not touch the ground.

How could she protect Connor from the disillusion he would feel when he knew that it was Roisin who had betrayed him? All the reasoning in the world would not make any difference to the pain. Even if his mind understood, his emotions would not. First Adair, now his own daughter.

And what would Liam make of it? He was confused, all his previous certainties were slipping away. His father, whom he had believed to be so strong he wavered in nothing, was losing control of his temper, being ordered around by men he despised, and he did nothing about it. Now his sister was the cause of it all, and for an emotion and a loyalty he could only guess at.

She yanked up the heavy pole, awkward, tipping in her hands from the weight of the wet sheets with the wind behind them. Suddenly it eased and she lurched forward, straight into Paddy.

"Sorry," he apologized, propping the pole up for her.

"Thank you," she said abruptly, realizing he had done it to help. The wind filled the sheets, bellying them high and wide, temporarily shielding them from view of the house.

"Your husband'll work it out that it was her," he said quietly. "You can't stop it."

"I know." She was not sure if she resented his understanding, or in an obscure way it was a comfort not to face it alone. No, that was absurd. Of course she was alone. Paddy was the enemy. Except that he too had been betrayed by someone he had trusted, and it had been very neatly done, using his own plan against him, enmeshing him in a double murder so he had no retreat. He must feel like a complete fool.

"It doesn't seem as if either of us can stop much, does it?" she said drily.

He looked at her with a black laughter in his eyes, self-mocking. He was trying to hide the hurt, and she knew in that instant that it was deep, and there were probably years of long and tangled debt behind it, and perhaps love of one sort or another. She was not sure if she wanted to know the story or not. She might understand it more than she could afford to.

She glanced at him again. He was staring out towards the horizon, his eyes narrowed against the light off the water, even though the sun was behind them.

"It didn't go where you expected, did it?" she said aloud.

"No," he admitted. "I never thought Connor would yield easily, but I thought he would, when he realized Adair had crossed over. I misjudged him. I guess the ransom for freeing him from old promises was too high. Too high for him, I mean."

"I know what you mean," she answered. "I'm not sure he knows how to escape now. He's more hostage to the past than he is to you. You're just more physically apparent, that's all. It's . . ." She thought how she was going to phrase what she wanted to say. She was thinking aloud, but if she spoke to anyone at all, it would be to Paddy.

"It's a matter of admitting it," he said for her, watching to see if she understood. "We've invested so much of ourselves, our reason for living, whatever it is that makes us think we matter, into a set of ideals. It takes a hell of a lot of courage to say that we didn't get it right—even in the silence of the small hours, staring up at the bedroom ceiling, let alone to all the angry men who've invested the same, and can't face it either. Some of us will die of pride, I think. If you don't believe in yourself, what have you got left?"

"Not much," she replied. "At least—not here. Ireland doesn't forgive—not politically. We're too good at remembering all the wrong things. We don't learn to forget and start again."

He smiled, turning to look at the water again. "Could we, do you think, then? There'd be a lot of things I'd do differently and dear God, but wouldn't I!" He swivelled suddenly to stare very directly at her. "What would you do differently, Bridget?"

She felt the colour rise up her face. His eyes were too frank, far too gentle, intruding into her thoughts, the hopes and sor-

rows she needed to keep locked inside herself. And yet she allowed him to go on looking at her, the wind streaming past them,
the sun bright, the gulls wheeling and crying above.

"You won't tell me, will you?" he said at
last, his voice urgent.

She lowered her gaze. "No, of course I
won't. None of it matters anyway, because
we can't."

"But I would like to have known," he said,
as she started to walk back in again, forgetting the laundry basket half hidden by the
blowing sheets.

She did not answer. He did know. He had
seen it in her face.

Inside the house the tension was almost un-
bearable. Everyone was in the kitchen, so
Dermot and Sean could watch them. Liam
was sitting at the table swinging his legs and
alternately kicking and missing the opposite
chair. Dermot was glaring at him, obviously
irritated. Now and then Liam looked up at
him, sullen and miserable, almost daring to
defy him, then backing off again.

Sean was standing in his usual place
against the door frame to the hall and the
bedrooms and bathroom. Connor stood by

the sink and the window to the side, and the long view of the path winding up over the hill, where he and Liam had gone fishing on the first day.

Roisin was looking through the store cupboards putting things in and out, as if it made any difference.

"Stop doing that," Connor told her. "Your mother knows what we've got. We'll have to live on potatoes, until Dermot here gets tired of them."

Roisin kept her back to him, and replaced the tins and packets, such as they were, exactly where she had found them. She was stiff, her fingers fumbling. Twice she lost her grip on a tin and knocked one over. Bridget realized she was waiting for Connor to piece the facts together and realize it was she who had betrayed them.

It was still early, but she wanted to break the prickling, near silence, the tiny, meaningless remarks.

"I'll make lunch," she said to no one in particular.

"Too soon," Dermot told her. "It's only half past eleven. Wait an hour."

"I'll make a fish pie," she answered. "It takes a while. And I could bake something at the same time. There's flour."

"Don't bake for them!" Connor ordered.

"Good idea," Dermot responded instantly. "You do that, Mrs. O'Malley. Bake us something. Can you do a cake?"

"Don't be ridiculous!" Connor moved forward as if he would stop her physically. "For God's sake, Bridget! Adair's betrayed us, told these terrorists where we are, so he can take my place and sell out the party! We're prisoners until God knows when, and you're going to bake a cake! Haven't you the faintest understanding of what's happening?"

She walked past him to the cupboard and bent down in front of it. She was aware of Paddy by the back door, and knew he was watching her. She needed to defend herself.

"Not eating isn't going to help," she replied. "And you may be perfectly happy to have potatoes for every meal, but I'd rather have something else as well. A cake is one of the few things we have the ingredients for. I'd rather bake than just stand here."

"You're playing into their hands! Don't you give a damn that Adair betrayed us? Billy and Ian are lying dead up there. Doesn't that mean something to you? You knew them for months! Ian helped you mend the gas. He stood in this kitchen only a couple of days ago." His voice was shaking. "How can you bake a cake, when this man tells you to?" He jerked his arm towards

Dermot. "Are you so afraid you'll do anything at all?"

She stood up slowly and turned around to face him. "No, Connor, I'm not. I'm baking a cake because I want to. I haven't forgotten what happened to Billy and Ian, but nothing's going to change that now. Maybe we could have when we had the chance, but now it's too late. And fighting over what we eat isn't brave, it's just stupid. Please move away from the bench, so I can use it."

Connor remained where he was.

Liam was watching them, his eyes wide, the muscles in his face drawn tight with fear.

"Please, Dad?" Roisin said urgently.

He raised his head and looked at her.

Bridget watched them. It was as if time stood still. She could hear the ticking of the clock on the wall as the secondhand jumped. She knew what was going to happen before it did, in the endless moment from one word to the next.

"You want me to do what he says?" Connor asked. "Why is that, Rosie? I told Adair we were going away for a week. I didn't tell him where to. Who did?"

Whether she could have lied or not, Bridget did not know, but Roisin must have felt her face give her away. The tide of colour must have burned.

"Eamonn!" Connor said bitterly. "You told him, and he told Adair!"

"No," Roisin looked straight back at him. "Adair never knew. He still doesn't, so far as I know. I told Paddy, because you won't listen and you won't change. I'm going to have a child, and I'm tired of endless fighting and killing from one generation to the next, with no hope of ever being different. I want peace for my children to grow up in. I don't want them afraid all the time, as I am, and everyone I know. No sooner do we build something than it's broken again. Everybody I know has lost someone, either dead, or maimed. Everybody's got to move. If you won't, then we need somebody else to lead us who will!"

"You did?" He said the words as if he could hardly believe them. He swayed a little, and gripped hard on the edge of the bench, his knuckles white. "You betrayed me, the cause? My own daughter? You got Billy and Ian murdered, and the rest of us, your mother and your brother held here at gunpoint—because you're going to have a baby? Great heaven, girl, do you think you're the only woman in Ireland to have a child?"

Bridget stepped forward. "Leave her alone, Connor. She did what she thought was right. She thought you'd change. She was wrong. But I think I'd have done the same thing in her place. We protect our children. We always have."

He stared at her. "You sound as if you agree with her?" It was an accusation.

Bridget heard Paddy move a little to her left, towards Connor, but closer to her also. She was afraid he was going to say something to protect her, then she realized how stupid that was, but the feeling was still there. She rushed into speech to prevent it. "I understand. It's not the same thing. Please, Connor, this isn't the time for us to quarrel, and not here."

His face twisted in scorn. "You mean in front of this lot?" he jabbed his elbow to indicate Dermot and Sean. "Do you think I give a damn what they think about me, or anything else?"

"Perhaps you don't," she replied. "Have you considered that I might? Or Roisin, or Liam?"

"Liam's with me," he stared at her icily. "As far as Roisin is concerned, she is no longer part of my family. She is Eamonn's wife, not my daughter. That's what she has chosen." He moved fractionally so he turned his shoulder away from Roisin, as if physically cutting her out of his sight, and his knowledge.

Bridget saw her face pale, and the tears fill her eyes, but she did not defend herself. Bridget understood why Connor had said it, she could feel his hurt as if it were a tangible thing in the room, but she still was angry with him for his reaction. He should have been larger, braver of heart than to cut Roisin off. She was not betraying for money or power, but because she believed differently, even though she had deceived him.

"What she did was wrong, at least the way she did it," she said aloud. "But you contributed to that also."

"I what?" he shouted.

"You contributed to that also! You don't listen. You never really listen to anybody else, unless they agree with you." She stopped abruptly as she saw Connor's face.

Behind her Dermot was applauding. She turned and saw his smile, a wide, curling leer. His hands were held up, clapping where the others could see them.

"It's a crusade of hate, with you, isn't it!" she said to him with disgust. "It's nothing to do with religion, or freedom, or any of the other things you talk about with such affected passion. It's about power and hate. The only way you can make anybody notice you is with a gun in your hand." Her contempt was so fierce, carrying her shame for

Connor, her pain for all of them, that her voice was laden with it.

Dermot swung his arm back to strike her, and Paddy lunged forward and took the blow on his forearm, sending him off balance a little, landing against the table.

Dermot swivelled to face him, his lips drawn back in a snarl. Then suddenly he stopped, and a hard, artificial smile replaced his anger. "Oh, very good!" he said sarcastically. "But I'm not that stupid, Paddy. A grandstand rescue isn't going to make any difference now. You're with us, like it or not. Remember Billy and whatever his name is, up on the hillside? You put them there just as much as we did, so you can forget trying to win Mrs. O'Malley over. She can't help you, and she won't."

"She's right," Paddy said bitterly. "You only know how to destroy."

"I know how to clear the ground, before I build," Dermot said between his teeth. "More than you do, Paddy. You're soft. You haven't the guts to go through with it, or the judgement to know who's strong and who's weak."

"Or who's honest and who isn't," Paddy added, but he did not move.

By the far door Sean relaxed a little. "I'm going to cook," Bridget said abruptly. "If you want to eat, you'll let me get on with it. If you don't, there's not much but raw potatoes. Take your choice." And without waiting for permission she went to the sink, filled the bowl with water, and took a dozen large potatoes out of the sack and began to scrub them.

Silence descended again until every movement she made sounded like a deliberate noise. The wind was rising. She heard Connor say he was going to the bathroom. There was a brief altercation with Dermot, and then he went.

She looked at Liam, still sitting at the kitchen table, and saw the misery in him. He glared back at her, as if she were the enemy. He was furious with her because she was not defending Connor. She had seen his defeat, and Liam could not forgive her for that. It confirmed it in his own mind, and made his confusion deeper. He so desperately wanted certainty, a cause to believe in and someone to admire, and in the space of a few days it had all been torn away and the flaws exposed, the fear and the weaknesses, the self-absorption.

She turned back at the potatoes. They were half done. She had to persuade Connor and Paddy both to run, in opposite directions. Paddy must know Dermot wasn't

going to let them live? Was that regret deep
enough in him for him to risk his life? Or
would he sacrifice them all for his own
chance?

And what about Connor? Would he risk
himself, to save his family? Or did he really
believe it was his duty to live, that only he
was fit to lead the cause? She remembered
him in her mind's eye as he had been when
they first met, his face smooth and eager, his
eyes full of dreams. There had been something beautiful in him then.

She was nearly finished with the potatoes.
How long had she got left before Dermot
made his decision? Once he moved it would
be too late. Little time, very little. She must
think of a way to persuade each person to
do what she needed them to. With Paddy
and Connor it would have to be without
their knowing.

She cut the potatoes into manageable
pieces, awkward with the one blunt slice
they had left her, and put them into the
largest saucepan, then covered them with
cold water. They were going to be very
bland. There was a little bacon left, and
some eggs, but she did not want to use them
now. It would betray the fact that she knew
that there was no tomorrow. She must behave as if she believed rescue, or at least re-

lease, was only a matter of time. There was no ideological difference between Connor and Eamonn, or Adair, only the means to attain the goal of Protestant safety. Just as there was none between Dermot and Paddy, only the means to unite Ireland under Catholic rule. No one expected anyone to cross the gulf between them. Their quarrels with each other were nothing compared with the enmity that stretched down the generations dividing Catholic from Protestant, Southern Ireland from the North. Paddy might not be on Dermot's side, but he would never be against him. There was all the difference in the world between those two things. She must not trust him.

But she did not have to tell the truth—to anyone!

She looked at the potatoes. They needed salt, and flavour. An idea began in her mind. It was small, not very good, but there was not time to spend waiting for something better. Dermot was nervous, shifting uneasily already. How much longer would it be before he decided to act? He could shoot them, her whole family, everyone she loved most in the world. Paddy would be upset, for a while, caught in an act of barbarity he had not intended, but violence was part of Irish life. Almost every week someone was killed. It would not make any difference to him, in the long run.

"Liam!" she said suddenly. "I want to move something in my room. Will you come and help me please?"

Sean looked up suspiciously.

"In my bedroom I'd rather have my son, thank you," she said sharply. "Liam!"

He stood up slowly, unwilling. He looked for a moment at his father, and received no response. He followed Bridget along the short corridor to the bedroom.

"What is it?" he said as soon as they were inside.

"Close the door," she told him.

He frowned.

"Be quick!"

"What is it?" He looked puzzled now, and a little alarmed, but he obeyed.

"Listen to me, Liam." She swallowed down the tension inside her, and deliberately banged the chair on the floor as if moving it. There was no time to think of the risk she was taking, or whether this might be the most costly mistake in her life. "Dermot can't afford to let us go. He killed Billy and Ian, and there isn't going to be any resolution to this. He'll realize it soon, and then he'll kill us."

His eyes were dark, wide with horror at what she had said, and the leap to denial.

"It's true," she said with as much firmness as she could put into her trembling voice. "One of us has to escape and get to the village."

"But, Mum . . ." he began.

"It has to be you," she cut across him. "There's no time to argue. Roisin can't do it, your father won't. I can't outrun them, but you might. I'm going to try and make Dermot think both Paddy and your father are escaping, in opposite directions, which should occupy Sean as well. When you see the chance, run for it. Don't go straight to the village, it's what they would expect. Go round the shore, and bring help back, as soon as you can. Do you understand?"

He stood silently, absorbing what she had said.

"Do you understand?" she repeated, her ears straining to catch the sound of Sean or Dermot in the passage outside. "There's no time to think of anything better."

"Are you sure?" he asked, his voice was tight, high pitched with fear.

"Yes. He can't let us go. Your father will hunt him down for ever. You know that!"

"Yes. Okay. When?"

"In a few minutes." She gulped. "If I can make Paddy and your father go in opposite directions—or I can make Dermot and Sean think they have."

"Does Dad know?"

"No. If I tell anyone else it'll raise their suspicions. Now go back and behave just the same. Go on."

He hesitated only a second, started to say something, then swallowed it back and went out. She followed a moment later.

In the kitchen everything was exactly as they had left it, Sean standing by the door, Dermot by the window behind the table, Roisin at the stove and Connor sitting on the hard-backed chair nearest to the back door. Bridget went back to the sink and ran the tap until it was hot, replaced the water over the potatoes, put in salt, and set them on the stove.

She must do it now, before thinking about it sapped away her courage. She had nothing to lose. She must keep that in mind all the time. If Dermot realized, and acted before she did, they would all be dead.

She started to speak, but her mouth was too dry. She licked her lips and started again. "This is going to be very bland. I need something with a bit of flavour to add to it." She turned to Connor. "There are some wild onions growing up the hillside, about a hundred yards or so. Can you go and dig them up?"

He looked surprised.

"Please?" She must not make it too urgent, or Dermot would suspect. Surely worrying about food would sound so normal, so sure of tomorrow and the next day?

"Send Liam," Connor replied, without moving from his seat.

Dermot straightened up. "You're neither of you going! Do you think I'm stupid? A hundred yards up the hill, and I'd never see you again. How do I know there even are onions up there?"

Liam raised his head. "There are," he replied, without looking at Bridget.

"Then Paddy can get them," Dermot said. He looked at Paddy. "Do you know an onion when you see it?"

"Probably not," Paddy said with a half smile. "But I can smell one, or taste it." He turned to Bridget. "Do you want them dug up, or pulled, or what?"

"Dig up two or three," she told him. "There's a small garden fork just outside the back door. Thank you." She could not meet his eyes for more than a moment, but by then he was gone anyway, closing the door after him.

Now she had to get Connor to go in the

other direction, or at the worst to make Dermot think he had. She glanced at Dermot. The slight sneer was still on his face. Could she trick him into doing what she wanted? Had she understood him?

She turned back to Connor. "Will you help me get the sheets in, please? It's a lot easier to fold them with two. Roisin, watch the potatoes."

"Liam can do it," Connor replied, remaining where he was.

Bridget let her annoyance show in her face. "Why can't you do something for once?" she answered back.

Liam's head turned from Bridget to Connor and back again. He was very pale.

"Liam, do as you're told," Connor said abruptly. "Help your mother with the laundry."

Uncertainly Liam started to climb to his feet.

"Sit down!" Dermot snapped. "O'Malley, she's right. You go and do something for a change. Help her fold the sheets! Move!"

Sean was smiling, leaning against the door to the passage, his gun also raised.

Slowly Connor rose to his feet, his face red, his lips in a tight, thin line. He opened the back door and Bridget followed him out. He walked ahead, without looking at her, and went straight to the line.

She hesitated. Now that the moment had come she found it desperately hard to do, almost too hard.

"Don't," she said as he unpegged the first end.

"What the hell's the matter now?" he snapped.

She moved closer to him, making him back behind the billowing sheet and he grabbed at it with his left hand.

"Connor, they won't let us go," she said levelly. "Dermot can't. And as soon as he realizes you aren't going to give in, which will be any moment, he'll shoot us. He has no choice. He'll go back over the border into Southern Ireland, and at least he'll have a head start before anybody even knows what's happened to us."

"They'll hunt him down like a rat," Connor said contemptuously.

"How? Who'll be alive to say it was him?"

The full horror of it dawned on him. She saw it in the void of his eyes.

There was a shout from the house. She could not tell from where, because the sheets were in the way, but it was Sean's voice. There was no time to hesitate.

"We've got to go! Now, while there's

time," she urged. Was Sean coming after them already? What about Paddy up the hill? If he'd kept on looking for the onions, which didn't exist, he should be over the slight rise and out of sight. Why wasn't one of them looking for him? Surely after their betrayal of him they couldn't trust him, could they? Not enough to let him out of their sight, this side of the border?

Then she heard Sean's voice again, calling Paddy's name, sharp and angry.

"Is this what you intend to do?" Connor demanded. "Turn and run, and leave Liam and Rosie to take Dermot's rage when he finds we've escaped? And you were the one who said you understood Rosie putting her baby before the cause, sacrificing her morality to save her child! You disgust me, Bridget. I thought I knew you, and you were better than that. You've betrayed not only me, but everything you said you believed in, everything you are."

"Don't stand there preaching!" She heard her voice rising out of control. "Run! While there's time! For the cause, if not for yourself!"

There was a shout of rage from up the hill, and then another. They both turned towards the sound, but they could see nothing. Then there was a scream, a shot, and then silence again.

The back door slammed open and for an instant she saw Dermot's head and shoulders outlined against the house, his arm raised.

"Run!" she yelled at Connor. Then in case Dermot had not heard her, she did it again.

This time Connor obeyed. At least they were drawing one of them away from the house, and there had been no shots inside. She caught up and grasped his hand, leaping over the sea grass and running down onto the beach, towards the low rise of the sandhills twenty yards away, where at least there was a little shelter.

They were racing over the beach near the tide line where it was hard and firm when the shot rang out. Connor stumbled and pitched forward, his hand going to the scarlet stain spreading across his chest and shoulder. He rolled over and over, carried by the impetus of his speed, then lay still.

Bridget stopped abruptly, and turned back. Dermot was standing on the soft sand just in front of the sea grass, the gun still held out stiffly in front of him. He could pull the trigger again any moment, all he had to do was tighten his grip.

She waited. Oddly, she did not feel a terrible loss. As long as Liam had got away, some-

thing was saved. Perhaps Rosie had even
gone with him, at least far enough to be out
of sight of the house. If they were alive, that
was enough. This was a clean way to go, here
on the wind-scoured sand, one shot, and
then oblivion. It was a bad time, but a good
place to die.

Dermot lowered the gun, not right down,
he still held it in his hand. He started walking towards her, slowly, evenly.

She did not know if Connor was dead or
not. A chest wound might be fatal, but it
looked to be closer to the shoulder. Just in
case he was still alive, she moved away from
him, and began to walk up towards Dermot.
If he came down for her, he might shoot
Connor again, to make sure. She increased
her speed. Strange how she could walk so
easily even where the wet sand changed to
dry, slithering under her feet. She stopped a
couple of yards from Dermot. He was smiling. "You don't care that I shot him, do
you!" he said, his eyes wide, his face pale,
with two spots of colour high on his cheeks.

"You have no idea what I care about," she
answered coldly.

"You'd rather have Paddy, wouldn't you!"
he said, his lip curling in disgust. "He'd use
you, and throw you away."

"It really doesn't matter what you think," she said wearily, surprised that now it was almost over, that was the exact truth. All she needed was time for Liam to get away, and Rosie if possible.

He jerked the gun towards the house. "Well, let's see, shall we? Is the Reverend O'Malley's wife as cold as she looks? Or his daughter, the pretty turncoat, Roisin?"

If she refused to move, she had no doubt he'd shoot her where she stood. Walking would gain a little more time, only minutes, but minutes might count. She obeyed slowly, passing him and walking ahead. She stepped carefully through the clumps of sea grass and onto the level stretch at the beginning of the lawn, or what passed for it. The sheets were still billowing. She had no idea where Paddy or Sean were. There was no sign of life from the house, and no sound.

She reached the sheets blowing towards her. The plastic laundry basket was just in front of her, empty. Why should she go into the house with him without a fight? It was ridiculous. Rosie might be in there. Even if she wasn't, why should Bridget herself let it be easy?

She picked up the laundry basket and

threw it at his feet just as he emerged between the sheets.

He had not had time to see it and dodge. It caught him below the knee, hard enough to cost him his balance. He stumbled forward, still clutching the gun. He was on his hands and knees, his face twisted with rage, already beginning to scramble up again.

She reached for the clothes prop, grasping it with both hands, yanking it out from the line and swinging it wide in a half circle, low and with all her weight behind it. The end of it caught him on the side of the head with a crack she felt all the way through her own body. He fell over sideways and lay motionless, the gun on the ground six inches away from his limp hand.

She scrambled over to him, her body shaking. She picked up the gun, then looked at him. The upper side of his head was bleeding, but not heavily. She knew from the angle of it that he had to be dead. His neck was broken.

She felt sick. But she still needed to face Sean and Paddy.

She walked shakily over to the back door and opened it. The kitchen was empty. "Roisin!" she called.

"Mum!"

The bedroom door crashed wide and Roisin came out, her eyes hollow with fear.

There was no time for hugging, for any kind of emotion. "Where's Liam?" Bridget asked. "And Sean?"

"Liam's gone, as you told him," Roisin answered. "Sean went up the hill after Paddy. I heard him shout. I don't think he came back. Where's Dad?" The look in her face betrayed that she knew.

"On the beach," Bridget replied. "Dermot's dead. I don't know how your father is, I hadn't time to look. Take the tea towels and see what you can do."

"What about you?"

"I've got the gun. I have to find Paddy and Sean."

"But . . ."

"I'll shoot them if I have to." She meant it. She could, to save herself and Roisin. "Go."

Roisin obeyed, and Bridget set off carefully up the slope, watching all the time, keeping both hands on the gun, ready to use it the moment she saw any kind of movement in the tussock and heather.

She had followed the track all the way to the ridge and beyond when she saw Paddy's body lying in a clear patch of grass, his shirt a pale blur against the green, except for the wide, bright red stain of blood across his chest, right in the middle.

Where was Sean? There was no time to allow herself grief now, or any understanding of the waste. She had heard only one shot. Sean was alive somewhere, maybe waiting, watching her right now. Then why had he not shot her too?

She turned around slowly, searching for him, expecting the noise and the shattering weight of the bullet any moment. But all she could hear was the distant sound of the waves, and bees in the heather. She could see where it had been broken, trampled down around Paddy as if there had been a fight there. Stems were snapped off, the damp earth gouged. The trail led to the edge of a little gully.

Very carefully she walked over towards it, holding the gun in front of her, ready to squeeze the trigger. She looked from right to left, and back again. If Sean was still here, why did he do nothing?

She came to the edge and looked over. She saw him immediately, lying on his back, his body twisted, hips and legs crooked, right thigh bent half under him. His eyes were still open and the gun was in his hand.

He shot at her, but it went wide. The angle was wrong, and he could not move to correct it.

She thought of shooting him, but it was cold-blooded, unnecessary. She also thought of saying something, but that was unnecessary too. His pelvis was broken, and at least one leg. He was not going to get out of the gully until someone came and carried him.

She turned away and walked back down the path to the house, and into the kitchen. It was empty. The pan of potatoes, half cooked, stood in the sink. Roisin had thought to take them off before she went into the bedroom.

She should go down to the sand and see if Connor was alive, and if she could do anything for him. At least she could help Roisin. She picked up a couple of bath towels and went out of the back door and past Dermot's body, over the edge of the sea grass and down the sand. Roisin was walking towards her, Connor lay beyond, where he had fallen, but she could not see clearly enough to know whether he was in exactly the same position or not.

Roisin stopped as Bridget reached her. Her face was wet with tears.

"He won't let me do anything," her voice choked. "He won't even listen to me."

So he was alive! And conscious. For an instant Bridget did not even know if she was glad or not. It was as if walls had closed around her again.

"Mum?"

Yes, of course she must be pleased. He didn't deserve to die. And she didn't have to stay inside the walls. It was her choice. If she paid her ransom she could escape. She must never forget that again.

"He may change his mind," she said gently, looking at Roisin. "But if he doesn't, you'll have to accept that. You made your choice, it's your husband and your child. It doesn't matter what I think, it's what you think. But if you care, I believe it's the right choice. And whether I like what you do or not, I shall always love you . . . as you will love your child." She touched Roisin for a moment, just the tips of her fingers to her cheek, then she walked on down the sand to Connor.

He looked at her as she knelt beside him. He was very white and there was a lot of blood on his shirt, but he seemed quite conscious. The tea towels were on the sand. She picked them up, rolled them into pads, and placed them firmly on the wound.

He winced and cried out.

"You should have let Rosie do it," she told him. "It would have cost you less blood."

"Never!" he said between clenched teeth, gasping as the pain washed through him in waves. "I don't have a daughter."

"That's your choice, Connor." She took one of the long towels to put it round him as well as she could to keep the pads in place. "I expect she'll forgive you for your part in this. Whether you forgive her or not is up to you, but I can tell you now, if you don't, you'll lose more than she will. By the way, you might like to know that Sean killed Paddy, but his own pelvis is broken, and he's lying up the hill in a gully. He'll be there until someone carries him out."

He stared at her as if he had never seen her before.

"And I killed Dermot." She could hardly believe her own words, though they were terribly, irrevocably true.

He blinked.

"Liam's gone for the police," she added. "I expect they'll be here soon. And a doctor."

"I can't feel my left arm," he said.

She rolled up the other towel and eased it under his head. "I'll go up to the house and get a blanket. You should be kept warm."

"No!" He breathed in and out slowly. "Stay with me!"

"Oh, I probably will," she replied. "But on my terms, Connor, not on yours. And I'm going to get the blanket. Shock can kill, if you get cold." She rose to her feet, smiling very slightly to herself, and walked back up the sand.

JOYCE CAROL OATES

From the publication of her first book of short stories, *By the North Gate*, in 1963, **Joyce Carol Oates** has been the most prolific of major American writers, turning out novels, short stories, reviews, essays, and plays in an unceasing flow as remarkable for its quality as its volume. Writers who are extremely prolific often risk not being taken as seriously as they should—if one can write it that fast, how good can it be? Oates, however, has largely escaped that trap, and even her increasing identification with crime fiction, at a time when the field has attracted a number of other mainstream literary figures, has not lessened her reputation as a formidable author in the least. Many of Oates's works contain at least some elements of crime and mystery, from the National Book Award winner *them*, through the Chappaquiddick fictionalization *Black Water* and the Jeffrey Dahmer-inspired serial-killer novel *Zombie*, to her controversial 738-page fictionalized biography of Marilyn Monroe, *Blonde*. The element of detection becomes explicit with the investigations of amateur sleuth Xavier Kilgarvan in the novel *The Mysteries of Winterthurn*, which, the author explains in an afterword to the 1985 paperback edition, "is the third in a quintet of experimental novels that deal, in genre form, with nineteenth- and early twentieth-century America." Why would a literary writer like Oates choose to work in such "deliberately confining structures"? Because "the formal discipline of 'genre' ... forces us inevitably to a radical re-visioning of the world and the craft of fiction." Oates, who numbers among her honors in a related genre the Bram Stoker Award of the Horror Writers of America, did not establish an explicit crime-fiction identity until *Lives of the Twins* appeared under the pseudonym

Rosamund Smith. Initially intended to be a secret, the identity of Smith was revealed almost immediately, and later novels were bylined Joyce Carol Oates (large print) writing as Rosamund Smith (smaller print). Her new pseudonym is Lauren Kelly, author most recently of *Blood Mask*. Other recent novels are *The Falls*, *Missing Mom*, and *Rape: A Love Story*.

THE CORN MAIDEN:
A LOVE STORY

Joyce Carol Oates

APRIL

YOU ASSHOLES!

Whywhy you're asking here's why her hair.*

I mean *her hair*! I mean like I saw it in the sun it's pale silky gold like corn tassels and in the sun sparks might catch. And her eyes that smiled at me sort of nervous and hopeful like she could not know (but who could know?) what is Jude's wish. For I am Jude the Obscure, I am the Master of Eyes. I am not to be judged by crude eyes like yours, assholes.

There was her mother. I saw them to-

*Note: The Sacrifice of the Corn Maiden is a composite drawn from traditional sacrificial rituals of the Iroquois, Pawnee, and Blackfoot Indian tribes.

gether. I saw the mother stoop to kiss *her*.
That arrow entered my heart. I thought *I
will make you see me.* I would not forgive.

Okay then. More specific. Some kind of
report you assholes will type up. Maybe
there's a space for the medical examiner's
verdict *cause of death.*

Assholes don't have a clue do you. If you
did you'd know it is futile to type up reports
as if such will grant you truth or even "facts."

Whywhy in the night at my computer
clickclickclicking through galaxies and
there was revealed on my birthday (March
11) the Master of Eyes granting me my wish
that is why. *All that you wish will be made man-
ifest in Time. If you are Master.*

Jude the Obscure he named me. In cyberspace we were twinned.

Here's why in sixth grade a field trip to
the museum of natural history and Jude
wandered off from the silly giggling children to stare at the Onigara exhibit of the
Sacrifice of the Corn Maiden. *This exhibit is
graphic in nature and not recommended for children younger than sixteen unless with parental
guidance* you stepped through an archway
into a fluorescent-lit interior of dusty dis-
play cases to stare at the Corn Maiden with
braided black bristles for hair and flat face
and blind eyes and mouth widened in an

expression of permanent wonder beyond
even terror and it was that vision that entered Jude's heart powerful as any arrow
shot into the Corn Maiden's heart that is
why.

Because it was an experiment to see if
God would allow it that is why.

Because there was no one to stop me that
is why.

DISCIPLES

We never thought Jude was serious!

We never thought it would turn out like
it did.

We never thought . . .

. . . just *didn't*!

Never meant . . .

. . . *never*!

Nobody had anything against . . .

. . . . .

(Jude said it's Taboo to utter that name.)

Jude was the Master of Eyes. She was
our leader all through school. Jude was
just so cool.

Fifth grade, Jude instructed us how to get
HIGH sniffing S. Where Jude got S., we
didn't know.

Seventh grade, Jude gave us E. Like the

older kids take. From her secret contact at the high school Jude got E.

When you're HIGH you love everybody but the secret is basically you don't give a damn.

That is what's so nice! HIGH floating above Skatskill like you could drop a bomb on Skatskill Day or your own house and there's your own family rushing out their clothes and hair on fire and screaming for help and you would smile because it would not touch you. That is HIGH.

Secrets no one else knew.

XXX videos at Jude's house.

Jude's grandmother Mrs. Trahern the widow of somebody famous.

Feral cats we fed. Cool!

Ritalin and Xanax Jude's doctors prescribed, Jude only just pretended to take that shit. In her bathroom, a supply of years.

Haagen Dazs French Vanilla ice cream we fed the Corn Maiden.

The Corn Maiden was sleepy almost at once, yawning. Ice cream tastes so good! Just one pill ground up, a half teaspoon. It was magic. We could not believe it.

Jude said you can't believe the magic you possess until somebody instructs how to unleash it.

The Corn Maiden had never been to Jude's house before. But Jude was friendly to her beginning back in March. Told us the Master of Eyes had granted her a wish on her birthday. And we were counted in that wish.

The plan was to *establish trust.*

The plan was to prepare for the Corn Maiden in the knowledge that one day there would be the magic hour when (Jude predicted) like a lightning flash lighting up the dark all would become clear.

This was so. We were in readiness, and the magic hour was so.

There is a rear entrance to the Trahern house. We came that way.

The Corn Maiden walked! On her own two feet the Corn Maiden walked, she was not forced, or carried.

Of her own volition Jude said.

It was not so in the Onigara Indian ceremony. There, the Corn Maiden did not come of her own volition but was kidnapped.

An enemy tribe would kidnap her. She would never return to her people.

The Corn Maiden would be buried, she would be laid among the corn seed in the sun and the earth covered over her. Jude told us of this like an old fairy tale to make you smile, but not to ask *Why.*

Jude did not like us to ask *Why.*

The Corn Maiden was never threatened. The Corn Maiden was treated with reverence, respect, and kindness.

(Except we had to scare her, a little. There was no other way Jude said.)

On Tuesdays and Thursdays she would come by the 7-Eleven store on the way home from school. Why this was, Jude knew. Mostly high school kids hang out there. Older kids, smoking. Crummy mini-mall on the state highway. Rug remnant store, hair and nails salon, Chinese takeout & the 7-Eleven. Behind are Dumpsters and a stink like something rotten.

Feral cats hide in the scrub brush behind the Dumpsters. Where it's like a jungle, nobody ever goes.

(Except Jude. To feed the feral cats she says are her Totem.)

At the 7-Eleven Jude had us walk separate so we would not be seen walking together.

Four girls together, somebody might notice.

A girl by herself, or two girls, nobody would notice.

Not that anybody was watching. We came by the back way.

Some old long-ago time when servants lived down the hill. When they climbed the hill to the big houses on Highgate Avenue.

Historic old Skatskill estate. That was where

Jude lived with just her grandmother. On TV it would be shown. In the newspapers. In *The New York Times* it would be shown on the front page. The house would be called *an eighteenth-century Dutch-American manor house.* We never knew about that. We never saw the house from the front. We only just went into Jude's room and a few other rooms. And there was the cellar.

From Highgate Avenue you can't see the Trahern house very well, there is a ten-foot stone wall surrounding it. This wall is old and crumbling but still you can't see over it. But through the gate that's wrought iron you can see if you look fast, while you're driving by.

Lots of people drive by now I guess.

NO PARKING NO PARKING NO PARKING on Highgate. Skatskill does not welcome strangers except to shop.

The Trahern estate it would be called. The property is eleven acres. But there is a short-cut from the rear. When we brought the Corn Maiden to the house, we came from the rear. Mostly the property is woods. Mostly it is wild, like a jungle. But there are old stone steps you can climb if you are careful. An old service road that's grown over with brambles and blocked off at the bottom of the hill by a concrete slab but you can walk around the slab.

This back way, nobody would guess. Three minutes' walk from the mini-mall.

Nobody would guess! The big old houses on Highgate, way up the hill, how the rear of their property slopes down to the state highway.

Jude warned *The Corn Maiden must be treated with reverence, respect, kindness, and firmness. The Corn Maiden must never guess the fate that will be hers.*

SUBURBAN SINGLE MOM, LATCHKEY DAUGHTER

"Marissa?"

The first signal something was wrong, no lights in the apartment.

The second, too quiet.

"Marissa, honey . . . ?"

Already there was an edge to her voice. Already her chest felt as if an iron band was tightening around it.

Stepped inside the darkened apartment. She would swear, no later than 8 P.M.

In a dreamlike suspension of emotion shutting the door behind her, switching on a light. Aware of herself as one might see oneself on a video monitor behaving with conspicuous normality though the circumstances have shifted, and are not normal.

A mother learns not to panic, not to betray weakness. Should a child be observing.

"Marissa? Aren't you . . . are you *home*?"

If she'd been home, Marissa would have the lights on. Marissa would be doing her homework in the living room with the TV on, loud. Or the CD player on, loud. When she was home alone Marissa was made uneasy by quiet.

Made her nervous she said. Made her think scary thoughts like about dying she said. Hear her own heartbeat she said.

But the apartment was quiet. In the kitchen, quiet.

Leah switched on more lights. She was still observing herself, she was still behaving calmly. Seeing, from the living room, down the hall to Marissa's room that the door to that room was open, darkness inside.

It was possible—it was! if only for a blurred desperate moment—to think that Marissa had fallen asleep on her bed, that was why . . . But Leah checked, there was no slender figure lying on the bed.

No one in the bathroom. Door ajar, darkness inside.

The apartment did not seem familiar

somehow. As if furniture had been moved. (It had not, she would determine later.) It was chilly, drafty as if a window had been left open. (No window had been left open.)

"Marissa? Marissa?"

There was a tone of surprise and almost-exasperation in the mother's voice. As if, if Marissa heard, she would know herself just mildly scolded.

In the kitchen that was empty, Leah set the groceries down. On a counter. Wasn't watching, the bag slumped slowly over. Scarcely saw, a container of yogurt fell out.

Marissa's favorite, strawberry.

So quiet! The mother, beginning to shiver, understood why the daughter hated quiet.

She was walking through the rooms, and would walk through the few rooms of the small first-floor apartment calling *Marissa? Honey?* in a thin rising voice like a wire pulled tight. She would lose track of time. She was the mother, she was responsible. For eleven years she had not lost her child, every mother's terror of losing her child, an abrupt physical loss, a theft, a stealing-away, a *forcible abduction.*

"No. She's here. Somewhere . . ."

Retracing her steps through the apartment. There were so few rooms for Marissa to be in! Again opening the bathroom door, wider. Opening a closet door. Closet doors. Stumbling against . . . Struck her shoulder on . . . Collided with Marissa's desk chair, stinging her thigh. "Marissa? Are you *hiding*?"

As if Marissa would be hiding. At such a time.

Marissa was eleven years old. Marissa had not hidden from her mother to make Mommy seek her out giggling and squealing with excitement in a very long time.

She would protest she was not a negligent mother.

She was a working mother. A single mother. Her daughter's father had disappeared from their lives, he paid neither alimony nor child support. How was it her fault, she had to work to support her daughter and herself, and her daughter required special education instruction and so she'd taken her out of public school and enrolled her at Skatskill Day . . .

They would accuse her. In the tabloids they would crucify her.

Dial 911 and your life is public fodder. Dial 911 and your life is not yours. Dial 911 and your life is forever changed.

Suburban Single Mom. Latchkey Daughter.

Eleven-Year-Old Missing, South Skatskill.

She would protest it was not that way at all! It was not.

Five days out of seven *it was not.*

Only Tuesdays and Thursdays she worked late at the clinic. Only since Christmas had Marissa been coming home to an empty apartment.

No. It was not ideal. And maybe she should have hired a sitter except . . .

She would protest she had no choice but to work late, her shift had been changed. On Tuesdays/Thursdays she began at 10:30 A.M. and ended at 6:30 P.M. Those nights, she was home by 7:15 P.M., by 7:30 P.M. at the latest she was home. She would swear, she was! Most nights.

How was it her fault, slow-moving traffic on the Tappan Zee Bridge from Nyack then north on route 9 through Tarrytown, Sleepy Hollow, to the Skatskill town limits, and route 9 under repair. Traffic in pelting rain! Out of nowhere a cloudburst, rain! She had wanted to sob in frustration, in fury at what her life had become, blinding headlights in her eyes like laser rays piercing her brain.

But usually she was home by 8 P.M. At the latest.

Before dialing 911 she was trying to think: to calculate.

Marissa would ordinarily be home by about 4 P.M. Her last class ended at 3:15 P.M. Marissa would walk home, five and a half suburban blocks, approximately a half mile, through (mostly) a residential neighborhood. (True, 15th Street was a busy street. But Marissa didn't need to cross it.) And she would walk with school friends. (Would she?) Marissa didn't take a school bus, there was no bus for private school children, and in any case Marissa lived near the school because Leah Bantry had moved to the Briarcliff Apts. in order to be near Skatskill Day.

She would explain! In the interstices of emotion over her *missing child* she would explain.

Possibly there had been something special after school that day, a sports event, choir practice, Marissa had forgotten to mention to Leah . . . Possibly Marissa had been invited home by a friend.

In the apartment, standing beside the phone, as if waiting for the phone to ring, trying to think what it was she'd just been thinking. Like trying to grasp water with her fingers, trying to think . . .

A friend! That was it.

What were the names of girls in Marissa's class . . . ?

Of course, Leah would telephone! She was shaky, and she was upset, but she would make these crucial calls before involving the police, she wasn't a hysterical mother. She might call Leah's teacher whose name she knew, and from her she would learn the names of other girls, she would call these numbers, she would soon locate Marissa, it would be all right. And the mother of Marissa's friend would say apologetically, *But I'd thought Marissa had asked you, could she stay for supper. I'm so very sorry!* And Leah would say quickly laughing in relief, *You know how children are, sometimes. Even the nice ones.*

Except: Marissa didn't have many friends at the school.

That had been a problem in the new, private school. In public school she'd had friends, but it wasn't so easy at Skatskill Day where most students were privileged, well-to-do. Very privileged, and very well-to-do. And poor Marissa was so sweet, trusting and hopeful and easy to hurt if other girls chose to hurt her.

Already in fifth grade it had begun, a perplexing girl-meanness.

In sixth grade, it had become worse.

"Why don't they like me, Mommy?"

"Why do they make fun of me, Mommy?"

For in Skatskill if you lived down the hill from Highgate Avenue and/or east of Summit Street you were known to be *working class*. Marissa had asked what it meant? Didn't everybody work? And what was a *class* was it like . . . a class in school? A class*room*?)

But Leah had to concede: even if Marissa had been invited home by an unknown school friend, she wouldn't have stayed away so long.

Not past 5 P.M. Not past dark.

Not without calling Leah.

"She isn't the type of child to . . ."

Leah checked the kitchen again. The sink was empty. No package of chicken cutlets defrosting.

Tuesdays/Thursdays were Marissa's evenings to start supper. Marissa loved to cook, Mommy and Marissa loved to cook together. Tonight they were having chicken jambalaya which was their favorite fun meal to prepare together. "Tomatoes, onions, peppers, cajun powder. Rice . . ."

Leah spoke aloud. The silence was unnerving.

If I'd come home directly. Tonight.

The 7-Eleven out on the highway. That's where she had stopped on the way home.

Behind the counter, the middle-aged Indian gentleman with the wise sorrowful eyes would vouch for her. Leah was a frequent customer, he didn't know her name but he seemed to like her.

Dairy products, a box of tissues. Canned tomatoes. Two six-packs of beer, cold. For all he knew, Leah had a husband. *He* was the beer drinker, the husband.

Leah saw that her hands were trembling. She needed a drink, to steady her hands.

"Marissa!"

She was thirty-four years old. Her daughter was eleven. So far as anyone in Leah's family knew, including her parents, she had been "amicably divorced" for seven years. Her former husband, a medical school drop-out, had disappeared somewhere in Northern California; they had lived together in Berkeley, having met at the university in the early 1990s.

Impossible to locate the former husband/father whose name was not Bantry.

She would be asked about him, she knew. She would be asked about numerous things.

She would explain: eleven is too old for day care. Eleven is fully capable of coming home alone . . . Eleven can be responsible for . . .

At the refrigerator she fumbled for a can of beer. She opened it and drank thirstily.

The liquid was freezing cold, her head began to ache immediately: an icy spot like a coin between her eyes. *How can you! At a time like this!* She didn't want to panic and call 911 before she'd thought this through. Something was staring her in the face, some explanation, maybe?

Distraught Single Mom. Modest Apartment.

Missing Eleven-Year-Old. "Learning Disabilities."

Clumsily Leah retraced her steps through the apartment another time. She was looking for . . . Throwing more widely open those doors she'd already opened. Kneeling beside Marissa's bed to peer beneath in a burst of desperate energy.

And finding—what? A lone sock.

As if Marissa would be hiding beneath a bed!

Marissa who loved her mother, would never never wish to worry or upset or hurt her mother. Marissa who was young for her age, never rebellious, sulky. Marissa whose idea of badness was forgetting to make her bed in the morning. Leaving the bathroom mirror above the sink splattered with water.

Marissa who'd asked Mommy, "Do I have a daddy somewhere like other girls, and he knows about me?"

Marissa who'd asked, blinking back tears,

"Why do they make fun of me, Mommy? Am I *slow*?"

In public school classes had been too large, her teacher hadn't had time or patience for Marissa. So Leah had enrolled her at Skatskill Day where classes were limited to fifteen students and Marissa would have special attention from her teacher and yet: still she was having trouble with arithmetic, she was teased, called "slow" . . . Laughed at even by girls she'd thought were her friends.

"Maybe she's run away."

Out of nowhere this thought struck Leah. Marissa had run away from Skatskill. From the life Mommy had worked so hard to provide for her.

"That can't be! Never."

Leah swallowed another mouthful of beer. Self-medicating, it was. Still her heart was beating in rapid thumps, then missing a beat. Hoped to God she would not faint . . .

"Where? Where would Marissa go? *Never.*"

Ridiculous to think that Marissa would run away!

She was far too shy, passive. Far too uncertain of herself. Other children, particularly older children, intimidated her. Because Marissa was unusually attractive, a beautiful child with silky blond hair to her shoulders, brushed by her proud mother until it shone, sometimes braided by her mother into elaborate plaits, Marissa often drew unwanted attention; but Marissa had very little sense of herself and of how others regarded her.

She had never ridden a bus alone. Never gone to a movie alone. Rarely entered any store alone, without Leah close by.

Yet it was the first thing police would suspect, probably: Marissa had run away.

"Maybe she's next door. Visiting the neighbors."

Leah knew this was not likely. She and Marissa were on friendly terms with their neighbors but they never visited one another. It wasn't that kind of apartment complex, there were few other children.

Still, Leah would have to see. It was expected of a mother looking for her daughter, to check with neighbors.

She spent some time then, ten or fifteen minutes, knocking on doors in the Briarcliff Apts. Smiling anxiously into strangers' startled faces. Trying not to sound desperate, hysterical.

"Excuse me . . ."

A nightmare memory came to her, of a distraught young mother knocking on their door, years ago in Berkeley when she'd first moved in with her lover who would become

Marissa's father. They'd been interrupted at
a meal, and Leah's lover had answered the
door, an edge of annoyance in his voice;
and Leah had come up behind him, very
young at the time, very blond and privileged, and she'd stared at a young Filipino
woman blinking back tears as she'd asked
them *Have you seen my daughter* . . . Leah
could not remember anything more.

Now it was Leah Bantry who was knocking on doors. Interrupting strangers at
mealtime. Apologizing for disturbing them,
asking in a tremulous voice *Have you seen my
daughter* . . .

In the barracks-like apartment complex
into which Leah had moved for economy's
sake two years before, each apartment
opened directly out onto the rear of the
building, into the parking area. This was a
brightly lit paved area, purely functional,
ugly. In the apartment complex there were
no hallways. There were no interior stairs,
no foyers. There were no meeting places for
even casual exchanges. This was not an attractive condominium village overlooking
the Hudson River but Briarcliff Apts, South
Skatskill.

Leah's immediate neighbors were sympathetic and concerned, but could offer no

help. They had not seen Marissa, and of course she hadn't come to visit them. They promised Leah they would "keep an eye out" and suggested she call 911.

Leah continued to knock on doors. A mechanism had been triggered in her brain, she could not stop until she had knocked on every door in the apartment complex. As she moved farther from her own first-floor apartment, she was met with less sympathy. One tenant shouted through the door to ask what she wanted. Another, a middle-aged man with a drinker's flushed indignant face, interrupted her faltering query to say he hadn't seen any children, he didn't know any children, and he didn't have time for any children.

Leah returned to her apartment staggering, dazed. Saw with a thrill of alarm she'd left the door ajar. Every light in the apartment appeared to be on. Almost, she thought Marissa must be home now, in the kitchen.

She hurried inside. "Marissa . . . ?"

Her voice was eager, piteous.

The kitchen was empty of course. The apartment was empty.

A new, wild idea: Leah returned outside, to the parking lot, to check her car which was parked a short distance away. She peered inside, though knowing it was locked and empty. Peered into the back seat.

Am I going mad? What is happening to me . . .

Still, she'd had to look. She had a power-ful urge, too, to get into the car and drive along 15th Street to Skatskill Day School, and check out the building. Of course, it would be locked. The parking lot to the rear . . .

She would drive on Van Buren. She would drive on Summit. She would drive along Skatskill's small downtown of bou-tiques, novelty restaurants, high-priced an-tique and clothing stores. Out to the highway past gas stations, fast-food restau-rants, mini-malls.

Expecting to see—what? Her daughter walking in the rain?

Leah returned to the apartment, thinking she'd heard the phone ring but the phone was not ringing. Another time, unable to stop herself she checked the rooms. This time looking more carefully through Marissa's small closet, pushing aside Marissa's neatly hung clothes. (Marissa had always been obsessively neat. Leah had not wished to wonder why.) Stared at Marissa's shoes. Such small shoes! Trying to remem-

ber what Marissa had worn that morning . . .
So many hours ago.

Had she plaited Marissa's hair that morning? She didn't think she'd had time. Instead she had brushed it, lovingly. Maybe
she was a little too vain of her beautiful
daughter and now she was being punished . . . No, that was absurd. You are not
punished for loving your child. She had
brushed Marissa's hair until it shone and
she had fastened it with barrettes, mother-
of-pearl butterflies.

"Aren't you pretty! Mommy's little angel."

"Oh, Mommy. I am not."

Leah's heart caught. She could not understand how the child's father had abandoned them both. She was sick with guilt, it
had to be her fault as a woman and a
mother.

She'd resisted an impulse to hug Marissa,
though. At eleven, the girl was getting too
old for spontaneous unexplained hugs from
Mommy.

Displays of emotion upset children, Leah
had been warned. Of course, Leah hadn't
needed to be warned.

Leah returned to the kitchen for another
beer. Before dialing 911. Just a few swallows,
she wouldn't finish the entire can.

She kept nothing stronger than beer in the apartment. That was a rule of her mature life.

No hard liquor. No men overnight. No exposure to her daughter, the emotions Mommy sometimes felt.

She knew: she would be blamed. For she was blameable.

Latchkey child. Working mom.

She'd have had to pay a sitter nearly as much as she made at the clinic as a medical assistant, after taxes. It was unfair, and it was impossible. She could not.

Marissa was not so quick-witted as other children her age but she was not *slow*! She was in sixth grade, she had not fallen behind. Her tutor said she was "improving." And her attitude was so hopeful. *Your daughter tries so hard, Mrs. Bantry! Such a sweet, patient child.*

Unlike her mother, Leah thought. Who wasn't sweet, and who had given up patience long ago.

"I want to report a child missing . . ."

She rehearsed the words, struck by their finality. She hoped her voice would not sound slurred.

Where was Marissa? It was impossible to think she wasn't somehow in the apartment. If Leah looked again . . .

Marissa knew: to lock the front door behind her, and to bolt the safety latch when she was home alone. (Mommy and Marissa had practiced this maneuver many times.) Marissa knew: not to answer the door if anyone knocked, if Mommy was not home. Not to answer the telephone immediately but to let the answering machine click on, to hear if it was Mommy calling.

Marissa knew: never let strangers approach her. No conversations with strangers. Never climb into vehicles with strangers or even with people she knew unless they were women, people Mommy knew or the mothers of classmates for instance.

Above all Marissa knew: come home directly from school.

Never enter any building, any house, except possibly the house of a classmate, a school friend . . . Even so, Mommy must be told about this beforehand.

(Would Marissa remember? Could an eleven-year-old be trusted to remember so much?)

Leah had totally forgotten; she'd intended to call Marissa's teacher. From Miss Fletcher, Leah would learn the names of Marissa's friends. This, the police would expect her to know. Yet she stood by the phone indecisively, wondering if she dared call the woman; for if she did, Miss Fletcher would know that something was wrong.

The ache between Leah's eyes had spread, her head was wracked with pain.

Four-year-old Marissa would climb up onto the sofa beside Leah, and stroke her forehead to smooth out the "worry lines." Wet kisses on Mommy's forehead. "Kiss to make go away!"

Mommy's vanity had been somewhat wounded, that her child saw worry lines in her face. But she'd laughed, and invited more kisses. "All right, sweetie. Kiss-to-make-go-away."

It had become their ritual. A frown, a grimace, a mournful look—either Mommy or Marissa might demand, "Kiss-to-make-go-away."

Leah was paging through the telephone directory. *Fletcher.* There were more than a dozen *Fletchers.* None of the initials seemed quite right. Marissa's teacher's first name was—Eve? Eva?

Leah dialed one of the numbers. A recording clicked on, a man's voice.

Another number, a man answered. Politely telling Leah no: there was no one named "Eve" or "Eva" at that number.

This is hopeless, Leah thought.

She should be calling ERs, medical cen-

ters, where a child might have been
brought, struck by a vehicle for instance
crossing a busy street . . .

She fumbled for the can of beer. She
would drink hurriedly now. Before the police arrived.

Self-medicating a therapist had called it.
Back in high school she'd begun. It was
her secret from her family, they'd never
known. Though her sister Avril had
guessed. At first Leah had drunk with her
friends, then she hadn't needed her
friends. It wasn't for the elevated sensation,
the buzz, it was to calm her nerves. To
make her less anxious. Less disgusted with
herself.

I need to be beautiful. More beautiful.

He'd said she was beautiful, many times.
The man who was to be Marissa's father.
Leah was beautiful, he adored her.

They were going to live in a seaside town
somewhere in northern California, Oregon.
It had been their fantasy. In the meantime
he'd been a medical student, resentful of
the pressure. She had taken the easier
route, nursing school. But she'd dropped
out when she became pregnant.

Later he would say sure she was beautiful,
but he did not love her.

Love wears out. People move on.

Still, there was Marissa. Out of their coupling, Marissa.

Gladly would Leah give up the man, any man, so long as she had her daughter back.

If she had not stopped on the way home from the clinic! If she had come directly home.

She knew this: she would have to tell police where she had been, before returning home. Why she'd been unusually late. She would have to confess that, that she had been late. Her life would be turned inside-out like the pockets of an old pair of pants. All that was private, precious, rudely exposed.

The single evening in weeks, months . . . She'd behaved out of character.

But she'd stopped at the 7-Eleven, too. It was a busy place in the early evening. This wasn't out of character, Leah frequently stopped at the convenience store which was two blocks from Briarcliff Apts. The Indian gentleman at the cash register would speak kindly of her to police officers. He would learn that her name was Leah Bantry and that her daughter was missing. He would learn that she lived close by, on 15th Street. He would learn that she was a single mother, she was not married. The numerous six-packs of Coors she bought had not been for a husband but for her.

He'd seen her with Marissa, certainly. And so he would remember Marissa. Shy blond child whose hair was sometimes in plaits. He would pity Leah as he'd never had reason to pity her in the past, only just to admire her in his guarded way, the blond shining hair, the American-healthy good looks.

Leah finished the beer, and disposed of the can in the waste basket beneath the sink. She thought of going outside and dumping all the cans into a trash can, for police would possibly search the house, but there was no time, she had delayed long enough waiting for Marissa to return and everything to be again as it had been. Thinking *Why didn't I get a cell phone for Marissa, why did I think the expense wasn't worth it?* She picked up the receiver, and dialed 911.

Her voice was breathless as if she'd been running.

"I want—I want—to report a child missing."

LONE WOLVES

I am meant for a special destiny. I am!

He lived vividly inside his head. She lived vividly inside her head.

He was a former idealist. She was an unblinking realist.

He was thirty-one years old. She was thirteen.

He was tall/lanky/ropey-muscled five feet ten inches (on his New York State driver's license he'd indicated 5'11"), weighing one hundred fifty-five pounds. She was four feet eleven, eighty-three pounds.

He thought well of himself, secretly. She thought very well of herself, not so secretly.

He was a substitute math teacher/"computer consultant" at Skatskill Day School. She was an eighth grader at Skatskill Day School.

His official status at the school was *part-time employee.*

Her official status at the school was *full-tuition pupil, no exceptions.*

Part-time employee meant no medical/dental insurance coverage, less pay per hour than full-time employees, and no possibility of tenure. *Full-tuition, no exceptions* meant no scholarship aid or tuition deferral.

He was a relatively new resident of Skatskill-on-Hudson, eight miles north of New York City. She was a longtime resident who'd come to live with her widowed grandmother when she was two years old, in 1992.

To her, to his face, he was *Mr. Zallman;* otherwise, *Mr. Z.*

To him, she had no clear identity. One of

those Skatskill Day girls of varying ages (elementary grades through high school) to whom he gave computer instructions and provided personal assistance as requested.

Even sixth grader Marissa Bantry with the long straight corn-tassel hair he would not recall, immediately.

The kids he called them. In a voice that dragged with reluctant affection; or in a voice heavy with sarcasm. *Those kids!*

Depending on the day, the week. Depending on his mood.

Those others she called them in a voice quavering with scorn.

They were an alien race. Even her small band of disciples she had to concede were losers.

In his confidential file in the office of the principal of Skatskill Day it was noted *Impressive credentials/recommendations, interacts well with brighter students. Inclined to impatience. Not a team player. Unusual sense of humor. (Abrasive?)*

In her confidential file (1998–present) in the principal's office it was noted in reports by numerous parties *Impressive background (maternal grandmother/legal guardian Mrs. A. Trahern, alumna/donor/trustee/ emeritus), im-*

pressive I.Q. (measured 149, 161, 113, 159 ages 6, 9, 10, 12), flashes of brilliance, erratic academic performance, lonely child, gregarious child, interacts poorly with classmates, natural leader, antisocial tendencies, lively presence in class, disruptive presence in class, hyperactive, apathetic, talent for "fantasy," poor communication skills, immature tendencies, verbal fluency, imagination stimulated by new projects, easily bored, sullen, mature for age, poor motor coordination skills, diagnosed Attention Deficit Syndrome age 5/prescribed Ritalin with good results/mixed results, diagnosed borderline dyslexic age 7, prescribed special tutoring with good results/mixed results, honor roll fifth grade, low grades/failed English seventh grade, suspended for one week Oct. 2002 "threatening" girl classmate, reinstated after three days/legal action brought against school by guardian/mandated psychological counseling with good/mixed results. (On the outside of the folder, in the principal's handwriting *A challenge!*)

He was swarthy skinned, with an olive complexion. She had pale translucent skin.

He was at the school Monday/Tuesday/Thursday unless he was subbing for another teacher which he did, on the average, perhaps once every five weeks. She was at the school five days a week, Skatskill Day was her turf!

Hate/love she felt for Skatskill Day. *Love/hate.*

(Often, as her teachers noted, she "disappeared" from classes and later "reappeared." Sulky/arrogant with no explanation.)

He was a lone wolf and yet: the great-grandson of immigrant German Jews who had come to the United States in the early 1900s. The grandson and son of partners at Cleary, McCorkle, Mace & Zallman, Wall Street brokers. She was the lone grandchild of New York State Supreme Court Justice Elias Trahern who had died before she was born and was of no more interest to her than the jut-jawed and bewigged General George Washington whose idealized image hung in the school rotunda.

His skin was dotted with moles. Not disfiguring exactly but he'd see people staring at these moles as if waiting for them to move.

Her skin was susceptible to angry-looking rashes. Nerve-rashes they'd been diagnosed, also caused by picking with her nails.

He was beginning to lose his thick-rippled dark hair he had not realized he'd been vain about. Receding at the temples so he wore it straggling over his collar. Her hair exploded in faded-rust fuzz like dandelion seed around her pointy pinched face.

He was Mikal. She was Jude.

He'd been born Michael but there were so many damn Michaels!

She'd been born Judith but—*Judith! Enough to make you want to puke.*

Lone wolves who scorned the crowd. Natural aristocrats who had no use for money, or for family connections.

He was estranged from the Zallmans. Mostly.

She was estranged from the Traherns. Mostly.

He had a quick engaging ironic laugh. She had a high-pitched nasal-sniggering laugh that surprised her suddenly, like a sneeze.

His favored muttered epithet was *What next?* Her favored muttered epithet was *Bor-ing!*

He knew: prepubescent/adolescent girls often have crushes on their male teachers. Yet somehow it never seemed very real to him, or very crucial. Mikal Zallman living in his own head.

She detested boys her own age. And most men, any age.

Making her disciples giggle and blush, at lunchtime flashing a paring knife in a swooping circular motion to indicate *cas-tra-tion:*

know what that is? as certain eighth grade boys passed noisily by carrying cafeteria trays.

Boys rarely saw her. She'd learned to go invisible like a playing card turned sideways.

He lived—smugly, it seemed to some observers—inside an armor of irony. (Except when alone. Staring at images of famine, war, devastation he felt himself blinking hot tears from his eyes. He'd shocked himself and others crying uncontrollably at his father's funeral in an Upper East Side synagogue the previous year.)

She had not cried in approximately four years. Since she'd fallen from a bicycle and cut a gash in her right knee requiring nine stitches.

He lived alone, in three sparely furnished rooms, in Riverview Heights, a condominium village on the Hudson River in North Tarrytown. She lived alone, except for the peripheral presence of her aging grandmother, in a few comfortably furnished rooms in the main wing of the Trahern estate at 83 Highgate Avenue; the rest of the thirty-room mansion had long been closed off for economy's sake.

He had no idea where she lived, as he had but the vaguest idea of who she was. She knew where he lived, it was three miles from 83 Highgate Avenue. She'd bicycled past Riverview Heights more than once.

He drove a not-new metallic blue Honda CR-V, New York license TZ 6063. She knew he drove a not-new metallic blue Honda CR-V, New York license TZ 6063.

Actually he didn't always think so well of himself. Actually she didn't always think so well of herself.

He wished to think well of himself. He wished to think well of all of humanity. He did not want to think *Homo sapiens is hopeless, let's pull the plug.* He wanted to think *I can make a difference in others' lives.*

He'd been an idealist who had *burnt out, crashed* in his late twenties. These were worthy clichés. These were clichés he had earned. He had taught in Manhattan, Bronx, and Yonkers public schools through his mid- and late twenties and after an interim of recovery he had returned to Columbia University to upgrade his credentials with a master's degree in computer science and he had returned to teaching for his old idealism yet clung to him like lint on one of his worn-at-the-elbow sweaters, one thing he knew he would never emulate his father in the pursuit of money, here in Skatskill-on-Hudson where he knew no one he could work part-time mostly helping kids with

computers and he would be respected here
or in any case his privacy would be respected, he wasn't an ambitious private
school teacher, wasn't angling for a permanent job, in a few years he'd move on but
for the present time he was contentedly em-
ployed, he had freedom to *feed my rat* as he
called it.

Much of the time she did not think so
well of herself. Secretly.

*Suicide fantasies are common to adolescents.
Not a sign of mental illness so long as they remain
fantasies.*

He'd had such fantasies, too. Well into his
twenties, in fact. He'd outgrown them now.
That was what *feeding my rat* had done for
Mikal Zallman.

Her suicide fantasies were cartoons, you
could say. A plunge from the Tappan Zee
Bridge/George Washington Bridge, footage
on the 6 P.M. news. A blazing fireball on a
rooftop. (Skatskill Day? It was the only roof
she had access to.) If you swallowed like five,
six Ecstasy pills your heart would explode
(maybe). If you swallowed a dozen barbitu-
rates you would fall asleep and then into a
coma and never wake up (maybe). With
drugs there was always the possibility of
vomiting, waking up in an ER your stomach
being pumped or waking up brain dam-

aged. There were knives, razor blades. Bleeding into a bathtub, the warm water gushing.

Eve of her thirteenth birthday and she'd been feeling shitty and her new friend/mentor the Master of Eyes (in Alaska, unless it was Antarctica) advised her why hate yourself Jude it's bor-ing. Better to hate *those others* who surround.

She never cried, though. Really really never cried.

Like Jude O's tear ducts are dried out. Cool!

Ducts reminded her of *pubes* she had first encountered as a word in a chat room, she'd looked up in the dictionary seeing *pubes* was a nasty word for those nasty crinkly/kinky hairs that had started to sprout in a certain place, between her legs. And in her armpits where she refused to apply *deodorant* until Grandmother nagnagged.

Grandmother Trahern was half blind but her sense of smell was acute. Grandmother Trahern was skilled at nagnagnagging, you might say it was the old woman's predominant skill in the eighth decade of her life.

Mr. Z! Maybe he'd smelled her underarms. She hoped he had not smelled her crotch.

Mr. Z. in computer lab making his way along the aisle answering kids' questions most of them pretty elementary/dumb ass she'd have liked to catch his eye and exchange a knowing smirk but Mr. Z. never seemed to be looking toward her and then she was stricken with shyness, blood rushing into her face as he paused above her to examine the confusion on her screen and she heard herself mutter with childish bravado *Guess I fucked up, Mr. Zallman, huh?* wiping her nose on the edge of her hand beginning to giggle and there was sexy/cool Mr. Z. six inches from her not breaking into a smile even of playful reproach giving not the slightest hint he'd heard the forbidden F-word from an eighth grade girl's innocent mouth.

In fact Mr. Z. had heard. Sure.

Never laugh, never encourage them. If they swear or use obscene or suggestive language.

And never touch them.

Or allow them to touch you.

The (subterranean) connection between them.

He had leaned over her, typed on her keyboard. Repaired the damage. Told her she was doing very well. Not to be discouraged! He didn't seem to know her name but maybe that was just pretense, his sense of humor. Moving on to the next raised hand.

Still, she'd known there was the (subterranean) connection.

As she'd known, first glimpsing the Corn Maiden in the seventh grade corridor. Silky blond corn-tassel hair. Shy, frightened.

A new girl. Perfect.

One morning she came early to observe the Corn Maiden's mother dropping her off at the curb. Good-looking woman with the same pale blond hair, smiling at the girl and hastily leaning over to kisskiss.

Some connections go through you like a laser ray.

Some connections, you just know.

Mr. Z. she'd sent an e-message *you are a master mister z.* Which was not like Jude O. to do because any message in cyberspace can never be erased. But Mr. Z. had not replied.

So easy to reply to a fucking e-message! But Mr. Z. had not.

Mr. Z. did not exchange a knowing smile/wink with her as you'd expect.

Ignored her!

Like he didn't know which one of them she was.

Like he could confuse her with *those others* her inferiors.

And so something turned in her heart like a rusty key and she thought calmly, *You will pay for this mister asshole Z and all your progeny.*

Thought of calling the FBI reporting a suspected terrorist, Mr. Z. was dark like an Arab, and shifty-eyed. Though probably he was a Jew.

Afterward vaguely he would recall *you are a master mister z* but of course he'd deleted it. So easy to delete an e-message.

Afterward vaguely he would recall the squirmy girl at the computer with the frizz hair and glassy staring eyes, a startling smell as of unwashed flesh wafting from her (unusual at Skatskill Day as it was unusual in the affluent suburban village of Skatskill) he had not known at the time, this was January/February, was Jude Trahern. He had no homeroom students, he met with more than one hundred students sometimes within days, couldn't keep track of them and had no interest in keeping track. Though a few days later he would come upon the girl in the company of a fattish friend, the two of them rummaging in a waste basket in the computer lab but he'd taken no special note of them as they'd hurried away embarrassed and giggling together as if he'd opened a door and seen them naked.

But he would remember: the same frizz-haired girl boldly seated at his computer after school one day frowning at the screen and click-clicking keys with as much authority as if the computer were her own and this time he'd spoken sharply to her, "Excuse me?" and she'd looked up at him cringing and blind-seeming as if she thought he might hit her. And so he joked, "Here's the famous hacker, eh?"——he knew it was the kindest as it was the wisest strategy to make a joke of the audacious/inexplicable behavior of adolescents, it wasn't a good idea to confront or embarrass. Especially not a girl. And this stunted-seeming girl hunched over like she was trying make herself smaller. Papery-thin skin, short upper lip exposing her front teeth, a guarded rodent look, furtive, anxious, somehow appealing. Her eyes were of the no-color of grit, moist and widened. Eyebrows and lashes scanty, near-invisible. She was so fiercely plain and her unbeautiful eyes stared at him so *rawly* . . . He felt sorry for her, poor kid. Bold, nervy, but in another year or so she'd be left behind entirely by her classmates, no boy would glance at her twice. He could not have guessed that the tremulous girl was the lone descendent of a family of reputation and privilege though possibly he might have guessed that her parents were long divorced from one another and perhaps from her as well. She was stammering some feeble explanation *Just needed to look something up, Mr. Zallman.* He laughed and dismissed her with a wave of his hand. Had an impulse, out of character for him, to reach out and tousle that frizzed floating hair as you'd rub a dog's head partly in affection and partly to chastise.

Didn't touch her, though. Mikal Zallman wasn't crazy.

"101 DALMATIANS"

Is she breathing, d'you think?

She is! Sure she is.

Oh God what if . . .

. . . she *is*. See?

The Corn Maiden slept by candlelight. The heavy open-mouthed sleep of the sedated.

We observed her in wonder. The Corn Maiden, in our power!

Jude removed the barrettes from her hair so we could brush it. Long straight pale blond hair. We were not jealous of the Corn Maiden's hair because *It is our hair now.*

The Corn Maiden's hair was spread out around her head like she was falling.

She was breathing, yes you could see. If you held a candle close to her face and throat you could see.

We had made a bed for the Corn Maiden, that Jude called a *bier*. Out of beautiful silk shawls and a brocaded bedspread, cashmere blanket from Scotland, goose-feather pillows. From the closed-off guest wing of the house Jude brought these, her face shining.

We fumbled to remove the Corn Maiden's clothes.

You pull off your own clothes without hardly thinking but another person, even a small girl who is lying flat on her back, arms and legs limp but heavy, that's different.

When the Corn Maiden was bare it was hard not to giggle. Hard not to snort with laughter ...

More like a little girl than she was like us.

We were shy of her suddenly. Her breasts were flat against her rib cage, her nipples were tiny as seeds. There were no hairs growing between her legs that we could see.

She was very cold, shivering in her sleep. Her lips were putty-colored. Her teeth were chattering. Her eyes were closed but you could see a thin crescent of white. So (almost!) you worried the Corn Maiden was watching us paralyzed in sleep.

It was Xanax Jude had prepared for the Corn Maiden. Also she had codeine and Oxycodone already ground to powder, in reserve.

We were meant to "bathe" the Corn Maiden, Jude said. But maybe not tonight.

We rubbed the Corn Maiden's icy fingers, her icy toes, and her icy cheeks. We were not shy of touching her suddenly, we wanted to touch her and touch and *touch*.

Inside here, Jude said, touching the Corn Maiden's narrow chest, there is a heart beating. An actual *heart*.

Jude spoke in a whisper. In the quiet you could hear the heart beat.

We covered the Corn Maiden then with silks, brocades, cashmere wool. We placed a goose-feather pillow beneath the Corn Maiden's head. Jude sprinkled perfume on the Corn Maiden with her fingertips. It was a blessing Jude said. The Corn Maiden would sleep and sleep for a long time and when she woke, she would know only our faces. The faces of her friends.

It was a storage room in the cellar beneath the guest wing we brought the Corn Maiden. This was a remote corner of the big old house. This was a closed-off corner of the house and the cellar was yet more remote, nobody would ever ever come here Jude said.

And you could scream your head off, nobody would ever hear.

Jude laughed, cupping her hands to her mouth like she was going to scream. But all that came out was a strangled choked noise.

There was no heat in the closed-off rooms of the Trahern house. In the cellar it was a damp cold like winter. Except this was meant to be a time of nuclear holocaust and no electricity we would have brought a space heater to plug in. Instead we had candles.

These were fragrant hand-dipped candles old Mrs. Trahern had been saving in a drawer since 1994, according to the gift shop receipt.

Jude said, Grandma won't miss 'em.

Jude was funny about her grandmother. Sometimes she liked her okay, other times she called her the old bat, said fuck her she didn't give a damn about Jude she was only worried Jude would embarrass her somehow.

Mrs. Trahern had called up the stairs, when we were in Jude's room watching a video. The stairs were too much for her, rarely she came upstairs to check on Jude. There was an actual elevator in the house (we had seen it) but Jude said she'd fucked it up, fooling with it so much when she was a little kid. Just some friends from school, Denise and Anita, Jude called back. You've met them.

Those times Mrs. Trahern saw us downstairs with Jude she would ask politely how we were and her snail-mouth would stretch in a grudging little smile but already she wasn't listening to anything we said, and she would never remember our names.

101 Dalmatians Jude played, one of her old videos she'd long outgrown. (Jude had a thousand videos she'd outgrown!) It was a young-kids' movie we had all seen but the Corn Maiden had never seen. Sitting cross-legged on the floor in front of the TV eating ice cream from a bowl in her lap and we finished ours and waited for her and Jude asked would she like a little more and the Corn Maiden hesitated just a moment then said *Yes thank you.*

We all had more Haagen Dazs French Vanilla ice cream. But it was not the same ice cream the Corn Maiden had not exactly!

Her eyes shining, so happy. Because we were her friends.

A sixth grader, friends with eighth graders. A guest in Jude Trahern's house.

Jude had been nice to her at school for a long time. Smiling, saying hello. Jude had a way of fixing you with her eyes like a cobra or something you could not look away. You were scared but sort of thrilled, too.

In the 7-Eleven she'd come inside to get a Coke and a package of nachos. She was on her way home from school and had no idea that two of us had followed her and one had run ahead, to wait. She was smiling to see Jude who was so friendly. Jude asked where was her mom and she said her mom was a nurse's aide across the river in Nyack and would not be home till after dark.

She laughed saying her mom didn't like her eating junk food but her mom didn't know.

Jude said what our moms don't know don't hurt them.

The Sacrifice of the Corn Maiden was a ritual of the Onigara Indians, Jude told us. In school we had studied Native Americans as they are called but we had not studied the Onigara Indians, Jude said had been extinct for two hundred years. The Iroquois had wiped out the Onigaras, it was survival of the fittest.

The Corn Maiden would be our secret. Beforehand we seemed to know it would be the most precious of our secrets.

Jude and the Corn Maiden walked ahead alone. Denise and Anita behind. Back of the stores, past the Dumpsters, we ran to catch up.

Jude asked would the Corn Maiden like to visit her house and the Corn Maiden said yes but she could not stay long. Jude said it was just a short walk. Jude pretended not to know where the Corn Maiden lived (but she knew: crummy apartments at 15th Street and Van Buren) and this was a ten-minute walk, approximately.

We climbed the back way. Nobody saw. Old Mrs. Trahern would be watching TV in her room, and would not see.

If she saw she would not seriously *see*. For at a distance her eyes were too weak.

The guest wing was a newer part of the house. It overlooked a swimming pool. But the pool was covered with a tarpaulin, Jude said nobody had swum in it for years. She could remember wading in the shallow end but it was long ago like the memory belonged to someone else.

The guest wing was never used either, Jude said. Most of the house was never used. She and her grandmother lived in just a few rooms and that was fine with them. Sometimes Mrs. Trahern would not leave the house for weeks. She was angry about something that had happened at church. Or maybe the minister had said something she found offensive. She had had to dismiss the black man who'd driven her "limo-zene." She had dismissed the black woman who'd been her cook and house cleaner for twenty years. Groceries were delivered to the house. Meals were mostly heat up in the microwave. Mrs. Trahern saw a few of her old friends in town, at the Village Woman's Club, the Hudson Valley Friends of History, and the Skatskill Garden Club. Her friends were not invited to the house to see her.

Do you love your mom? Jude asked the Corn Maiden.

The Corn Maiden nodded yes. Sort of embarrassed.

Your mom is real pretty. She's a nurse, I guess?

The Corn Maiden nodded yes. You could see she was proud of her mom but shy to speak of her.

Where is your dad? Jude asked.

The Corn Maiden frowned. She did not know.

Is your dad living?

Did not know.

When did you see your dad last?

Was not sure. She'd been so little . . .

Did he live around here, or where?

California, the Corn Maiden said. Berkeley.

My mom is in California, Jude said. Los Angeles.

The Corn Maiden smiled, uncertainly.

Maybe your dad is with my dad now, Jude said.

The Corn Maiden looked at Jude in wonderment.

In Hell, Jude said.

Jude laughed. That way she had, her teeth glistening.

Denise and Anita laughed. The Corn Maiden smiled not knowing whether to laugh. Slower and slower the spoon was being lifted to her mouth, her eyelids were drooping.

We would carry the Corn Maiden from Jude's room. Along a corridor and through a door into what Jude called the guest wing, where the air was colder, and stale. And down a stairway in the guest wing and into a cellar to the storage room.

The Corn Maiden did not weigh much. Three of us, we weighed so much more.

On the outside of the storage room door, a padlock.

Anita and Denise had to leave by 6 P.M., to return to their houses for supper. So boring!

Jude would remain with the Corn Maiden for much of the night. To *watch over*. A *vigil*. She was excited by the candle flames, the incense-smell. The pupils of her eyes were dilated, she was highhigh on Ecstasy. She would not bind the Corn Maiden's wrists and ankles, she said, until it was necessary.

Jude had a Polaroid camera, she would take pictures of the Corn Maiden sleeping on her bier.

As the Corn Maiden was being missed the next morning we would all be at school as usual. For nobody had seen us, and nobody would think of *us*.

Some pre-vert they'll think of, Jude said. We can help them with that.

Remember, the Corn Maiden has come as our guest, Jude said. It is not *kidnapping*.

The Corn Maiden came to Jude on the Thursday before Palm Sunday, in April of the year.

BREAKING NEWS

Dial 911 your life is no longer your own.
   Dial 911 you become a beggar.
   Dial 911 you are stripped naked.

She met them at the curb. Distraught mother awaiting police officers in the rain outside Briarcliff Apts., 15th St., South Skatskill, 8:20 P.M. Approaching officers as they emerged from the patrol car pleading, anxious, trying to remain calm but her voice rising, Help me please help my daughter is missing! I came home from work, my daughter isn't here, Marissa is eleven years old, I have no idea where she is, nothing like this has ever happened, please help me find her, I'm afraid that someone has taken my daughter!—Caucasian female, early thirties, blond, bare-headed, strong smell of beer on her breath.

They would question her. They would repeat their questions, and she would repeat her answers. She was calm. She tried to be calm. She began to cry. She began to be angry. She knew her words were being recorded, each word she uttered was a matter of public record. She would face TV cameras, interviewers with microphones outthrust like scepters. She would see herself performing clumsily and stumbling over her lines in the genre *missing child/pleading mother*. She would see how skillfully the TV screen leapt from her anxious drawn face and bloodshot eyes to the smiling innocent wide-eyed Marissa, sweet-faced Marissa with gleaming blond hair, eleven years old, sixth grader, the camera lingered upon each of three photos of Marissa provided by her mother; then, as

the distraught mother continued to speak,
you saw the bland sandstone facade of the
"private"—"exclusive"—Skatskill Day School
and next you were looking at the sinister
nighttime traffic of 15th Street, South
Skatskill along which, as a neutral-sounding
woman's voice explained, eleven-year-old
Marissa Bantry normally walked home to let
herself into an empty apartment and begin
to prepare supper for her mother (who
worked at a Nyack medical clinic, would not
be home until 8 P.M.) and herself; then you
were looking at the exterior, rear of Briarcliff Apts. squat and ugly as an army barracks
in the rain, where a few hardy residents
stood curious staring at police officers and
camera crews; then you saw again the
mother of the missing girl Leah Bantry,
thirty-four, obviously a negligent mother, a
sick-with-guilt mother publicly pleading If
anyone has seen my daughter, if anyone has
any idea what might have happened to
Marissa . . .

Next news item, tractor-trailer overturned
on the New Jersey Turnpike, pile-up involving eleven vehicles, two drivers killed, eight
taken by ambulance to Newark hospital.

So ashamed! But I only want Marissa back.

It was BREAKING NEWS! which means exciting news and by 10 P.M. of that Thursday in April each of four local TV stations was carrying the *missing Marissa* story, and would carry it at regular intervals for as long as there were developments and as long as local interest remained high. But really it was not "new" news, everyone had seen it before. All that could be "new" were the specific players and certain details to be revealed in time, with the teasing punctuality of a suspense film.

It was a good thing, the distraught mother gathered, that cases of missing/abducted children were relatively rare in the affluent Hudson Valley suburbs north of New York City, as crimes of violence in these communities were rare. This meant dramatically focused police attention, cooperation with neighboring police departments in Tarrytown, Sleepy Hollow, Irvington. This meant dramatically focused media coverage, replication of Marissa Bantry's likeness, public concern and participation in the search. *Outpouring of sympathy*, it would be called. *Community involvement.* You would not find such a response in a high-crime area, Leah was told.

"Something to be grateful for. Thank you!"

She wasn't speaking ironically. Tears shone in her bloodshot eyes, she wanted only to be believed.

It was in the distraught mother's favor, too, that, if her daughter had been abducted and hadn't simply run away of her own volition, hers would be the first such case in Skatskill's history.

That was remarkable. That was truly a novelty.

"But she didn't run away. Marissa did not run away. I've tried to explain . . ."

Another novelty in the affluent Hudson Valley suburbs was the mysterious/suspicious circumstance of the "considerable" time lapse between the child's probable disappearance after school and the recorded time the mother reported her missing at 8:14 P.M. The most vigilant of the local TV stations was alert to the dramatic possibilities here. *Skatskill police will neither confirm nor deny that the department is said to be considering charging Bantry, who has no previous police record, with child endangerment.*

And how it would be leaked to this same TV station, the distraught mother had evidenced signs of "inebriation" when police arrived at her home, no one at the station was in a position to say.

So ashamed! I want to die.
If I could exchange my life for Marissa's.

Hours, days. Though each hour was singular, raw as a stone forced down the throat. And what were days but unchartable and unfathomable durations of time too painful to be borne except as singular hours or even minutes. She was aware of a great wheel turning, and of herself caught in this wheel, helpless, in a state of suspended panic and yet eager to cooperate with the very turning of the wheel, if it might bring Marissa back to her. For she was coming to feel, possibly yes there was a God, a God of mercy and not just justice, and she might barter her life for Marissa's.

Through most of it she remained calm. On the surface, calm. She believed she was calm, she had not become hysterical. She had called her parents in Spokane, Washington, for it could not be avoided. She had called her older sister in Washington, D.C. She had not seemed to hear in their shocked and incredulous voices any evidence of reproach, accusation, disgust; but she understood that that was to come, in time.

I am to blame. I know.

It doesn't matter about me.

She believed she was being damned calm! Answering their impudent questions and re-answering them and again repeating as in a deranged tape loop the answers that were all she had in the face of their suspicion, their doubt. She answered the officers' questions with the desperation of a drowning woman clutching a rope already fraying to haul herself into a lifeboat already leaking water. She had no idea, she had told them immediately she had no idea where Marissa's father was, for the past seven years there had been no contact between them, she had last seen him in Berkeley, California, thousands of miles away and he had had no interest in Marissa, he had sought no interest in his own daughter, and so truly she did not believe she could not believe that there was any likelihood of that man having abducted Marissa, truly she did not want to involve him, did not wish to seem in the most elliptical way to be accusing him . . . Yet they continued to question her. It was an interrogation, they sensed that she had something to hide, had she? And what was that, and why? Until finally she heard herself say in a broken defeated voice all right, yes I will give you his name and his last-known address and telephone number that was surely inoperative after so long, all right I will tell you: we were never married, his name is not my child's name, he'd pretended even to doubt that Marissa was his child, we had only lived together, he had no interest in marriage, are you satisfied now?

Her shame, she'd never told her parents. Never told her sister.

Now they would know Leah's pathetic secret. It would be another shock, a small one set beside the other. It would cause them to think less of her, and to know that she was a liar. And now she must telephone to tell them before they discovered it in the media. *I lied to you, I was never married to Andrew. There was no marriage, and there was no divorce.*

Next, they needed to know exactly where she'd been after she had left the Nyack clinic at 6:30 P.M. of the day her daughter had disappeared. Now they knew she was a liar, and a desperate woman, now they had scented blood. They would track the wounded creature to its lair.

At first Leah had been vague about time. In the shock of her daughter missing, it had been natural for the mother to be vague, confused, uncertain about time.

She'd told them that she had been stuck in traffic returning home from Nyack. The Tappan Zee Bridge, route 9 and road repair and rain but yes, she had stopped at the 7-Eleven store near her apartment to buy a few things as she often did . . .

And was that all, had that been her only stop?

Yes. Her only stop. The 7-Eleven. The clerk at the cash register would recognize her.

This was a question, a probing, that had to do with Leah Bantry's male friends. If she had any, who would have known Marissa. Who would have met Marissa. Who might simply have glimpsed Marissa.

Any male friend of the missing girl's mother who might have been attracted to the girl. Might have "abducted" her.

For Marissa might have willingly climbed into a vehicle, if it was driven by someone she knew. Yes?

Calmly Leah insisted no, no one.

She had no male friends at the present time. No serious involvements.

No one she was "seeing"?

Leah flared up, angry. In the sense of—what? What did "seeing" mean?

She was being adamant, and she was speaking forcibly. Yet her interrogators seemed to know. Especially the female de-

tective seemed to know. An evasiveness in
Leah's bloodshot eyes that were the eyes of
a sick, guilty mother. A quavering in Leah's
voice even as she spoke impatiently, defi-
antly. I told you! God damn I have told you.

There was a pause. The air in the room
was highly charged.

There was a pause. Her interrogators
waited.

It was explained to Leah then that she
must answer the officers' questions fully and
truthfully. This was a police investigation,
she would be vulnerable to charges of ob-
struction of justice if she lied.

If she lied.

A known liar.

An exposed, humiliated liar.

And so, another time, Leah heard her
voice break. She heard herself say all right,
yes. She had not gone directly to the 7-
Eleven store from Nyack, she had stopped
first to see a friend and, yes he was a close
male friend, separated from his wife and uncertain of his future and he was an intensely
private man whose identity she could not re-
veal for he and Leah were not exactly lovers
though, yes they had made love . . .

Just once, they had made love. One time.

On Sunday evening, the previous Sunday
evening they had made love.

For the first time they had made love. And it wasn't certain that . . . Leah had no way of knowing whether . . .

She was almost pleading now. Blood seemed to be hemorrhaging into her swollen face.

The police officers waited. She was wiping at her eyes with a wadded tissue. There was no way out of this was there! Somehow she had known, with the sickening sensation of a doomed cow entering a slaughter chute, she had known that a part of her life would be over, when she'd dialed 911.

Your punishment, for losing your daughter.

Of course, Leah had to provide the police officers with the man's name. She had no choice.

She was sobbing, crushed. Davitt would be furious with her.

Davitt Stoop, M.D. Director of the medical clinic. He was Dr. Stoop, her superior. Her employer. He was a kindly man, yet a short-tempered man. He was not in love with Leah Bantry, she knew; nor was Leah in love with him, exactly; and yet, they were relaxed together, they got along so very well together, both were parents of single children of about the same age, both had been hurt and deceived in love, and were wary of new involvements.

Davitt was forty-two, he had been married for eighteen years. He was a responsible husband and father as he had a reputation at the clinic for being an exacting physician and it had been his concern that he and Leah might be seen together prematurely. He did not want his wife to know about Leah, not yet. Still less did he want Leah's coworkers at the clinic to know. He dreaded gossip, innuendo. He dreaded any exposure of his private life.

It was the end, Leah knew.

Before it had begun between them, it would end.

They would humiliate him, these police officers. They would ask him about Leah Bantry and Leah's missing daughter, did he know the child, how well did he know the child, had he ever seen the child without the mother present, had he ever been alone with the child, had he ever given the child a ride in his car for instance this past Thursday?

Possibly they would want to examine the car. Would he allow a search, or would he insist upon a warrant?

Davitt had moved out of his family home in February and lived in an apartment in Nyack, the very apartment Leah Bantry had visited on Thursday evening after her shift.

Impulsively she had dropped by. Davitt might have expected her, it hadn't been certain. They were in the early stages of a romance, excited in each other's presence but uncertain.

This apartment. Had Marissa ever been there?

No! Certainly not.

In a faltering voice telling the officers that Davitt scarcely knew Marissa. Possibly he'd met her, once. But they had spent no time together, certainly not.

Leah had stayed in Davitt's apartment approximately a half hour.

Possibly, forty minutes.

No. They had not had sex.

Not exactly.

They had each had a drink. They had been affectionate, they had talked.

Earnestly, seriously they had talked! About the clinic, and about their children. About Davitt's marriage, and Leah's own.

(It would be revealed, Leah had led Davitt Stoop to believe she had been married, and divorced. It had seemed such a trivial and inconsequential lie at the time.)

Leah was saying, stammering, Davitt would never do such a thing! Not to Marissa, not to any child. He was the father

of a ten-year-old boy, himself. He was not
the type . . .

The female detective asked bluntly what
did Leah mean, "type"? Was this a "type" she
believed she could recognize?

Davitt forgive me! I had no choice.

*I could not lie to police. I had to tell them about
you. I am so very sorry, Davitt, you can understand can't you I must help them find Marissa I
had no choice.*

Still, Marissa remained missing.

"People who do things like this, take children, they're not rational. What they do,
they do for their own purposes. We can only
track them. We can try to stop them. We
can't understand them."

And, "When something like this happens,
it's natural for people to want to cast blame.
You'd be better off not watching TV or reading the papers right now, Miss Bantry."

One of the Skatskill detectives spoke so
frankly to her, she could not believe he too
might be judging her harshly.

There were myriad calls, e-mail messages.
Blond-haired Marissa Bantry had been
sighted in a car exiting the New York
Thruway at Albany. She had been sighted in
the company of "hippie-type males" on West
Houston Street, New York City. A Skatskill
resident would recall, days after the fact,
having seen "that pretty little pig-tailed
blond girl" getting into a battered-looking
van driven by a Hispanic male in the parking lot of the 7-Eleven store a few blocks
from her home.

Still, Marissa remained missing.

. . . hours in rapid succession jarring and dis-
continuous as a broken film projected upon
a flimsy screen she would not sleep for more
than two or three hours even with sedatives
and she slept without dreaming like one
who has been struck on the head with a mal-
let and she woke hollow-headed and parch-
mouthed and her heart beating in her chest
like something with a broken wing.

Always as she woke in that split-second before awareness rushed upon her like a

mouthful of filthy water *My daughter is gone, Marissa is lost* there was a sense of grace, a confusion in time like a prayer *It has not happened yet has it? Whatever it will be.*

HAVE YOU SEEN ME?

Like a sudden bloom of daffodils there appeared overnight, everywhere in Skatskill, the smiling likeness of MARISSA BANTRY, 11.

In store windows. On public bulletin boards, telephone poles. Prominent in the foyers of the Skatskill Post Office, the Skatskill Food Mart, the Skatskill Public Library. Prominent though already dampening in April rain, on the fences of construction sites.

MISSING SINCE APRIL 10. SKATSKILL DAY SCHOOL/15TH ST. AREA.

Hurriedly established by the Skatskill police department was a MARISSA Web site posting more photos of the missing blond girl, a detailed description of her, background information. ANYONE KNOWING ANYTHING ABOUT MARISSA BANTRY PLEASE CONTACT SKATSKILL POLICE AT THIS NUMBER.

Initially, no reward was posted. By Friday evening, an anonymous donor (prominent Skatskill philantropist, retired) had come forward to offer fifteen thousand dollars.

It was reported by the media that Skatskill
police were working *round the clock*. They
were *under intense pressure*, they were investigating *all possible leads*. It was reported that
known pedophiles, sex offenders, child molesters
in the area were being questioned. (Information about such individuals was confidential of course. Still, the most vigilant of
area tabloids learned from an anonymous
source that a sixty-year-old Skatskill resident, a retired music teacher with a sexual
misdemeanor record dating back to 1987,
had been visited by detectives. Since this individual refused to speak with a reporter, or
consent to be photographed, the tabloid
published a photograph of his front door at
12 Amwell Circle on its cover, beneath the
strident headline LOCAL SEX OFFENDER
QUERIED BY COPS: WHERE IS MARISSA?)

Each resident of Briarcliff Apts. was questioned, some more than once. Though no
search warrants had been issued, several residents cooperated with police allowing both
their apartments and their motor vehicles to
be searched.

Storekeepers in the area of the Skatskill
Day School and along Marissa Bantry's
route home were questioned. At the 7-

Eleven store in the mini-mall on the highway, so often frequented by young people, several clerks examined photographs of the missing girl, solemnly shook their heads and told police officers no, they did not believe that Marissa Bantry had been in the store recently, or ever. "There are so many children . . ." Questioned about Leah Bantry, whose photograph they were also shown, the eldest clerk said, carefully, that yes, he recognized this woman, she was a friendly woman; friendlier than most of his customers; but he could not say with certainty if she had been in his store on Thursday, with or without her daughter. "There are so many customers. And so many of them, they look like one another especially if they are blond."

Detectives queried teenagers, most of them from Skatskill High, and some no longer in school, who hung out at the mini-mall. Most of them stiffened at the approach of police officers and hurriedly shook their heads no, they had not seen the little blond girl who was missing, or anyway could not remember seeing her. A striking girl with electric blue hair and a glittering pin in her left eyebrow frowned at the photo and said finally yeah she'd maybe seen Marissa "like with her mother? But when, like maybe it wasn't yesterday because I don't think I was here yesterday, might've been last week? I don't know."

Skatskill Day School was in a stage of siege. TV crews on the front walk, reporters and press photographers at all the entrances. Crisis counsellors met with children in small groups through the day following Marissa's disappearance and there was an air in all the classrooms of shock, as if in the wake of a single violent tremor of the earth. A number of parents had kept their children home from school, but this was not advised by school authorities: "There is no risk at Skatskill Day. Whatever happened to Marissa did not happen on school grounds, and would never have happened on school grounds." It was announced that school security had been immediately strengthened, and new security measures would be begun on Monday. In Marissa Bantry's sixth grade class children were subdued, uneasy. After the counsellor spoke, and asked if anyone had a question, the class sat silent until a boy raised his hand to ask if there would be a search party "like on TV, people going through woods and fields until they find the body?"

Not after a counsellor spoke with eighth graders, but later in the day, an eighth-grade girl named Anita Helder came forward hesitantly to speak with her teacher. Anita was a heavyset girl with a low C average who rarely spoke in class, and often asked to be excused for mysterious health reasons. She was a suspected drug-taker, but had never been caught. In class, she exuded a sulky, defiant manner if called upon by her teacher. Yet now she was saying, in an anxious, faltering voice, that maybe she had seen Marissa Bantry the previous day, on 15h Street and Trinity, climbing into a minivan after school.

". . . I didn't know it was her then for sure, I don't know Marissa Bantry at all but I guess now it must've been her. Oh God I feel so bad I didn't try to stop her! I was like close enough to call out to her, 'Don't get in!' What I could see, the driver was leaning over and sort of pulling Marissa inside. It was a man, he had real dark hair kind of long on the sides but I couldn't see his face. The minivan was like silver-blue, the license plate was something like TZ 6 . . . Beyond that, I can't remember."

Anita's eyes welled with tears. She was visibly trembling, the memory so upset her.

By this time Skatskill detectives had questioned everyone on the school staff except for Mikal Zallman, thirty-one years old, computer consultant and part-time employee, who wasn't at the Skatskill Day School on Fridays.

FEEDING MY RAT

It was an ugly expression. It was macho-ugly, the worst kind of ugly. It made him smile.

Feeding my rat. Alone.

IN CUSTODY

Alone he'd driven out of Skatskill on Thursday afternoon immediately following his final class of the week. Alone driving north in his trim Honda minivan along the Hudson River where the river landscape so mesmerizes the eye, you wonder why you'd ever given a damn for all that's petty, inconsequential. Wondering why you'd ever given a damn for the power of others to hurt you. Or to accuse you with tearful eyes of hurting them.

He'd tossed a valise, his backpack, a few books, hiking boots and a supply of trail food into the back of the van. Always he traveled light. As soon as he left Skatskill he ceased to think of his life there. It was of little consequence really, a professional life arranged to provide him with this freedom. *Feeding my rat.*

There was a woman in Skatskill, a married woman. He knew the signs. She was lonely in her marriage and yearning to be saved from her loneliness. Often she invited him as if impulsively, without premeditation. *Come to dinner, Mikal? Tonight?* He had been vague about accepting, this time. He had not wanted to see the disappointment in her eyes. He felt a tug of affection for her, he recognized her hurt, her resentment, her confusion, she was a colleague of his at the Skatskill School whom he saw often in the company of others, there was a rapport between them, Zallman acknowledged, but he did not want to be involved with her or with any woman, not now. He was thirty-one, and no longer naive. More and more he lived for *feeding my rat.*

It was arrogant, was it, this attitude? Selfish. He'd been told so, more than once. Living so much in his own head, and for himself.

He hadn't married, he doubted he would ever marry. The prospect of children made his heart sink: bringing new lives into the uncertainty and misery of this world, in the early twenty-first century!

He much preferred his secret life. It was an innocent life. Running each morning, along the river. Hiking, mountain climbing. He did not hunt or fish, he had no need to destroy life to enhance his own. Mostly it was exulting in his body. He was only a moderately capable hiker. He hadn't the endurance or the will to run a marathon. He wasn't so fanatic, he wanted merely to be alone where he could exert his body pleasurably. Or maybe to the edge of pain.

One summer in his mid-twenties he'd gone backpacking alone in Portugal, Spain, northern Morocco. In Tangier he'd experimented with the hallucinatory *kif* which was the most extreme form of aloneness and the experience had shaken and exhilarated him and brought him back home to reinvent himself. Michael, now Mikal.

Feeding my rat meant this freedom. Meant he'd failed to drop by her house as she had halfway expected he would. And he had not telephoned, either. It was a way of allowing the woman to know he didn't want to be involved, he would not be involved. In turn, she and her her husband would not provide Mikal Zallman with an alibi for those crucial hours.

———

When, at 5:18 P.M. of Friday, April 11, returning to his car along a steep hiking trail, he happening to see what appeared to be a New York State troopers' vehicle in the parking lot ahead, he had no reason to think *They've come for me.* Even when he saw that two uniformed officers were looking into the rear windows of his minivan, the lone vehicle in the lot parked near the foot of the trail, because it had been the first vehicle of the day parked in the lot, the sight did not alarm or alert him. So confident in himself he felt, and so guiltless.

"Hey. What d'you want?"

Naively, almost conversationally he called to the troopers, who were now staring at him, and moving toward him.

Afterward he would recall how swiftly and unerringly the men moved. One called out, "Are you Mikal Zallman" and the other called, sharply, before Zallman could reply, "Keep your hands where we can see them, sir."

Hands? What about his hands? What were they saying about his hands?

He'd been sweating inside his T-shirt and khaki shorts and his hair was sticking against the nape of his neck. He'd slipped and fallen on the trail once, his left knee was scraped, throbbing. He was not so exuberant as he'd been in the fresh clear air of morning. He held his hands before him, palms uplifted in a gesture of annoyed supplication.

What did these men want with *him*? It had to be a mistake.

. . . staring into the back of the minivan. He'd consented to a quick search. Trunk, interior. Glove compartment. What the hell, he had nothing to hide. Were they looking for drugs? A concealed weapon? He saw the way in which they were staring at two paperback books he'd tossed onto the rear window ledge weeks ago, Roth's The Dying Animal *and Ovid's* The Art of Love. *On the cover of the first was a sensuously reclining Modligliani nude in rich flesh tones, with prominent pink-nippled breasts. On the cover of the other was a classical nude, marmoreal white female with a full, shapely body and blank, blind eyes.*

TABOO

It was Taboo to utter aloud the Corn Maiden's name.

It was Taboo to touch the Corn Maiden except as Jude guided.

For Jude was the Priest of the Sacrifice. No one else.

What does Taboo mean, it means death. If you disobey.

Jude took Polaroid pictures of the Corn Maiden sleeping on her bier. Arms crossed on her flat narrow chest, cornsilk hair spread like pale flames around her head. Some pictures, Jude was beside the Corn Maiden. We took pictures of her smiling, and her eyes shiny and dilated.

For posterity, Jude said. For the record.

It was Taboo to utter the Corn Maiden's actual name aloud and yet: everywhere in Skatskill that name was being spoken! And everywhere in Skatskill her face was posted!

Missing Girl. Abduction Feared. State of Emergency.

It is so easy, Jude said. To make the truth your own.

But Jude was surprised too, we thought. That it was so real, what had only been for so long Jude O's *idea*.

Ju*dith*!

Mrs. Trahern called in her whiny old-woman voice, we had to troop into her smelly bedroom where she was propped up in some big old antique brass bed like a nutty queen watching TV where footage of the *missing Skatskill Day girl* was being shown. Chiding, You girls! Look what has happened to one of your little classmates! Did you know this poor child?

Jude mumbled no Grandma.

Well. You would not be in a class with a retarded child, I suppose.

Jude mumbled no Grandma.

Well. See that you never speak with strangers, Judith! Report anyone who behaves strangely with you, or is seen lurking around the neighborhood. Promise me!

Jude mumbled okay. Grandma, I promise.

Denise and Anita mumbled Me, too, Mrs. Trahern. For it seemed to be expected.

Next, Mrs. Trahern made Jude come to her bed, to take Jude's hands in her clawy old-woman hands. I have not always been a good grandma, I know. As the judge's widow there are so many demands on my time. But I am your grandma, Judith. I am your only blood kin who cares for you, dear. You know that, I hope?

Jude mumbled Yes Grandma, I know.

THE WORLD AS WE HAVE KNOWN IT

Has vanished.

We are among the few known survivors.

. . . terrorist attack. Nuclear war. Fires.

New York City is a gaping hole. The George Washington Bridge is crashed into the river. Washington, D.C., is gone.

So the Corn Maiden was told. So the Corn Maiden believed in her Rapture.

Many times we said these words. Jude had made us memorize. The world as we have known it has vanished. There is no TV now. No newspapers. No electricity. We are among the few known survivors. We must be brave, everyone else is gone. All the adults are gone. All our mothers.

The Corn Maiden opened her mouth to shriek but she had not the strength. Her eyes welled with tears, lapsing out of focus.

All our mothers. So exciting!

Only candles to be lighted, solemnly. To keep away the night.

The Corn Maiden was informed that we had

to ration our food supplies. For there were no stores now, all of Skatskill was gone. The Food Mart was gone. Main Street was gone. The Mall.

Jude knew, to maintain the Rapture the Corn Maiden must be fed very little. For Jude did not wish to bind her wrists and ankles, that were so fragile-seeming. Jude did not wish to gag her, to terrify her. For then the Corn Maiden would fear us and not trust and adore us as her protectors.

The Corn Maiden must be treated with reverence, respect, kindness, and firmness. She must never guess the fate that will be hers.

The Corn Maiden's diet was mostly liquids. Water, transparent fruit juices like apple, grapefruit. And milk.

It was Taboo Jude said for the Corn Maiden to ingest any foods except white foods. And any foods containing bones or skins.

These foods were soft, crumbly or melted foods. Cottage cheese, plain yogurt, ice cream. The Corn Maiden was not a retarded child as some of the TV stations were saying but she was not shrewd-witted, Jude said. For these foods we fed her were refrigerated, and she did not seem to know.

Of course, finely ground in these foods were powdery-white tranquilizers, to maintain the Rapture.

The Corn Maiden of the Onigara Sacrifice was to pass into the next world in a Rapture. Not in fear.

We took turns spooning small portions of food into the Corn Maiden's mouth that sucked like an infant's to be fed. So hungry, the Corn Maiden whimpered for more. No, no! There is no more she was told.

(How hungry we were, after these feedings! Denise and Anita went home to stuff-stuff their faces.)

Jude did not want the Corn Maiden to excrete solid waste she said. Her bowels must be clean and pure for the Sacrifice. Also we had to take her outside the storage room for this, half-carrying her to a bathroom in a corner of the cobwebby cellar that was a "recreation room" of some bygone time Jude said the 1970s that is ancient history now.

Only two times did we have to take the Corn Maiden to this bathroom, half-carried out, groggy and stumbling and her head lolling on her shoulders. All other times the Corn Maiden used the pot Jude had brought in from one of the abandoned greenhouses. A fancy Mexican ceramic pot, for the Corn Maiden to squat over, as we held her like a clumsy infant.

The Corn Maiden's pee! It was hot, bubbly. It had a sharp smell different from our own.

Like a big infant the Corn Maiden was becoming, weak and trusting all her bones. Even her crying when she cried saying she wanted to go home, she wanted her mommy, where was her mommy she wanted her mommy was an infant's crying, with no strength or anger behind it.

Jude said all our mommies are gone, we must be brave without them. She would be safe with us Jude said stroking her hair. See, we would protect her better than her mommy had protected her.

Jude took Polaroid pictures of the Corn Maiden sitting up on her bier her face streaked with tears. The Corn Maiden was chalky white and the colors of the bier were so rich and silky. The Corn Maiden was so thin, you could see her collarbone jutting inside the white muslin nightgown Jude had clothed her in.

We did not doubt Jude. What Jude meant to do with the Corn Maiden we would not resist.

In the Onigara ceremony Jude said the Corn Maiden was slowly starved and her bowels cleaned out and purified and she was tied on an altar still living and a priest shot an arrow that had been blessed into her heart. And the heart was scooped out with a knife that had been blessed and touched to the lips of the priest and others of the tribe to bless them. And the heart and the Corn Maiden's body were then carried out into a field and buried in the earth to honor the Morning Star which is the sun and the Evening Star which is the moon and beg of them their blessing for the corn harvest.

Will the Corn Maiden be killed we wished to know but we could not ask Jude for Jude would be angered.

To ourselves we said Jude will kill the Corn Maiden, maybe! We shivered to think so. Denise smiled, and bit at her thumbnail, for she was jealous of the Corn Maiden. Not because the Corn Maiden had such beautiful silky hair but because Jude fussed over the Corn Maiden so, as Jude would not have fussed over Denise.

The Corn Maiden wept when we left her. When we blew out the candles and left her in darkness. We had to patrol the house we said. We had to look for fires and "gas leak-

age" we said. For the world as we have
known it has come to an end, there were no
adults now. We were the adults now.

We were our own mommies.

Jude shut the door, and padlocked it. The
Corn Maiden's muffled sobs from inside.
Mommy! Mommy! the Corn Maiden wept but
there was no one to hear and even on the
steps to the first floor you could no longer
hear.

OUT THERE

HATEHATEHATE you assholes Out There.
The Corn Maiden was Jude O's perfect re-
venge.

At Skatskill Day we saw our hatred like
scalding-hot lava rushing through the corri-
dors and into the classrooms and cafeteria
to burn our enemies alive. Even girls who
were okay to us mostly would perish for they
would rank us below the rest, wayway below
the Hot Shit Cliques that ran the school and
also the boys—all the boys. And the teachers, some of them had pissed us off and deserved death. Jude said Mr. Z. had "dissed"
her and was the "target enemy" now.

Sometimes the vision was so fierce it was a
rush better than E!

Out There it was believed that the *missing Skatskill girl* might have been kidnapped. A ransom note was awaited.

Or, it was believed the *missing girl* was the victim of a "sexual predator."

On TV came Leah Bantry, the mother, to appeal to whoever had taken her daughter saying, Please don't hurt Marissa, please release my daughter I love her so, begging please in a hoarse voice that sounded like she'd been crying a lot and her eyes haggard with begging so Jude stared at the woman with scorn.

Not so hot-shit now, are you Mrs. Brat-tee! Not so pretty-pretty.

It was surprising to Denise and Anita, that Jude hated Leah Bantry so. We felt sorry for the woman, kind of. Made us think how our mothers would be, if we were gone, though we hated our mothers we were thinking they'd probably miss us, and be crying, too. It was a new way of seeing our moms. But Jude did not have a mom even to hate. Never spoke of her except to say she was Out West in L.A. We wanted to think that Jude's mom was a movie star under some different name, that was why she'd left Jude with Mrs. Trahern to pursue a film career. But we would never say this to Jude, for sure.

Sometimes Jude scared us. Like she'd maybe hurt *us*.

Wild! On Friday 7 P.M. news came BULLETIN— BREAKING NEWS—SKATSKILL SUSPECT IN CUSTODY. It was Mr. Zallman!

We shrieked with laughter. Had to press our hands over our mouths so old Mrs. Trahern would not hear.

Jude is flicking through the channels and there suddenly is Mr. Z. on TV! And some broadcaster saying in an excited voice that this man had been apprehended in Bear Mountain State Park and brought back to Skatskill to be questioned in the disappearance of Marissa Bantry and the shocker is: Mikal Zallman, thirty-one, is on the faculty of the Skatskill Day School.

Mr. Zallman's jaws were scruffy like he had not shaved in a while. His eyes were scared and guilty-seeming. He was wearing a T-shirt and khaki shorts like we would never see him at school and this was funny, too. Between two plainclothes detectives being led up the steps into police headquarters and at the top they must've jerked him under the arms, he almost turned his ankle.

We were laughing like hyenas. Jude

crouched in front of the TV rocking back and forth, staring.

"Zallman claims to know nothing of Marissa Bantry. Police and rescue workers are searching the Bear Mountain area and will search through the night if necessary."

There was a cut to our school again, and 15th Street traffic at night. ". . . unidentified witness, believed to be a classmate of Marissa Bantry, has told authorities that she witnessed Marissa being pulled into a Honda CR-V at this corner, Thursday after school. This vehicle has been tentatively identified as . . ."

Unidentified witness. That's me! Anita cried.

And a second "student witness" had come forward to tell the school principal that she had seen "the suspect Zallman" fondling Marissa Bantry, stroking her hair and whispering to her in the computer lab when he thought no one was around, only last week.

That's *me!* Denise cried.

And police had found a mother-of-pearl butterfly barrette on the ground near Zallman's parking space, behind his condominium residence. This barrette had been "absolutely identified" by Marissa Bantry's mother as a barrette Marissa had been wearing on Thursday.

We turned to Jude who was grinning.

We had not known that Jude had planned *this*. On her bicycle she must've gone, to drop the barrette where it would be found.

We laughed so, we almost wet ourselves. Jude was just so *cool*.

But even Jude seemed surprised, kind of. That you could make the wildest truth your own and every asshole would rush to believe.

DESPERATE

Now she knew his name: *Mikal Zallman*.

The man who'd taken Marissa. One of Marissa's teachers at the Skatskill Day School.

It was a nightmare. All that Leah Bantry had done, what exertion of heart and soul, to enroll her daughter in a private school in which a pedophile was allowed to instruct elementary school children.

She had met Zallman, she believed. At one of the parents' evenings. Something seemed wrong, though: Zallman was young. You don't expect a young man to be a pedophile. An attractive man though with a hawkish profile, and not very warm. Not with Leah. Not that she could remember.

The detectives had shown her Zallman's

photograph. They had not allowed her to speak with Zallman. Vaguely yes she did remember. But not what he'd said to her, if he had said anything. Very likely Leah has asked him about Marissa but what he'd said she could not recall.

And then, hadn't Zallman slipped away from the reception, early? By chance she'd seen him, the only male faculty member not to be wearing a necktie, hair straggling over his collar, disappearing from the noisy brightly lighted room.

He'd taken a polygraph, at his own request. The results were "inconclusive."

If I could speak with him. Please.

They were telling her no, Mrs. Bantry. Not a good idea.

This man who took Marissa if I could speak with him *please*.

In her waking state she pleaded. She would beg the detectives, she would throw herself on their mercy. Her entire conscious life was now begging, pleading, and bartering. And waiting.

Zallman is the one, isn't he? You have him, don't you? An eyewitness said she saw him.

Saw him pull Marissa into a van with him. In broad daylight! And you found Marissa's barrette by his parking space *isn't that proof!*

To her, the desperate mother, it was certainly proof. The man had taken Marissa, he knew where Marissa was. The truth had to be wrung from him before it was too late.

On her knees she would beg to see Zallman promising not to become emotional and they told her no, for she would only become emotional in the man's presence. And Zallman, who had a lawyer now, would only become more adamant in his denial.

Denial! How could he . . . deny! He had taken Marissa, he knew where Marissa was.

She would beg *him*. She would show Zallman pictures of Marissa as a baby. She would plead with this man for her daughter's life if only if only if only for God's sake they would allow her.

Of course, it was impossible. The suspect was being questioned following a procedure, a strategy, to which Leah Bantry had no access. The detectives were professionals, Leah Bantry was an amateur. She was only the mother, an amateur.

———

The wheel, turning.

It was a very long Friday. The longest Friday of Leah's life.

Then abruptly it was Friday night, and then it was Saturday morning. And Marissa was still gone.

Zallman had been captured, yet Marissa was still gone.

He might have been tortured, in another time. To make him confess. The vicious pedophile, whose "legal rights" had to be honored.

Leah's heart beat in fury. Yet she was powerless, she could not intervene.

Saturday afternoon: approaching the time when Marissa would be missing for forty-eight hours.

Forty-eight hours! It did not seem possible.

She has drowned by now, Leah thought. She has suffocated for lack of oxygen.

She is starving. She has bled to death. Wild creatures on Bear Mountain have mutilated her small body.

She calculated: it would soon be fifty hours since Leah had last seen Marissa. Kissed her hurriedly good-bye in the car, in front of the school Thursday morning at eight. And (she forced herself to remember, she would not escape remembering) Leah hadn't troubled to watch her daughter run up the walk, and into the school. Pale gold hair shimmering behind her and just possibly (possibly!) at the door, Marissa had turned to wave good-bye to Mommy but Leah was already driving away.

And so, she'd had her opportunity. She would confess to her sister Avril *I let Marissa slip away.*

The great wheel, turning. And the wheel was Time itself, without pity.

She saw that now. In her state of heightened awareness bred of terror she saw. She had ceased to give a damn about "Leah Bantry" in the public eye. The distraught/negligent mother. Working mom, single mom, mom-with-a-drinking-problem. She'd been exposed as a liar. She'd been exposed as a female avid to sleep with another woman's husband and that husband her boss. She knew, the very police who were searching for Marissa's abductor were investigating her, too. Crude tabloids, TV journalism. Under a guise of sympathy, pity for her "plight."

None of this mattered, now. What the jackals said of her, and would say. She was bartering her life for Marissa's. Appealing to God in whom she was trying in desperation to believe. *If You would. Let Marissa be alive. Return Marissa to me. If You would hear my plea.* So there was no room to give a damn about herself, she had no scruples now, no shame. Yes she would consent to be interviewed on the cruelest and crudest of the New York City TV stations if that might help Marissa, somehow. Blinking into the blinding TV lights, baring her teeth in a ghastly nervous smile.

Never would she care again for the pieties of ordinary life. When on the phone her own mother began crying, asking why, why on earth had Leah left Marissa alone for so many hours, Leah had interrupted the older woman coldly, "That doesn't matter now, Mother. Good-bye."

Neither of the elder Bantrys was in good health, they would not fly east to share their daughter's vigil. But Leah's older sister Avril flew up immediately from Washington to stay with her.

For years the sisters had not been close. There was a subtle rivalry between them, in which Leah had always felt belittled.

Avril, an investment attorney, was brisk and efficient answering the telephone, screening all e-mail. Avril checked the *Marissa*

Web site constantly. Avril was on frank terms with the senior Skatskill detective working the case, who spoke circumspectly and with great awkwardness to Leah.

Avril called Leah to come listen to a voice-mail message that had come in while they'd been at police headquarters. Leah had told Avril about Davitt Stoop, to a degree.

It was Davitt, finally calling Leah. In a slow stilted voice that was not the warm intimate voice Leah knew he was saying *A terrible thing . . . This is a . . . terrible thing, Leah. We can only pray this madman is caught and that . . .* A long pause. You would have thought that Dr. Stoop had hung up but then he continued, more forcibly, *I'm sorry for this terrible thing but Leah please don't try to contact me again. Giving my name to the police! The past twenty-four hours have been devastating for me. Our relationship was a mistake and it can't be continued, I am sure you understand. As for your position at the clinic I am sure you understand the awkwardness among all the staff if . . .*

Leah's heart beat in fury, she punched *erase* to extinguish the man's voice. Grateful that Avril, who'd tactfully left the room, could be relied upon not to ask about Davitt Stoop, nor even to offer sisterly solicitude.

*Take everything from me. If You will leave me
Marissa, the way we were.*

EMISSARIES

"Mommy!"

It was Marissa's voice, but muffled, at a distance.

Marissa was trapped on the far side of a barrier of thick glass, Leah heard her desperate cries only faintly. Marissa was pounding the glass with her fists, smearing her damp face against it. But the glass was too thick to be broken. "Mommy! Help me, Mommy . . ." And Leah could not move to help the child, Leah was paralyzed. Something gripped her legs, quicksand, tangled ropes. If she could break free . . .

Avril woke her, abruptly. There was someone to see her, friends of Marissa's they said they were.

"H-Hello, Mrs. Branty . . . Bant*ry*. My name is . . ."

Three girls. Three girls from Skatskill Day. One of them, with faded-rust-red hair and glistening stone-colored eyes, was holding out to Leah an astonishing large bouquet of dazzling white flowers: long-stemmed roses, carnations, paperwhites, mums. The sharp astringent fragrance of the paper-whites prevailed.

The bouquet must have been expensive, Leah thought. She took it from the girl and tried to smile. "Why, thank you."

It was Sunday, midday. She'd sunk into a stupor after twenty hours of wakefulness. Seeing it was a warm, incongruously brightly sunny April day beyond the partly-drawn blinds on the apartment windows.

She would have to focus on these girls. She'd been expecting, from what Avril had said, younger children, Marissa's age. But these were adolescents. Thirteen, fourteen. In eighth grade, they'd said. Friends of Marissa's?

The visit would not last long. Avril, disapproving, hovered near.

Possibly Leah had invited them, the girls were seated in her living room. They were clearly excited, edgy. They glanced about like nervous birds. Leah supposed she should offer them Cokes but something in her resisted. Hurriedly she'd washed her face, dragged a comb through her snarled hair that no longer looked blond, but dust-colored. How were these girls Marissa's friends? Leah had never seen them before in her life.

Nor did their names mean anything to her. "Jude Trahern," "Denise . . ." The third name she'd failed to catch.

The girls were moist-eyed with emotion. So many neighbors had dropped by to express their concern, Leah supposed she had to endure it. The girl who'd given Leah the bouquet, Jude, was saying in a faltering nasal voice how sorry they were for what had happened to Marissa and how much they liked Marissa who was just about the nicest girl at Skatskill Day. If something like this had to happen too bad it couldn't happen to—well, somebody else.

The other girls giggled, startled at their friend's vehemence.

"But Marissa is so nice, and so sweet. Ma'am, we are praying for her safe return, every minute."

Leah stared at the girl. She had no idea how to reply.

Confused, she lifted the bouquet to her face. Inhaled the almost too rich paperwhite smell. As if the purpose of this visit was to bring Leah . . . What?

The girls were staring at her almost rudely. Of course, they were young, they knew no better. Their leader, Jude, seemed to be a girl with some confidence, though she wasn't the eldest or the tallest or the most attractive of the three.

Not attractive at all. Her face was fiercely plain as if she'd scrubbed it with steel wool. Her skin was chalky, mottled. You could sense the energy thrumming through her like an electric current, she was wound up so tightly.

The other girls were more ordinary. One was softly plump with a fattish pug face, almost pretty except for something smirky, insolent in her manner. The other girl had a sallow blemished skin, limp grease-colored hair and oddly quivering, parted lips. All three girls wore grubby blue jeans, boys' shirts, and ugly square-toed boots.

". . . so we were wondering, Mrs. Bran-, Bantry, if you would like us to, like, pray with you? Like, now? It's Palm Sunday. Next Sunday is Easter."

"What? Pray? Thank you but . . ."

"Because Denise and Anita and me, we have a feeling, we have a really strong feeling, Mrs. Bantry, that Marissa is alive. And Marissa is depending on us. So, if—"

Avril came forward quickly, saying the visit was ended.

"My sister has been under a strain, girls. I'll see you to the door."

The flowers slipped through Leah's fingers. She caught at some of them, clumsily. The others fell to the floor at her feet.

Two of the girls hurried to the door, held open by Avril, with frightened expressions. Jude, pausing, continued to smile in her earnest, pinched way. She'd taken a small black object out of her pocket. "May I take a picture, Mrs. Bantry?"

Before Leah could protest, she raised the camera and clicked the shutter. Leah's hand had flown up to shield her face, instinctively.

Avril said sharply, "Please. The visit is over, girls."

Jude murmured, on her way out, "We will pray for you anyway, Mrs. Bantry. 'Bye!"

The other girls chimed in *Bye! bye!* Avril shut the door behind them.

Leah threw the flowers away in the trash. White flowers!

At least, they hadn't brought her calla lilies.

———

DUTCHWOMAN

. . . in motion. Tracing and retracing The Route. Sometimes on foot, sometimes in her car. Sometimes with Avril but more often alone. "I need to get out! I can't breathe in here! I need to see what Marissa saw."

These days were very long days. And yet, in all of the hours of these days, nothing happened.

Marissa was still gone, still gone.

Like a clock's ticking: still, still gone. Each time you checked, still gone.

She had her cell phone of course. If there was news.

She walked to the Skatskill Day School and positioned herself at the front door of the elementary grades wing, which was the door Marissa would have used, would have left by on Thursday afternoon. From this position she began The Route.

To the front sidewalk and east along Pinewood. Across Pinewood to Mahopac Avenue and continue east past 12th Street, 13th Street, 14th Street, 15th Street. At 15th and Trinity, the witness had claimed to see Mikal Zallman pull Marissa Bantry into his Honda CR-V van, and drive away.

Either it had happened that way, or it had not.

There was only the single witness, a Skatskill Day student whom police would not identify.

Leah believed that Zallman was the man and yet: there was something missing. Like a jigsaw puzzle piece. A very small piece, yet crucial.

Since the girls' visit. Since the bouquet of dazzling white flowers. That small twitchy smile Leah did not wish to interpret as taunting, of the girl named Jude.

We will pray for you anyway, Mrs. Bantry. Bye!

Important for Leah to walk briskly. To keep in motion.

There is a deep-sea creature, perhaps a shark, that must keep in motion constantly, otherwise it will die. Leah was becoming this creature, on land. She believed that news of Marissa's death would come to her only if she, the mother, were still; there was a kind of deadness in being still; but if she was in motion, tracing and retracting Marissa's route . . . "It's like Marissa is with me. Is *me*."

She knew that people along The Route were watching her. Everyone in Skatskill knew her face, her name. Everyone knew why she was out on the street, tracing and retracing The Route. A slender woman in shirt, slacks, dark glasses. A woman who had made a merely perfunctory attempt to disguise herself, dusty-blond hair partly hidden beneath a cap.

She knew the observers were pitying her. And blaming her.

Still, when individuals spoke to her, as a few did each time she traced The Route, they were invariably warm, sympathetic. Some of them, both men and women, appeared to be deeply sympathetic. Tears welled in their eyes. *That bastard* they spoke of Zallman. *Has he confessed yet?*

In Skatskill the name *Zallman* was known now, notorious. That the man was—had been—a member of the faculty at the Skatskill Day School had become a local scandal.

The rumor was, Zallman had a record of prior arrests and convictions as a sexual predator. He'd been fired from previous teaching positions but had somehow managed to be hired at the prestigious Skatskill School. The school's beleaguered principal had given newspaper and TV interviews vigorously denying this rumor, yet it prevailed.

Bantry, Zallman. The names now luridly linked. In the tabloids photos of the missing girl and "suspect" were printed side by side. Several times, Leah's photograph was included as well.

In her distraught state yet Leah was able

to perceive the irony of such a grouping: a mock family.

Leah had given up hoping to speak with Zallman. She supposed it was a ridiculous request. If he'd taken Marissa he was a psychopath and you don't expect a psychopath to tell the truth. If he had not taken Marissa . . .

"If it's someone else. They will never find him."

The Skatskill police had not yet arrested Zallman. Temporarily, Zallman had been released. His lawyer had made a terse public statement that he was "fully cooperating" with the police investigation. But what he had told them, what could possibly be of worth that he had told them, Leah didn't know.

Along The Route, Leah saw with Marissa's eyes. The facades of houses. On 15th Street, storefronts. No one had corroborated the eyewitness's testimony about seeing Marissa pulled into a van in full daylight on busy 15th Street. Wouldn't anyone else have seen? And who had the eyewitness been? Since the three girls had dropped by to see her, Leah was left with a new sensation of unease.

Not Marissa's friends. Not those girls.

She crossed Trinity and continued. This was a slight extension of Marissa's route home from school. It was possible, Marissa dropped by the 7-Eleven to buy a snack on Tuesdays/Thursdays when Leah returned home late.

Taped to the front plate-glass door of the 7-Eleven was

HAVE YOU SEEN ME?
MARISSA BANTRY, 11
MISSING SINCE APRIL 10

Marissa's smiling eyes met hers as Leah pushed the door open.

Inside, trembling, Leah removed her dark glasses. She was feeling dazed. Wasn't certain if this was full wakefulness or a fugue state. She was trying to orient herself. Staring at a stack of thick Sunday *New York Times.* The front page headlines were of U.S.-Iraq issues and for a confused moment Leah thought *Maybe none of it has happened yet.*

Maybe Marissa was outside, waiting in the car.

The gentlemanly Indian clerk stood behind the counter in his usual reserved, yet attentive posture. He was staring at her strangely, Leah saw, as he would never have done in the past.

Of course, he recognized her now. Knew her name. All about her. She would never be an anonymous customer again. Leah saw, with difficulty, for her eyes were watering, a second HAVE YOU SEEN ME? taped conspicuously to the front of the cash register.

Wanting to embrace the man, wordless. Wanted to press herself into his arms and burst into tears.

Instead she wandered in one of the aisles. How like an overexposed photograph the store was. So much to see, yet you saw nothing.

Thank God, there were no other customers at the moment.

Saw her hand reach out for—what? A box of Kleenex.

Pink, the color Marissa preferred.

She went to the counter to pay. Smiled at the clerk who was smiling very nervously at her, clearly agitated by the sight of her. His always-so-friendly blond customer! Leah was going to thank him for having posted the notices, and she was going to ask him if he'd ever seen Marissa in his store alone, without her, when suddenly the man said, to her astonishment, "Mrs. Bantry, I know of your daughter and what has happened, that is so terrible. I watch all the time, to see what will come of it." Behind the counter was a small portable TV, volume turned down. "Mrs. Bantry, I want to say, when the police came here, I was nervous and not able to remember so well, but now I do remember, I am more certain, yes I did see your daughter that day, I believe. She did come into the store. She was alone, and then there was another girl. They went out together."

The Indian clerk spoke in a flood of words. His eyes were repentant, pleading.

"When? When was—"

"That day, Mrs. Bantry. That the police have asked about. Last week."

"Thursday? You saw Marissa on Thursday?"

But now he was hesitating. Leah spoke too excitedly.

"I think so, yes. I can not be certain. That is why I did not want to tell the police, I did not want to get into trouble with them. They are impatient with me, I don't know English so well. The questions they ask are not so easy to answer while they wait staring at you."

Leah didn't doubt that the Indian clerk was uneasy with the Caucasian Skatskill police, she was uneasy with them herself.

She said, "Marissa was with a girl, you say? What did this girl look like?"

The Indian clerk frowned. Leah saw that he was trying to be as accurate as possible. He had probably not looked at the girls very closely, very likely he could not distinguish among most of them. He said, "She was older than your daughter, I am sure. She was not too tall, but older. Not so blond-haired."

"You don't know her, do you? Her name?"

"No. I do not know their names any of them." He paused, frowning. His jaws tightened. "Some of them, the older ones, I think this girl is one of them, with their friends they come in here after school and take things. They steal, they break. They rip open bags, to eat. Like pigs they are. They think I can't see them but I know what they do. Five days a week they come in here, many of them. They are daring me to shout at them, and if I would touch them—"

His voice trailed off, tremulous.

"This girl. What did she look like?"

". . . a white skin. More than yours, Mrs. Bantry. A strange color of hair like . . . a color of something red, faded."

He spoke with some repugnance. Clearly, the mysterious girl was not attractive in his eyes.

Red-haired. Pale-red-haired. Who?

Jude Trahern. The girl who'd brought the

flowers. The girl who spoke of praying for Marissa's safe return.

Were they friends, then? Marissa had had a friend?

Leah was feeling light-headed. The fluorescent lighting began to tilt and spin. There was something here she could not grasp. *Pray with you. Next Sunday is Easter.* She had more to ask of this kindly man but her mind had gone blank.

"Thank you. I . . . have to leave now."

"Don't tell them, Mrs. Bantry? The police? Please?"

Blindly Leah pushed through the door.

"Mrs. Bantry?" The clerk hurried after her, a bag in his hand. "You are forgetting."

The box of pink Kleenex.

Flying Dutchman. Dutchwoman. She was becoming. Always in motion, terrified of stopping. Returning home to her sister.

Any news?

None.

Behind the drab little mini-mall she was drifting, dazed. She would tell the Skatskill detectives what the Indian clerk had told her—she must tell them. If Marissa had been in the store on Thursday afternoon, then Marissa could not have been pulled into a minivan on 15th Street and Trinity, two blocks back toward school. Not by Mikal Zallman, or by anyone. Marissa must have continued past Trinity. After the 7-Eleven she would have circled back to 15th Street again, and walked another half block to home.

Unless she'd been pulled into the minivan on 15th Street and Van Buren. The eyewitness had gotten the streets wrong. She'd been closer to home.

Unless the Indian clerk was confused about days, times. Or, for what purpose Leah could not bear to consider, lying to her.

"Not him! Not him, too."

She refused to think that was a possibility. Her mind simply shut blank, in refusal.

She was walking now slowly, hardly conscious of her surroundings. A smell of rancid food assailed her nostrils. Only a few employees' cars were parked behind the mini-mall. The pavement was stained and littered, a single Dumpster overflowing trash. At the back of the Chinese takeout several scrawny cats were rummaging in food scraps and froze at Leah's approach before running away in panic.

"Kitties! I'm not going to hurt you."

The feral cats' terror mocked her own. Their panic was hers, misplaced, to no purpose.

Leah wondered: what were the things Marissa did, when Leah wasn't with her? For years they had been inseparable: mother, daughter. When Marissa had been a very small child, even before she could walk, she'd tried to follow her mother everywhere, from room to room. *Mom-my! Where Mom-my going!* Now, Marissa did many things by herself. Marissa was growing up. Dropping by the 7-Eleven, with other children after school. Buying a soft drink, a bag of something crunchy, salty. It was innocent enough. No child should be punished for it. Leah gave Marissa pocket change, as she called it, for just such impromptu purchases, though she disapproved of junk food.

Leah felt a tightening in her chest, envisioning her daughter in the 7-Eleven store the previous Thursday, buying something from the Indian clerk. Then, he had not known her name. A day or two later, everyone in Skatskill knew Marissa Bantry's name.

Of course it probably meant nothing. That Marissa had walked out of the store with a classmate from school. Nothing unusual about that. She could imagine with what polite stiff expressions the police would respond to such a "tip."

In any case, Marissa would still have returned to 15th Street on her way home. So busy, dangerous at that hour of day.

It was there on 15th Street that the "unidentified" classmate had seen Marissa being pulled into the Honda. Leah wondered if the witness was the red-haired Jude.

Exactly what the girl had told police officers, Leah didn't know. The detectives exuded an air, both assuring and frustrating, of knowing more than they were releasing at the present time.

Leah found herself at the edge of the paved area. Staring at a steep hill of uncultivated and seemingly worthless land. Strange how in the midst of an affluent suburb there yet remain these stretches of vacant land, uninhabitable. The hill rose to Highgate Avenue a half mile away, invisible from this perspective. You would not guess that "historical" old homes and mansions were located on the crest of this hill, property worth millions of dollars. The hill was profuse with crawling vines, briars, and stunted trees. The accumulation of years of wind-blown litter and debris made it look like an informal dump. There was a scurrying sound somewhere just inside the tangle of briars, a furry shape that appeared and disappeared so swiftly Leah scarcely saw it.

Behind the Dumpster, hidden from her view, the colony of wild cats lived, foraged for food, fiercely interbred, and died the premature deaths of feral creatures. They would not wish to be "pets"—they had no capacity to receive the affection of humans. They were, in clinical terms, undomesticable.

Leah was returning to her car when she heard a nasal voice in her wake:

"Mrs. Ban-try! H'lo."

Leah turned uneasily to see the frizz-haired girl who'd given her the flowers.

Jude. Jude Trahern.

Now it came to Leah: there was a Trahern Square in downtown Skatskill, named for a Chief Justice Trahern decades ago. One of the old Skatskill names. On Highgate, there was a Trahern estate, one of the larger houses, nearly hidden from the road.

This strange glistening-eyed girl. There was something of the sleek white rat about her. Yet she smiled uncertainly at Leah, clumsily straddling her bicycle.

"Are you following me?"

"Ma'am, no. I . . . just saw you."

Wide-eyed the girl appeared sincere, uneasy. Yet Leah's nerves were on edge, she spoke sharply: "What do you want?"

The girl stared at Leah as if something very bright glared from Leah's face that was both blinding and irresistible. She wiped nervously at her nose. "I . . . I want to say I'm sorry, for saying dumb things before. I guess I made things worse."

Made things worse! Leah smiled angrily, this was so absurd.

"I mean, Denise and Anita and me, we wanted to help. We did the wrong thing, I guess. Coming to see you."

"Were you the 'unidentified witness' who saw my daughter being pulled into a minivan?"

The girl blinked at Leah, blank-faced. For a long moment Leah would have sworn that she was about to speak, to say something urgent. Then she ducked her head, wiped again at her nose, shrugged self-consciously and muttered what sounded like, "I guess not."

"All right. Good-bye. I'm leaving now."

Leah frowned and turned away, her heart beating hard. How badly she wanted to be alone! But the rat-girl was too obtuse to comprehend. With the dogged persistence of an overgrown child she followed Leah at an uncomfortably close distance of about three feet, pedaling her bicycle awkwardly. The bicycle was an expensive Italian make of the kind a serious adult cyclist might own.

At last Leah paused, to turn back. "*Do* you have something to tell me, Jude?"

The girl looked astonished.

" 'Jude'! You remember my name?"

Leah would recall afterward this strange moment. The exultant look in Jude Trahern's face. Her chalky skin mottled with pleasure.

Leah said, "Your name is unusual, I remember unusual names. If you have something to tell me about Marissa, I wish you would."

"Me? What would I know?"

"You aren't the witness from school?"

"What witness?"

"A classmate of Marissa's says she saw a male driver pull Marissa into his minivan on 15th Street. But you aren't that girl?"

Jude shook her head vehemently. "You can't always believe 'eyewitnesses,' Mrs. Bantry."

"What do you mean?"

"It's well known. It's on TV all the time, police shows. An eyewitness swears she sees somebody, and she's wrong. Like, with Mr. Zallman, people are all saying it's him but, like, it might be somebody else."

The girl spoke rapidly, fixing Leah with her widened shining eyes.

"Jude, what do you mean, somebody else? Who?"

Excited by Leah's attention, Jude lost her balance on the bicycle, and nearly stumbled. Clumsily she began walking it again. Gripping the handlebars so tightly her bony knuckles gleamed white.

She was breathing quickly, lips parted. She spoke in a lowered conspiratorial voice.

"See, Mrs. Bantry, Mr. Zallman is like notorious. He comes on to girls if they're pretty-pretty like Marissa. Like some of the kids were saying on TV, he's got these laser-eyes." Jude shivered, thrilled.

Leah was shocked. "If everybody knows about Zallman, why didn't anybody tell? Before this happened? How could a man like that be allowed to teach?" She paused, anxious. Thinking *Did Marissa know? Why didn't she tell me?*

Jude giggled. "You got to wonder why any of them *teach*. I mean, why'd anybody want to hang out with *kids*! Not just some weird guy, but females, too." She smiled, seeming not to see how Leah stared at her. "Mr. Z. is kind of fun. He's this 'master'—he calls himself. On-line, you can click onto him he's 'Master of Eyes.' Little kids, girls, he'd come on to after school, and tell them be sure not to tell anybody, see. Or they'd be 'real sorry.'" Jude made a twisting motion with her hands as if wringing an invisible neck. "He likes girls with nice long hair he can brush."

"Brush?"

"Sure. Mr. Zallman has this wire brush, like. Calls it a little-doggy-brush. He runs it through your hair for fun. I mean, it used to be fun. I hope the cops took the brush when they arrested him, like for evidence. Hell, he never came on to me, I'm not pretty-pretty."

Jude spoke haughtily, with satisfaction. Fixing Leah with her curious stone-colored eyes.

Leah knew that she was expected to say, with maternal solicitude, *Oh, but you are pretty, Jude! One day, you will be.*

In different circumstances she was meant to frame the rat-girl's hot little face in her cool hands, comfort her. *One day you will be loved, Jude. Don't feel bad.*

"You were saying there might be— somebody else? Not Zallman but another person?"

Jude said, sniffing, "I wanted to tell you before, at your house, but you seemed, like, not to want to hear. And that other lady was kind of glaring at us. She didn't want us to stay."

"Jude, please. Who is this person you're talking about?"

"Mrs. Branly, Bant-ry, like I said Marissa is a good friend of mine. She is! Some kids make fun of her, she's a little slow they say but I don't think Marissa is slow, not really. She tells me all kinds of secrets, see?" Jude paused, drawing a deep breath. "She said, she missed her dad."

It was as if Jude had reached out to pinch her. Leah was speechless.

"Marissa was always saying she hates it here in Skatskill. She wanted to be with her dad, she said. Some place called 'Berkeley'—in California. She wanted to go there to live."

Jude spoke with the ingratiating air of one child informing on another to a parent. Her lips quivered, she was so excited.

Still Leah was unable to respond. Trying to think what to say except her brain seemed to be partly shutting down as if she'd had a small stroke.

Jude said innocently, "I guess you didn't know this, Mrs. Bantry?" She bit at her thumbnail, squinting.

"Marissa told you that? She told you— those things?"

"Are you mad at me, Mrs. Bantry? You wanted me to tell."

"Marissa told you—she wanted to live

with her 'dad'? Not with her mother but
with her 'dad'?"

Leah's peripheral vision had narrowed.
There was a shadowy funnel-shape at the
center of which the girl with the chalky skin
and frizzed hair squinted and grinned, in a
show of repentance.

"I just thought you would want to know,
see, Mrs. Bantry? Like, maybe Marissa ran
away? Nobody is saying that, everybody
thinks it's Mr. Zallman, like the cops are
thinking it's got to be him. Sure, maybe it is.
But—maybe!—Marissa called her dad, and
asked him to come get her? Something
weird like that? And it was a secret from
you? See, a lot of times Marissa would talk
that way, like a little kid. Like, not thinking
about her mother's feelings. And I told her,
'Your mom, she's real nice, she'd be hurt
real bad, Marissa, if you—' "

Leah couldn't hold back the tears any
longer. It was as if she'd lost her daughter
for the second time.

MISTAKES

His first was to assume that, since he knew
nothing of the disappearance of Marissa
Bantry, he could not be "involved" in it.

His second was not to contact a lawyer immediately. As soon as he realized exactly why he'd been brought into police headquarters for questioning.

His third seemed to be to have lived the wrong life.

Pervert. Sex offender. Pedophile.
Kidnapper/rapist/murderer.
Mikal Zallman, thirty-one. Suspect.

"Mother, it's Mikal. I hope you haven't seen the news already, I have something very disturbing to tell you . . ."

Nothing! He knew nothing.

The name MARISSA BANTRY meant nothing to him.

Well, not initially. He couldn't be sure.

In his agitated state, not knowing what the hell they were getting at with their questions, he couldn't be sure.

"Why are you asking me? Has something happened to 'Marissa Bantry'?"

Next, they showed him photographs of the girl.

Yes: now he recognized her. The long

blond hair, that was sometimes plaited. One of the quieter pupils. Nice girl. He recognized the picture but could not have said the girl's name because, look: "I'm not these kids' teacher, exactly. I'm a 'consultant.' I don't have a homeroom. I don't have regular classes with them. In the high school, one of the math instructors teaches computer science. I don't get to know the kids by name, like their other instructors do."

He was speaking quickly, an edge to his voice. It was uncomfortably cold in the room, yet he was perspiring.

As in a cartoon of police interrogation. *They sweated it out of the suspect.*

Strictly speaking, it wasn't true that Zallman didn't know students' names. He knew the names of many students. Certainly, he knew their faces. Especially the older students, some of whom were extremely bright, and engaging. But he had not known Marissa Bantry's name, the shy little blond child had made so little an impression on him.

Nor had he spoken with her personally. He was certain.

"Why are you asking me about this girl? If she's missing from home what is the connection with *me?*"

That edge to Zallman's voice. Not yet angry, only just impatient.

He was willing to concede, yes: if a child has been missing for more than twenty-four hours that was serious. If eleven-year-old Marissa Bantry was missing, it was a terrible thing.

"But it has nothing to do with *me*."

They allowed him to speak. They were tape recording his precious words. They did not appear to be passing judgment on him, he was not receiving the impression that they believed him involved with the disappearance, only just a few questions to put to him, to aid in their investigation. They explained to him that it was in his best interests to cooperate fully with them, to straighten out the misunderstanding, or whatever it was, a misidentification perhaps, before he left police headquarters.

"Misidentification"? What was that?

He was becoming angry, defiant. Knowing he was God-damned innocent of any wrongdoing, no matter how trivial: traffic violations, parking tickets. *He was innocent!* So he insisted upon taking a lie-detector test.

Another mistake.

Seventeen hours later an aggressive stranger now retained as Mikal Zallman's criminal lawyer was urging him, "Go home, Mikal. If you can, sleep. You will need your sleep. Don't speak with anyone except people you know and trust and assume yourself under surveillance and whatever you do, man—don't try to contact the missing girl's mother."

Please understand I am not the one. Not the madman who has taken your beautiful child. There has been some terrible misunderstanding but I swear I am innocent, Mrs. Bantry, we've never met but please allow me to commiserate with you, this nightmare we seem to be sharing.

Driving home to North Tarrytown. Oncoming headlights blinding his eyes. Tears streaming from his eyes. Now the adrenaline rush was subsiding, leaking out like water in a clogged drain, he was beginning to feel a hammering in his head that was the worst headache pain he'd ever felt in his life.

Jesus! What if it was a cerebral hemorrhage . . .

He would die. His life would be over. It would be judged that his guilt had provoked the hemorrhage. His name would never be cleared.

He'd been so cocky and arrogant coming into police headquarters, confident he'd be released within the hour, and now. A wounded animal limping for shelter. He could not keep up with traffic on route 9, he was so sick. Impatient drivers sounded their horns. A massive SUV pulled up to within inches of Zallman's rear bumper.

He knew! Ordinarily he was an impatient driver himself. Disgusted with overly cautious drivers on route 9 and now he'd become one of these, barely mobile at twenty miles an hour.

Whoever they were who hated him, who had entangled him in this nightmare, they had struck a first, powerful blow.

Zallman's bad luck, one of his fellow tenants was in the rear lobby of his building, waiting for the elevator, when Zallman staggered inside. He was unshaven, disheveled, smelling frankly of his body. He saw the other man staring at him, at first startled, recognizing him; then with undisguised repugnance.

But I didn't! I am not the one.

The police would not have released me if.

Zallman let his fellow tenant take the elevator up, alone.

Zallman lived on the fifth floor of the so-called condominium village. He had never thought of his three sparely furnished rooms as "home" nor did he think of his mother's Upper East Side brownstone as "home" any longer: it was fair to say that Zallman had no home.

It was near midnight of an unnamed day. He'd lost days of his life. He could not have stated with confidence the month, the year. His head throbbed with pain. Fumbling with the key to his darkened apartment he heard the telephone inside ringing with the manic air of a telephone that has been ringing repeatedly.

Released for the time being. Keep your cell phone with you at all times for you may be contacted by police. Do not REPEAT DO NOT leave the area. A bench warrant will be issued for your arrest in the event that you attempt to leave the area.

"It isn't that I am innocent, Mother. I know that I am innocent! The shock of it is, people seem to believe that I might not be. A lot of people."

It was a fact. A lot of people.

He would have to live with that fact, and what it meant of Mikal Zallman's place in the world, for a long time.

Keep your hands in sight, sir.
That had been the beginning. His wounded brain fixed obsessively upon that moment, at Bear Mountain.

The state troopers. Staring at him. As if.

(Would they have pulled their revolvers and shot him down, if he'd made a sudden ambiguous gesture? It made him sick to think so. It should have made him grateful that it had not happened but in fact it made him sick.)

Yet the troopers had asked him politely enough if they could search his vehicle. He'd hesitated only a moment before consenting. Sure it annoyed him as a private citizen who'd broken no laws and as a (lapsed) member of the ACLU but why not, he knew there was nothing in the minivan to catch the troopers' eyes. He didn't even smoke marijuana any longer. He'd never carried a concealed weapon, never even owned a gun. So the troopers looked through the van, and found nothing. No idea what the hell they were looking for but he'd felt a gloating sort of relief that they hadn't found it. Seeing the way they were staring at the covers of the paperback books in the back seat he'd tossed there weeks ago and had more or less forgotten.

Female nudes, and so what?

"Good thing it isn't kiddie porn, officers, eh? That stuff is illegal."

Even as a kid Zallman hadn't been able to resist wisecracking at inopportune moments.

Now, he had a lawyer. "His" lawyer.

A criminal lawyer whose retainer was fifteen thousand dollars.

They are the enemy.

Neuberger meant the Skatskill detectives, and beyond them the prosecutorial staff of the district, whose surface civility Zallman had been misinterpreting as a tacit sympathy with him, his predicament. It was a fact they'd sweated him, and he'd gone along with it naively, frankly. Telling him he was not *under arrest* only just *assisting in their investigation.*

His body had known, though. Increasingly anxious, restless, needing to urinate every twenty minutes. He'd been flooded with adrenaline like a cornered animal.

His blood pressure had risen, he could feel pulses pounding in his ears. Damned stupid to request a polygraph at such a time but—he was an innocent man, wasn't he?

Should have called a lawyer as soon as they'd begun asking him about the missing child. Once it became clear that this was a serious situation, not a mere misunderstanding or misidentification by an unnamed "eyewitness." (One of Zallman's own students? Deliberately lying to hurt him? For Christ's sake *why?*) So at last he'd called an older cousin, a corporation attorney, to whom he had not spoken since his father's funeral, and explained the situation to him, this ridiculous situation, this nightmare situation, but he had to take it seriously since obviously he was a suspect and so: would Joshua recommend a good criminal attorney who could get to Skatskill immediately, and intercede for him with the police?

His cousin had been so stunned by Zallman's news he'd barely been able to speak. "Y-you? Mikal? You're arrested—?"

"No. I am not arrested, Andrew."

He believes I might be guilty. My own cousin believes I might be a sexual predator.

Still, within ninety minutes, after a flurry of increasingly desperate phone calls, Zallman had retained a Manhattan criminal lawyer named Neuberger who didn't blithely assure him, as Zallman halfway expected he would, that there was nothing to worry about.

**TARRYTOWN RESIDENT QUESTIONED
IN ABDUCTION OF 11-YEAR-OLD**

**SEARCH FOR MARISSA CONTINUES
SKATSKILL DAY INSTRUCTOR
IN POLICE CUSTODY**

**6TH GRADER STILL MISSING
SKATSKILL DAY INSTRUCTOR
QUESTIONED BY POLICE
TENTATIVE IDENTIFICATION OF MINIVAN
BELIEVED USED IN ABDUCTION**

**MIKAL ZALLMAN, 31,
COMPUTER CONSULTANT
QUESTIONED BY POLICE IN
CHILD ABDUCTION**

**ZALLMAN: "I AM INNOCENT"
TARRYTOWN RESIDENT QUESTIONED
BY POLICE IN CHILD ABDUCTION CASE**

Luridly spread across the front pages of the newspapers were photographs of the missing girl, the missing girl's mother, and "alleged suspect Mikal Zallman."

It was a local TV news magazine. Neuberger had warned him not to watch TV, just as he should not REPEAT SHOULD NOT answer the telephone if he didn't have caller I.D., and for sure he should not answer his door unless he knew exactly who was there. Still, Zallman was watching TV fortified by a half dozen double-strength Tylenols that left him just conscious enough to stare at the screen disbelieving what he saw and heard.

Skatskill Day students, their faces blurred to disguise their identities, voices eerily slurred, telling a sympathetic female broadcaster their opinions of Mikal Zallman.

Mr. Zallman, he's cool. I liked him okay.

Mr. Zallman is kind of sarcastic I guess. He's okay with the smart kids but the rest of us it's like he's trying real hard and wants us to know.

I was so surprised! Mr. Zallman never acted like that, you know—weird. Not in computer lab.

Mr. Zallman has, like, these laser eyes? I always knew he was scary.

Mr. Zallman looks at us sometimes! It makes you shiver.

Some kids are saying he had, like, a hairbrush? To brush the girls' hair? I never saw it.

This hairbrush Mr. Zallman had, it was so weird! He never used it on me, guess I'm not pretty-pretty enough for him.

He'd help you in the lab after school if you asked. He was real nice to me. All this stuff about Marissa, I don't know. It makes me want to cry.

And there was Dr. Adrienne Cory, principal of Skatskill Day, grimly explaining to a skeptical interviewer that Mikal Zallman whom she had hired two and a half years previously had excellent credentials, had come highly recommended, was a conscientious and reliable staff member of whom there had been no complaints.

No complaints! What of the students who'd just been on the program?

Dr. Cory said, twisting her mouth in a semblance of a placating smile, "Well. We never knew."

And would Zallman continue to teach at Skatskill Day?

"Mr. Zallman has been suspended with pay for the time being."

His first, furious thought was *I will sue.*

His second, more reasonable thought was *I must plead my case.*

He had friends at Skatskill Day, he believed. The young woman who thought herself less-than-happily married, and who'd several times invited Zallman to dinner; a male math teacher, whom he often met at the gym; the school psychologist, whose sense of humor dovetailed with his own; and Dr. Cory herself, who was quite an intelligent woman, and a kindly woman, who had always seemed to like Zallman.

He would appeal to them. They must believe him!

Zallman insisted upon a meeting with Dr. Cory, face to face. He insisted upon being allowed to present his side of the case. He was informed that his presence at the school was "out of the question" at the present time; a mere glimpse of Zallman, and faculty members as well as students would be "distracted."

If he tried to enter the school building on Monday morning, Zallman was warned, security guards would turn him away.

"But why? What have I done? What have I done that is anything more than rumor?"

Not what Zallman had done but what the public perceived he might have done, that was the issue. Surely Zallman understood?

He compromised, he would meet Dr.

Cory on neutral territory, 8 A.M. Monday in the Trahern Square office of the school's legal counsel. He was told to bring his own legal counsel but Zallman declined.

Another mistake, probably. But he couldn't wait for Neuberger, this was an emergency.

"I need to work! I need to return to school as if nothing is wrong, in fact *nothing is wrong*. I insist upon returning."

Dr. Cory murmured something vaguely supportive, sympathetic. She was a kind person, Zallman wanted to believe. She was decent, well-intentioned, she liked him. She'd always laughed at his jokes!

Though sometimes wincing, as if Zallman's humor was a little too abrasive for her. At least publicly.

Zallman was protesting the decision to suspend him from teaching without "due process." He demanded to be allowed to meet with the school board. How could he be suspended from teaching for no reason—wasn't that unethical, and illegal? Wouldn't Skatskill Day be liable, if he chose to sue?

"I swear I did not—*do it. I am not involved.* I scarcely know Marissa Bantry, I've had virtually no contact with the girl. Dr. Cory—

Adrienne—these 'eyewitnesses' are lying. This 'barrette' that was allegedly found by police behind my building—someone must have placed it there. Someone who hates me, who wants to destroy me! This has been a nightmare for me but I'm confident it will turn out well. I mean, it can't be proven that I'm involved with—with—whatever has happened to the girl—because I am not involved! I need to come back to work, Adrienne, I need you to demonstrate that you have faith in me. I'm sure that my colleagues have faith in me. Please reconsider! I'm prepared to return to work this morning. I can explain to the students—something! Give me a chance, will you? Even if I'd been arrested—which I am not, Adrienne—under the law I am innocent until proven guilty and I can't possibly be proven guilty because I—I did not—*I did not do anything wrong.*"

He was struck by a sudden stab of pain, as if someone had driven an ice pick into his skull. He whimpered and slumped forward gripping his hand in his hands.

A woman was asking him, in a frightened voice, "Mr. Zallman? Do you want us to call a doctor?—an ambulance?"

UNDER SURVEILLANCE

He needed to speak with her. He needed to console her.

On the fifth day of the vigil it became an overwhelming need.

For in his misery he'd begun to realize how much worse it was for the mother of Marissa Bantry, than for him who was merely the suspect.

It was Tuesday. Of course, he had not been allowed to return to teach. He had not slept for days except fitfully, in his clothes. He ate standing before the opened refrigerator, grabbing at whatever was inside. He lived on Tylenols. Obsessively he watched TV, switching from channel to channel in pursuit of the latest news of the missing girl and steeling himself for a glimpse of his own face, haggard and hollow-eyed and disfigured by guilt as by acne. *There he is! Zallman!* The only suspect in the case whom police had actually brought into custody, paraded before a phalanx of photographers and TV cameramen to arouse the excited loathing of hundreds of thousands of spectators who would not have the opportunity to see Zallman, and to revile him, in the flesh.

In fact, the Skatskill police had other suspects. They were following other "leads." Neuberger had told him he'd heard that they had sent men to California, to track down the elusive father of Marissa Bantry who had emerged as a "serious suspect" in the abduction.

Yet, in the Skatskill area, the search continued. In the Bear Mountain State Park, and in the Blue Mountain Reserve south of Peekskill. Along the edge of the Hudson River between Peekskill and Skatskill. In parkland and wooded areas east of Skatskill in the Rockefeller State Park. These were search and rescue teams comprised of both professionals and volunteers. Zallman had wanted to volunteer to help with the search for he was desperate to do something but Neuberger had fixed him with a look of incredulity. "Mikal, that is not a good idea. Trust me."

There had been reports of men seen "dumping" mysterious objects from bridges into rivers and streams and there had been further "sightings" of the living girl in the company of her captor or captors at various points along the New York State Thruway and the New England Expressway. Very blond fair-skinned girls between the ages of eight and thirteen resembling Marissa Bantry were being seen everywhere.

Police had received more than one thousand calls and Web site messages and in the media it was announced that *all leads will be followed* but Zallman wondered at this. *All* leads?

He himself called the Skatskill detectives, often. He'd memorized their numbers. Often, they failed to return his calls. He was made to understand that Zallman was no longer their prime suspect—maybe. Neuberger had told him that the girl's barrette, so conspicuously dropped by Zallman's parking space, had been wiped clean of fingerprints: "An obvious plant."

Zallman had had his telephone number changed to an unlisted number yet still the unwanted calls—vicious, obscene, threatening, or merely inquisitive—continued and so he'd had the phone disconnected and relied now upon his cell phone exclusively, carrying it with him as he paced through the shrinking rooms of his condominium apartment. From the fifth floor, at a slant, Zallman could see the Hudson River on overcast days like molten lead but on clear days possessed of an astonishing slate-blue beauty. For long minutes he lost himself in contemplation of the view: beauty that was pure, unattached to any individual, destined to outlive the misery that had become his life.

Nothing to do with me. Nothing to do with human evil.

Desperately he wanted to share this insight with the mother of Marissa Bantry. It was such a simple fact, it might be overlooked.

He went to 15th Street where the woman lived, he'd seen the exterior of the apartment building on TV numerous times. He had not been able to telephone her. He wanted only to speak with her for a few minutes.

It was near dusk of Tuesday. A light chill mist-rain was falling. For a while he stood indecisively on the front walk of the barracks-like building, in khaki trousers, canvas jacket, jogging shoes. His damp hair straggled past his collar. He had not shaved for several days. A sickly radiance shone in his face, he knew he was doing the right thing now crossing the lawn at an angle, to circle to the rear of the building where he might have better luck discovering which of the apartments belonged to Leah Bantry.

Please I must see you.

We must share this nightmare.

Police came swiftly to intercept him, grabbing his arms and cuffing his wrists behind his back.

———

SACRIFICE

Is she breathing?

   . . . Christ!

   She isn't . . . is she? *Is* she?

   She is. She's okay.

   . . . like maybe she's being . . . poisoned?

We were getting so scared! Anita was crying a lot, then Anita was laughing like she couldn't stop. Denise had this eating-thing, she was hungry all the time, stuffing her mouth at meals and in the cafeteria at school then poking a finger down her throat to make herself vomit into a toilet flush-flush-flushing the toilet so if she was at home nobody in her family would hear or if she was at school other girls wouldn't hear and tell on her.

More and more we could see how they were watching us at school, like *somehow they knew.*

Since giving the white flowers to the Corn Maiden's mother nothing felt right. Denise knew, and Anita. Jude maybe knew but would not acknowledge it.

Mothers don't give a shit about their kids. See, it's all pretend.

Jude believed this. She hated the Corn

Maiden's mother worse than she hated anybody, just about.

Anita was worried the Corn Maiden was
being poisoned, all the strong drugs Jude
was making her swallow. The Corn Maiden
was hardly eating anything now, you had to
mush it up like cottage cheese with vanilla
ice cream, open her jaws and spoon it into
her mouth then close her jaws and try to
make her to swallow, but half the time the
Corn Maiden began choking and gagging
and the white mush just leaked out of her
mouth like vomit.

We were begging, Jude maybe we
better . . .

. . . we don't want her to die, like do we?
Jude? *Jude?*

The fun was gone now. Seeing TV news, and
all the newspapers even *The New York Times*,
and the posters HAVE YOU SEEN ME? and the
fifteen-thousand-dollar reward, and all that,
that made us laugh like hyenas just a few
days ago but wasn't anything to laugh at
now, or anyway not much. Jude still scorned
the assholes, she called them, and laughed
at how they ran around looking for the
Corn Maiden practically under their noses
out Highgate Avenue.

Jude was doing these weird things. On Monday she came to school with one of the Corn Maiden's butterfly barrettes she was going to wear in her hair but we told her Oh no better not! and she laughed at us but didn't wear it.

Jude talked a lot about fire, "immolation." On the Internet she looked up some things like Buddhists had done a long time ago.

The Sacrifice of the Corn Maiden called for the heart of the captive cut out, and her blood collected in sacred vessels, but you could burn the Corn Maiden, too, and mix her ashes with the soil Jude said.

Fire is a cleaner way, Jude said. It would only hurt at the beginning.

Jude was taking Polaroids all the time now. By the end, Jude would have like fifty of these. We believed that Jude intended to post them on the Internet but that did not happen.

What was done with them, if the police took them away we would not know. They were not ever printed. Maybe they were destroyed.

These were pictures to stare at! In some of them the Corn Maiden was lying on her back in the bier in the beautiful silky fabrics and brocades and she was *so little*. Jude

posed her naked and with her hair fanned
out and her legs spread wide so you could
see the little pink slip between her legs Jude
called her cut.

The Corn Maiden's cut was not like ours,
it was a little-girl cut and nicer, Jude said. It
would never grow *pubic hairs* Jude said, the
Corn Maiden would be spared that.

Jude laughed saying she would send the
TV stations these pictures they could not use.

Other poses, the Corn Maiden was sitting
up or kneeling or on her feet if Jude could
revive her, and slap-slap her face so her eyes
were open, you would think she was awake,
and smiling this wan little smile leaning
against Jude, their heads leaning together
and Jude grinning like Jude O and the Corn
Maiden were floating somewhere above the
earth in some Heaven where nobody could
reach them, only just look up at them wondering how they'd got there!

Jude had us take these pictures. One of
them was her favorite, she said she wished
the Corn Maiden's mother could see it and
maybe someday she would.

That night, we thought the Corn Maiden
would die.

She was shivering and twitching in her sleep like she'd been mostly doing then suddenly she was having like an epileptic fit, her mouth sprang open *Uh-uh-uh* and her tongue protruded wet with spittle and really ugly like a freak and Anita was backing off and whimpering She's going to die! oh God she's going to die! Jude do something she's going to die! and Jude slapped Anita's face to shut her up, Jude was so disgusted. Fat ass, get away. What the fuck do you know. Jude held the Corn Maiden down, the Corn Maiden's skinny arms and legs were shaking so, it was like she was trying to dance laying down and her eyes came open unseeing like a doll's dead glass eyes and Jude was kind of scared now and excited and climbed up onto the bier to lay on her, for maybe the Corn Maiden was cold, so skinny the cold had gotten into her bones, Jude's arms were stretched out like the Corn Maiden's arms and her hands were gripping the Corn Maiden's hands, her legs quivering stretched out the Corn Maiden's legs, and the side of her face against the Corn Maiden's face like they were twin girls hatched from the same egg. I am here, I am Jude I will protect you, in the Valley of the Shadow of Death I will protect you forever AMEN. Till finally the Corn Maiden ceased convulsing and was only just breathing in this long shuddering way, but she was breathing, she would be okay.

Still, Anita was freaked. Anita was trying not to laugh this wild hyena laugh you'd hear from her at school sometimes, like she was being tickled in a way she could not bear so Jude became disgusted and slapped Anita SMACK-SMACK on both cheeks calling her fat ass and stupid cunt and Anita ran out of the storage room like a kicked dog crying, we heard her on the stairs and Jude said, She's next.

On darkspeaklink.com where Jude O bonded with the Master of Eyes Jude showed us IF THERE IS A PERSON THERE IS A PROBLEM. IF THERE IS NO PERSON THERE IS NO PROBLEM. (STALIN)

Jude had never told the Master of Eyes that she was female or male and so the Master of Eyes believed her to be male. She had told him she had taken her captive, did he give her permission to Sacrifice? and the Master of Eyes shot back you are precocious/precious if 13 yrs old & where do you live Jude O? but the thought came to Jude suddenly the Master of Eyes was not her friend who dwelled in several places of the earth si-

multaneously but an FBI agent pretending
to be her soul mate in order to capture her so
Jude O disappeared from darkspeaklink.com
forever.

YOU ASSHOLES! A SUICIDE NOTE

Jude O knew, it was ending. Four days pre-
ceding the Sacrifice and this was the sixth
day. No turning back.

Denise was breaking down. Dull/dazed
like she'd been hit over the head and in
morning homeroom the teacher asked,
Denise are you ill and at first Denise did not
hear then shaking her head almost you
could not hear her *no*.

Anita had not come to school. Anita was
hiding away at home, and would betray
Jude. And there was no way to get to Anita
now, Jude was unable to silence the traitor.

Jude's disciples, she had trusted. Yet she
had not truly trusted them knowing they
were inferiors.

Denise was begging, Jude I think we
better . . .

. . . let the Corn Maiden go?

Because because if she, if . . .

The Corn Maiden becomes Taboo. The
Corn Maiden can never be released. Except

if somebody takes the Corn Maiden's place the Corn Maiden can never be released.

You want to take the Corn Maiden's place?

Jude, she isn't the Corn Maiden she's M-Marissa Ban—

A flame of righteous fury came over Jude O, SMACK-SMACK with the palm and back of her hand she slapped the offensive face.

When spotted hyenas are born they are usually twins. One twin is stronger than the other and at once attacks the other hoping to tear out its throat and why, because the other would try to kill it otherwise. There is no choice.

At the table at the very rear of the cafeteria where Jude O and her disciples perceived as pathetic misfit losers by their Skatskill Day classmates usually ate their lunches together except today only Jude O and Denise Ludwig, and it was observed how Denise was whimpering and pleading with Jude wiping at her nose in a way repellent to the more fastidious girl who said through clenched jaws I forbid you to cry, I forbid you to make a spectacle of yourself, but Denise continued, and Denise whimpered and begged, and at last a flame of indignation swept over Jude who slapped Denise and Denise stumbled from the table overturning her chair, ran blubbering from the cafeteria in full view of staring others, and in that same instant it seemed that wily Jude O fled through a rear exit running crouched over to the middle school bicycle rack, and fueled by that same passion of indignation Jude bicycled 2.7 miles home to the old Trahern house on Highgate Avenue several times nearly struck by vehicles that swerved to avoid the blind-seeming cyclist and she laughed for she was feeling absolutely no fear now like a hawk riding the crest of an updraft scarcely needing to move its wings to remain aloft, and lethal. A hawk! Jude O was a hawk! If her bicycle had been struck and crushed, if she'd died on Highgate Avenue the Corn Maiden would molder in her bier of silks and brocades, unseen. No one would find the Corn Maiden for a long time.

It is better this way, we will die together.

She would not have requested a jury trial, you had to utter such bullshit to sway a jury. She would have requested a judge merely.

A judge is an aristocrat. Jude O was an aristocrat.

She would have been tried as an adult! Would have insisted.

In the gardener's shed there was a rusted old lawnmower. A can of gasoline half full. You poured the gasoline through the funnel if you could get it open. Jude had experimented, she could get it open.

Her grandmother's old silver lighter engraved with the initials *G.L.T.* Click-click-click and a transparent little bluish-orange flame appeared pretty as a flicking tongue.

She would immolate the Corn Maiden first.

No! Better to die together.

Telling herself calmly *It will only hurt at first. Just for a few seconds and by then it will be too late.*

She laughed to think of it. Like already it was done.

Stealthily entering the house by the rear door. So the old woman watching afternoon TV would not hear.

She was very excited! She was determined to make no error. Already forgetting that perhaps she had erred, allowing both her disciples to escape when she'd known that they were weakening. And confiding in the Master of Eyes believing she could trust him as her twin not recalling the spotted hyena twin, of course you could not trust.

Well, she had learned!

Forced herself to compose the Suicide Note. In her thoughts for a long time (it seemed so, now!) Jude had been composing this with care knowing its importance. It was addressed to *you assholes* for there was no one else.

Smiling to think how *you assholes* would be amazed.

On TV and on-line and in all the papers including *The New York Times* front page.

Whywhy you're asking here's why her hair.

I mean *her hair*! I mean like I saw it in the sun . . .

So excited! Heart beating fast like she'd swallowed a dozen E's. Unlocking the padlock with trembling hands. If Denise had told, already! *Should have killed them both last night. When I had the chance.* Inside the storage room, the Corn Maiden had shifted from the lying-on-her-side position in which Jude had left her that morning after making her eat. This was proof, the Corn Maiden was shrewdly pretending to be weaker than she was. Even in her sickness there was deceit.

Jude left the storage room door open, to let in light. She would not trouble to light the scented candles, so many candles there was not time. And flame now would be for a different purpose.

Squatting breathless over the Corn Maiden, with both thumbs lifting the bruised eyelids.

Milky eyes. Pupils shrunken.

Wake up! It's time it's time.

Feebly the Corn Maiden pushed at Jude. She was frightened, whimpering. Her breath smelled of something rotted. She had not been allowed to brush her teeth since coming to Jude's house, she had not been allowed to bathe herself. Only as Jude and her disciples had bathed her with wetted soapy washclothes.

Know what time it is it's time it's time it's timetimetime!

Don't hurt me please let me go . . .

Jude was the Taboo Priest. Seizing the Corn Maiden's long silky hair in her fist and forcing her down onto the bier scolding No no no no no *no* like you would scold a baby.

A baby that is flesh of your flesh but you must discipline.

The immolation would have to be done swiftly, Jude knew. For that traitor-cunt Denise had babbled by now. Fat ass Anita had babbled. Her disciples had betrayed her, they were unworthy of her. They would be so sorry! She would not forgive them, though. Like she would not forgive the Corn Maiden's mother for staring at her

like she was a bug or something, loathsome.
What she regretted was she would not have
time to cut out the Corn Maiden's heart as
the Sacrifice demanded.

Lay still, I said it's *time*.

A new thought was coming to her now.
She had not hold of it yet, the way you have
not yet hold of a dream until it is fully
formed like a magnificent bubble inside
your head.

Jude had dragged the gasoline can into
the storage room, and was spilling gasoline
in surges. This could be the priest blessing
the Corn Maiden and her bier. The stink of
gasoline was strong, that was why the Corn
Maiden was revived, her senses sharpening.

No! no! Don't hurt me let me go! I want
my mother.

Jude laughed to see the Corn Maiden so
rebellious. Actually pushing free of Jude, so
weak she could not stand but on hands and
knees naked crawling desperately toward
the door. Never had Jude left the door open
until now and yet the Corn Maiden saw, and
comprehended this was escape. Jude smiled
seeing how desperate the Corn Maiden,
stark naked and her hair trailing the floor
like an animal's mane. Oh so skin-and-
bones! Her ribs, bony hips, even the ankle
bones protruding. Skinny haunches no big-

ger than Jude's two hands fitted together. And her hinder. *Hinder* was a funny word, a word meant to make you smile. A long time ago a pretty curly-haired woman had been humming and singing daubing sweet-smelling white powder onto Jude's little *hinder* before drawing up her rubber underpants, pulling down Jude's smock embroidered with dancing kittens or maybe it had been a nightgown, and the underpants had been a diaper.

Jude watched, fascinated. She had never seen the Corn Maiden disobey her so openly! It was like a baby just learning to crawl. She had not known the Corn Maiden so desired to live. Thinking suddenly *Better for her to remain alive, to revere me. And I have made my mark on her she will never forget.*

The Priest was infused with the power. The power of life-and-death. She would confer life, it was her decision. Climbing onto the bier spilling gasoline in a sacred circle around her. The stink of gasoline made her sensitive nostrils constrict, her eyes were watering so she could barely see. But she had no need to see. All was within, that she wished to see. *It will only hurt at first. Then it will be too late.* Click-click-clicking the silver lighter with gasoline-slippery fingers until the bright little flame-tongue leapt out.

See what I can do assholes, you never could.

SEPTEMBER

The Little Family

It was their first outing together, at the Croton Falls Nature Preserve. The three of them, as a family.

Of course, Zallman was quick to concede, not an actual *family*.

For the man and woman were not married. Their status as friends/lovers was yet undefined. And the girl was the woman's child, alone.

Yet if you saw them, you would think *family*.

It was a bright warm day in mid-September. Zallman who now measured time in terms of before/after was thinking the date was exactly five months *after*. But this was a coincidence merely.

From Yonkers, where he now lived, Zallman drove north to Mahopac to pick up Leah Bantry and her daughter Marissa at their new home. Leah and Marissa had prepared a picnic lunch. The Croton Falls Nature Preserve, which Leah had only recently discovered, was just a few miles away.

A beautiful place, Leah had told Zallman. So quiet.

Zallman guessed this was a way of saying *Marissa feels safe here.*

Leah Bantry was working now as a medical technician at Woman/Space, a clinic in Mahopac, New York. Mikal Zallman was temporarily teaching middle school math at a large public school in Yonkers where he also assisted the soccer/basketball/baseball coach.

Marissa was enrolled in a small private school in Mahopac without grades or a formal curriculum in which students received special tutoring and counseling as needed.

Tuition at the Mahopac Day School was high. Mikal Zallman was helping with it.

No one can know what you and your daughter went through. I feel so drawn to you both, please let me be your friend!

Before Zallman had known Leah Bantry, he had loved her. Knowing her now he was confirmed in his love. He vowed to bear this secret lightly until Leah was prepared to receive it.

She wanted no more emotion in her life, Leah said. Not for a long time.

Zallman wondered: what did that mean? And did it mean what it meant, or was it simply a way of saying *Don't hurt me! Don't come near.*

He liked it that Leah encouraged Marissa to call him Uncle Mikal. This suggested he might be around for a while. So far, in Zallman's presence at least, Marissa did not call him anything at all.

Zallman saw the girl glance at him, sometimes. Quick covert shy glances he hesitated to acknowledge.

There was a tentative air about them. The three of them.

As if (after the media nightmare, this was quite natural) they were being observed, on camera.

Zallman felt like a tightrope walker. He was crossing a tightrope high above a gawking audience, and there was no safety net beneath. His arms were extended for balance. He was terrified of falling but he must go forward. If at this height your balance is not perfect, it will be lethal.

In the nature preserve in the bright warm autumnal sunshine the adults walked together at the edge of a pond. To circle the pond required approximately thirty minutes. There were other visitors to the preserve on this Sunday afternoon, families and couples.

The girl wandered ahead of the adults, though never far ahead. Her behavior was more that of a younger child than a child of eleven. Her movements were tentative, sometimes she paused as if she were out of breath. Her skin was pale and appeared translucent. Her eyes were deep-socketed, wary. Her pale blond hair shimmered in the sun. It had been cut short, feathery, falling to just below her delicate eggshell ears.

After her ordeal in April, Marissa had lost much of her beautiful long hair. She'd been hospitalized for several weeks. Slowly she had regained most of the weight she'd lost so abruptly. Still she was anemic, Leah was concerned that there had been lasting damage to Marissa's kidneys and liver. She suffered from occasional bouts of tachycardia, of varying degrees of severity. At such times, her mother held her tight, tight. At such times the child's runaway heartbeat and uncontrollable shivering seemed to the mother a demonic third presence, a being maddened by terror.

Both mother and daughter had difficulty sleeping. But Leah refused prescription drugs for either of them.

Each was seeing a therapist in Mahopac. And Marissa also saw Leah's therapist for a joint session with her mother, once a week.

Leah confided in Zallman, "It's a matter of time. Of healing. I have faith, Marissa will be all right."

Leah never used such terms as *normal, recovered*.

Mikal Zallman had been the one to write to Leah Bantry of course. He had felt the desperate need to communicate with her, even if she had not the slightest wish to communicate with him.

I feel that we have shared a nightmare. We will never understand it. I don't know what I can offer you other than sympathy, commiseration. During the worst of the nightmare I had almost come to think that I was responsible . . .

After Marissa was discharged from the hospital, Leah took her away from Skatskill. She could not bear living in that apartment another day, she could not bear all that reminded her of the nightmare. She was surrounded by well-intentioned neighbors, and through the ordeal she had made several friends; she had been offered work in the area. If she'd wished to return to work at the Nyack Clinic, very likely Davitt Stoop would have allowed her to return. He had reconciled with his wife, he was in a forgiving mood. But Leah had no wish to see the man again, ever. She had no wish to drive across the Tappan Zee Bridge again, ever.

Out of the ordeal had come an unexpected alliance with her sister Avril. While Marissa was in the hospital, Avril had continued to stay in Skatskill; one or the other of the two sisters was always in Marissa's hospital room. Avril had taken an unpaid leave from her job in Washington, she helped Leah find another job and to relocate in Mahopac, fifty miles north in hilly Putnam County.

Enough of Westchester County! Leah would never return.

She was so grateful for Avril's devotion, she found herself at a loss for words.

"Leah, come on! It's what any sister would do."

"No. It is not what any sister would do. It's what my sister would do. God damn I love you, Avril."

Leah burst into tears. Avril laughed at her. The sisters laughed together, they'd become ridiculous in their emotions. Volatile and unpredictable as ten-year-olds.

Leah vowed to Avril, she would never take anyone for granted again. Never anything. Not a single breath! Never again.

When they'd called her with the news: *Marissa is alive.*

That moment. Never would she forget that moment.

In their family only Avril knew: police had tracked Marissa's elusive father to Coos Bay, Oregon. There, he had apparently died in 1999 in a boating mishap. The medical examiner had ruled the cause of death "inconclusive." There had been speculation that he'd been murdered . . .

Leah hadn't been prepared for the shock she'd felt, and the loss.

Now, he would never love her again. He would never love his beautiful daughter again. He would never make things right between them.

She had never spoken his name aloud to Marissa. She would never speak it aloud. As a younger child Marissa used to ask Where is Daddy? When will Daddy come back? But now, never.

The death of Marissa's father in Coos Bay, Oregon, was a mystery, but it was a mystery Leah Bantry would not pursue. She was sick of mystery. She wanted only clarity, truth. She would surround herself with good decent truthful individuals for the remainder of her life.

Mikal Zallman agreed. No more mysteries!

You become exhausted, you simply don't care. You care about surviving. You care about the banalities of life: *closure, moving on.* Before the nightmare he'd have laughed at such TV talk-show jargon but now, no.

Of Leah Bantry and Mikal Zallman, an unlikely couple, Zallman was the more verbal, the more edgy. He was from a tribe of talkers, he told Leah. Lawyers, financiers, high-powered salesmen. A rabbi or two. For Zallman, just to wake up in the morning in Yonkers, and not in Skatskill, was a relief. And not in April, during that siege of nightmare. To lift his head from the pillow and not wince with pain as if broken glass were shifting inside his skull. To be able to open a newspaper, switch on TV news, without seeing his own craven likeness. To breathe freely, not-in-police-custody. Not the object of a mad girl's vengeance.

Mad girl was the term Zallman and Leah used, jointly. Never would they utter the name *Jude Trahern.*

Why had the mad girl abducted Marissa? Why, of all younger children she might have preyed upon, had she chosen Marissa? And why had she killed herself, why in such a gruesome way, self-immolation like a martyr? These questions would never be answered. The cowed girls who'd conspired with her in the abduction had not the slightest clue. Something about an Onigara Indian sacrifice! They could only repeat brainlessly that they hadn't thought the mad girl was serious. They had only just followed her direction, they had wanted to be her friend.

To say that the girl had been *mad* was only a word. But the word would suffice.

Zallman said in disgust, "To know all isn't to forgive all. To know all is to be sickened by what you know." He was thinking of the Holocaust, too: a cataclysm in history that defied all explanation.

Leah said, wiping at her eyes, "I would not forgive her, under any circumstances. She wasn't 'mad,' she was evil. She took pleasure in hurting others. She almost killed my daughter. I'm glad that she's dead, she's removed herself from us. But I don't want to talk about her, Mikal. Promise me."

Zallman was deeply moved. He kissed Leah Bantry then, for the first time. As if to seal an understanding.

Like Leah, Zallman could not bear to live in the Skatskill area any longer. Couldn't breathe!

Without exactly reinstating Zallman, the principal and board of trustees of Skatskill Day had invited him back to teach. Not immediately, but in the fall.

A substitute was taking his place at the school. It was believed to be most practical for the substitute to finish the spring term.

Zallman's presence, so soon after the ugly publicity, would be "distracting to students." Such young, impressionable students. And their anxious parents.

Zallman was offered a two-year renewable contract at his old salary. It was not a very tempting contract. His lawyer told him that the school feared a lawsuit, with justification. But Zallman said the hell with it. He'd lost interest in combat.

And he'd lost interest in computers, overnight.

Where he'd been fascinated by the technology, now he was bored. He craved something more substantial, of the earth and time. Computers were merely technique, like bodiless brains. He would take a temporary job teaching math in a public school, and he would apply to graduate schools to study history. A Ph.D. program in

American studies. At Columbia, Yale, Princeton.

Zallman didn't tell Leah what revulsion he sometimes felt, waking before dawn and unable to return to sleep. Not for computers but for the Zallman who'd so adored them.

How arrogant he'd been, how self-absorbed! The lone wolf who had so prided himself on aloneness.

He'd had enough of that now. He yearned for companionship, someone to talk with, make love with. Someone to share certain memories that would otherwise fester in him like poison.

In late May, after Leah Bantry and her daughter Marissa had moved away from Skatskill—a departure excitedly noted in the local media—Zallman began to write to her. He'd learned that Leah had taken a position at a medical clinic in Mahopoc. He knew the area, to a degree: an hour's drive away. He wrote a single-page, thoughtfully composed letter to her not expecting her to reply, though hoping that she might. *I feel so close to you! This ordeal that has so changed our lives.* He'd studied her photographs in the papers, the grieving mother's drawn, exhausted face. He knew that Leah Bantry was a few years older than he, that she was no longer in contact with Marissa's father. He sent her postcards of works of art: Van Gogh's sunflowers, Monet's water lilies, haunted landscapes of Caspar David Friedrich and gorgeous autumnal forests of Wolf Kahn. In this way Zallman courted Leah Bantry. He allowed this woman whom he had never met to know that he revered her. He would put no pressure on her to see him, not even to respond to him.

In time, Leah Bantry did respond.

They spoke on the phone. They made arrangements to meet. Zallman was nervously talkative, endearingly awkward. He seemed overwhelmed by Leah's physical presence. Leah was more wary, reticent. She was a beautiful woman who looked her age, she wore no makeup, no jewelry except a watch; her fair blond hair was threaded with silver. She smiled, but she did not speak much. She liked it that this man would do the talking, as men usually did not. Mikal Zallman was a personality of a type Leah knew, but at a distance. Very New York, very intense. Brainy, but naive. She guessed that his family had money, naturally Zallman scorned money. (But he'd been reconciled with his family, Zallman said, at the time of the ordeal. They had been outraged on his behalf and had insisted upon paying his lawyer's exorbitant fees.) During their conversation, Leah recalled how they'd first met at the Skatskill school, and how Zallman the computer expert had walked away from her. So arrogant! Leah would tease him about that, one day. When they became lovers perhaps.

Zallman's hair was thinning at the temples, there was a dented look to his cheeks. His eyes were those of a man older than thirty-one or -two. He'd begun to grow a beard, a goatee, to disguise his appearance, but you could see that it was a temporary experiment, it would not last. Yet Leah thought Mikal Zallman handsome, in his way rather romantic. A narrow hawkish face, brooding eyes. Quick to laugh at himself. She would allow him to adore her, possibly one day she would adore him. She was not prepared to be hurt by him.

Eventually she would tell him the not-quite-true *I never believed you were the one to take Marissa, Mikal. Never!*

The little family, as Zallman wished to think them, ate their picnic lunch, and what a delicious lunch it was, on a wooden table on the bank of a pond, beneath a willow tree so exquisitely proportioned it looked like a work of art in a children's storybook. He noted that Marissa still had trouble with food, ate slowly and with an air of caution, as if, with each mouthful, she was expecting to encounter broken glass. But she ate most of a sandwich, and half an apple Leah peeled for her, since "skins" made her queasy. And afterward tramping about the pond admiring snowy egrets and great blue herons and wild swans. Everywhere were lushly growing cattails, rushes, flaming sumac. There was a smell of moist damp earth and sunlight on water and in the underbrush red-winged blackbirds were flocking in a festive cacophony. Leah lamented, "But it's too soon! We're not ready for winter." She sounded genuinely hurt, aggrieved.

Zallman said, "But Leah, snow can be nice, too."

Marissa, who was walking ahead of her mother and Mr. Zallman, wanted to think this was so: *snow, nice.* She could not clearly remember snow. Last winter. Before April, and after April. She knew that she had lived for eleven years and yet her memory was a windowpane covered in cobwebs. Her therapists were kindly soft-spoken women who asked repeatedly about what had happened to her in the cellar of the old house, what the bad girls had done to her, for it was healthy to remember, and to speak of what she remembered, like draining an absess they said, and she should cry, too, and be angry; but it was difficult to have such emotions when she couldn't remember clearly. What are you feeling, Marissa, she was always being asked, and the answer was *I don't know* or *Nothing!* But that was not the right answer.

Sometimes in dreams she saw, but never with opened eyes.

With opened eyes, she felt blind. Sometimes.

The bad girl had fed her, she remembered. Spoon-fed. She'd been so hungry! So grateful.

All adults are gone. All our mothers.

Marissa knew: that was a lie. The bad girl had lied to her.

Still, the bad girl had fed her. Brushed her hair. Held her when she'd been so cold.

The sudden explosion, flames! The burning girl, terrible shrieks and screams— Marissa had thought at first it was herself, on fire and screaming. She was crawling upstairs but was too weak and she fainted and someone came noisy and shouting to lift her in his arms and it was three days later

Mommy told her when she woke in the hospital, her head so heavy she could not lift it.

Mommy and Mr. Zallman. She was meant to call him "Uncle Mikal" but she could not.

Mr. Zallman had been her teacher in Skatskill. But he behaved as if he didn't remember any of that. Maybe Mr. Zallman had not remembered her, Marissa had not been one of the good students. He had only seemed to care for the good students, the others were invisible to him. He was not "Uncle Mikal" and it would be wrong to call him that.

At this new school everybody was very nice to her. The teachers knew who she was, and the therapists and doctors. Mommy said they had to know or they could not help her. One day, when she was older, she would move to a place where nobody knew Marissa Bantry. Away out in California.

Mommy would not wish her to leave. But Mommy would know why she had to leave.

At this new school, that was so much smaller than Skatskill Day, Marissa had a few friends. They were shy wary thin-faced girls like herself. They were girls who, if you only just glanced at them, you would think they were missing a limb; but then you would see, no they were not. They were *whole girls*.

Marissa liked her hair cut short. Her long silky hair the bad girls had brushed and fanned out about her head, it had fallen out in clumps in the hospital. Long hair made her nervous now. Through her fingers at school sometimes lost in a dream she watched girls with hair rippling down their backs like hers used to, she marveled they were oblivious to the danger.

They had never heard of the Corn Maiden! The words would mean nothing to them.

Marissa was a reader now. Marissa brought books everywhere with her, to hide inside. These were storybooks with illustrations. She read slowly, sometimes pushing her finger beneath the words. She was fearful of encountering words she didn't know, words she was supposed to know but did not know. Like a sudden fit of coughing. Like a spoon shoved into your mouth before you were ready. Mommy had said Marissa was safe now from the bad girls and from any bad people, Mommy would take care of her but Marissa knew from reading stories that this could not be so. You had only to turn the page, something would happen.

Today she had brought along two books from the school library: *Watching Birds!* and *The Family of Butterflies.* They were books for readers younger than eleven, Marissa knew. But they would not surprise her.

Marissa is carrying these books with her, wandering along the edge of the pond a short distance ahead of Mommy and Mr. Zallman. There are dragonflies in the cattails like floating glinting needles. There are tiny white moth-butterflies, and beautiful large orange monarchs with slow-pulsing wings. Behind Marissa, Mommy and Mr. Zallman are talking earnestly. Always they are talking, it seems. Maybe they will be married and talk all the time and Marissa will not need to listen to them, she will be invisible.

A red-winged blackbird swaying on a cattail calls sharply to her.

In the Valley of the Shadow of Death I will protect you AMEN.

SHARYN MCCRUMB

Sharyn McCrumb holds degrees from the University of North Carolina and Virginia Tech. She lives in Virginia's Blue Ridge Mountains but travels the United States and the world lecturing on her work, most recently leading a writer's workshop in Paris in summer 2001. Her Ballad series, beginning with *If Ever I Return, Pretty Peggy-O* (1990), has won her numerous honors, including the Appalachian Writers Association's Award for Outstanding Contribution to Appalachian Literature and several listings as *New York Times* and *Los Angeles Times* notable books. In the introduction to her short-story collection *Foggy Mountain Breakdown and Other Stories*, she details the family history in North Carolina and Tennessee that contributed to her Appalachian fiction. One of the continuing characters, Sheriff Spencer Arrowood, takes his surname from ancestors on her father's side, while Frankie Silver ("the first woman hanged for murder in the state of North Carolina"), whose story McCrumb would incorporate in *The Ballad of Frankie Silver*, was a distant cousin. "My books are like Appalachian quilts," she writes. "I take brightly colored scraps of legends, ballads, fragments of rural life, and local tragedy, and I place them together into a complex whole that tells not only a story, but also a deeper truth about the nature of the mountain south." The seventh and most recent title in the Ballad series, *Ghost Riders*, appeared in 2003. Her most recent novel is *St. Dale*.

THE RESURRECTION MAN

Sharyn McCrumb

Haloed in lamplight the young man stands swaying on the threshold for an instant, perhaps three heartbeats, before the scalpel falls from his fingers, and he pitches forward into the dark hallway, stumbling toward the balcony railing where the stairwell curves around the rotunda. From where he stands outside the second floor classroom, it is thirty feet or more to the marble floor below.

The old man in the hall is not surprised. He has seen too many pale young men make just such a dash from that room, from its stench of sweet decay, hardly leavened by the tobacco spit that coats the wooden floor. They chew to mask the odor—this boy is new, and does not yet know that trick. The tobacco will make him as sick as the other at first. It is all one.

He makes no move to take hold of the sufferer. They are alone in the building, but even so, these days such a thing would not be proper. The young man might take offense, and there is his own white linen suit to be thought of. He is not working tonight. He only came to see why there was a light in the upstairs window. More to the point, he has long ago lost the desire to touch human flesh. He stays in the shadows and watches the young man lunge for cold air in the cavernous space beneath the dome.

But the smell of the dissecting room is not escaped so easily, and the old man knows what will happen if the student does not get fresh air soon. Somebody will have to clean up the hall floor. It won't be the old man. He is too grand for that, but it will be one of the other employees, some acquaintance of his, and it is easy enough to spare a cleaner more work and the young man more embarrassment. Easy enough to offer the fire bucket as an alternative.

A gallon bucket of sand has been set outside the dissection room in case a careless student overturns an oil lamp, and in one fluid motion he hoists it, setting it in front of the iron railing, directly in the path of the young man, who has only to bend over and exhale to make use of it, which he does, for a long time. He coughs and retches until he can manage only gasps and dry heaves. By the time he is finished he is on his knees, hunched over the bucket, clutching it with both hands. The retching turns to sobbing and then to soft cursing.

A few feet away the old man waits, courteously and without much interest in the purging process. If the student should feel too ill to return to his work, he will call someone to tend to him. He will not offer his shoulder unless the tottering young man insists. He does not care to touch people: The living are not his concern. Most of the students know him, and would shrink from him, but this one is new. He may not know whom he has encountered in the dark hallway. For all the boy's momentary terror and revulsion, he will be all right. He will return to his task, if not tonight then tomorrow. It is the night before his first dissection class, after all, and many a queasy novice has conquered his nerves and gone on to make a fine doctor.

The young man wipes his face with a linen handkerchief, still gulping air as if the motion *in* will prevent the motion *out*. "I'm all right," he says, aware of the silent presence a few feet away.

"Shouldn't come alone," the old man says. "They make you work together for a reason. 'Cause you joke. You prop up one another's nerve. Distractions beguile the mind, makes it easier, if you don't think too much."

The young man looks up then, recognizing the florid speech and the lilt of a Gullah accent beneath the surface. Pressing the handkerchief to his mouth, he takes an involuntary step backward. He does know who this is. He had been expecting to see a sweeper, perhaps, or one of the professors working here after hours, but this apparition, suddenly recognized, legendary and ancient even in his father's student days, fills him with more terror than the shrouded forms in the room he has just quit.

He is standing in the hall, beside a bucket filled with his own vomit, and his only companion is this ancient black man, still straight and strong-looking in a white linen suit, his grizzled hair shines about his head in the lamplight like a halo, and the student knows that he looks a fool in front of this old man who has touched more dead people than live ones. He peers at the wrinkled face to see if there is some trace of scorn in the impassive countenance.

"I was here because I was afraid," he says,

glancing back at the lamp-lit room of shrouded tables. He does not owe this man an explanation, and if asked, he might have replied with a curt dismissal, but there is only silence, and he needs to feel life in the dark hall. "I thought I might make a fool of myself in class tomorrow——" He glances toward the bucket, and the old man nods. "——And so I came along tonight to try to prepare myself. To see my——well, to see it. Get it over with. Put a cloth over its eyes." He dabbed at his mouth with the soiled handkerchief. "You understand that feeling, I guess."

"I can't remember," said the old man. He has always worked alone. He pulls a bottle out of the pocket of his black coat, pulls out the cork, and passes it to the young man. It is half full of grain alcohol, clear as water.

The young man takes a long pull on the bottle and wipes his mouth with the back of his hand. The two of them look at each other and smile. Not all of the students would drink from the same bottle as a black man. Not in this new century. Maybe once, but not now. The prim New Englanders would not, for his race is alien to them, and while they preach equality, they shrink from proximity. The crackers would not, because they must always be careful to enforce their

precarious rank on the social ladder, even
more so since Reconstruction. But this boy
is planter class, and he has no need for such
gestures. He has traded sweat and spit with
Negroes since infancy, and he has no self-
consciousness, no need for social barriers. It
is the way of his world. They understand
each other.

"You don't remember?" The young man
smiles in disbelief as he hands back the bottle. "But how could you not recall the first
time you touched the dead?"

Because it has been nigh on sixty years, the
old man thinks. He points to the bucket.
"Do you remember the first time you ever
did that?"

His life is divided into *before the train* and *after the train*. Not after the war. Things for
him did not so much change after the war as
this new century's white folks might suppose. The landmark of his life was that train
ride down from Charleston. He remembers
some of his earliest life, or perhaps he has
imagined parts of it for so long that they
have taken on a reality in his mind. He remembers a rag quilt that used to lay atop his
corn shuck mattress. It had been pieced together from scraps of cloth—some of the

pieces were red and shiny, probably scavenged from silk dresses worn by the ladies up at the house. His memories are a patchwork as well: a glimpse of dark eyes mirroring firelight; the hollowed shell of a box turtle . . . someone, an old man, is making music with it, and people are dancing . . . he is very young, sitting on a dirt floor, watching legs and calico skirts flash past him, brushing him sometimes, as the dancers stamped and spun, the music growing louder and faster . . .

There was a creek, too . . . He is older by then . . . Squatting on a wet rock a little way out into the water, waiting for the frog . . . waiting . . . So still that the white birds come down into the field for the seeds as if he were not there . . . Then crashing through the cattails comes Dog, reeking of creek water and cow dung, licking his face, thrashing the water with his muddy tail . . . frogs scared into kingdom come. What was that dog's name? It is just sounds now, that name, and he isn't sure he remembers them right, but once they meant something inside his head, those sounds . . . He has never heard them since.

Older still . . . Now he has seen the fields for what they are: not a place to play. Sun up to sun down . . . Water in a bucket, dispensed from a gourd hollowed out to make a dipper . . . the drinking gourd. He sits in the circle of folks in the dark field, where a young man with angry eyes is pointing up at the sky. The *drinking gourd* is a pattern of stars. They are important. They lead you somewhere, as the Wise Men followed stars . . . But he never set off to follow those stars, and he does not know what became of the angry young man who did. It is long ago, and he resolved to have nothing to do with drinking gourds—neither stars nor rice fields.

He listened to the old people's stories, of how the trickster rabbit smiled and smiled his way out of danger, and how the fox never saw the trap for the smile, and he reckoned he could do that. He could smile like honey on a johnny cake. Serenity was his shield. You never looked sullen, or angry, or afraid. Sometimes bad things happened to you anyway, but at least, if they did, you did not give your tormentor the gift of your pain as well. So he smiled in the South Carolina sunshine and waited for a door to open somewhere in the world, and presently it did.

The sprawling white house sat on a cobblestone street near the harbor in Charleston. It had a shady porch that ran the length of the house, and a green front door with a polished brass door knocker in the shape of a lion's head, but that door did not open to the likes of him. He used the back door, the one that led to the kitchen part of the house.

The old woman there was kind. To hear anyone say otherwise would have astonished her. She kept slaves as another woman might have kept cats—with indulgent interest in their habits, and great patience with their shortcomings. Their lives were her theatre. She was a spinster woman, living alone in the family house, and she made little enough work for the cook, the maid, and the yard man, but she must have them, for the standards of Charleston's quality folk must be maintained.

The old woman had a cook called Rachel. A young girl with skin the color of honey, and still so young that the corn pone and gravy had not yet thickened her body. She was not as pretty as some, but he could tell by her clothes and the way she carried herself that she was a cherished personage in some fine house. He had met her at church, where he always took care to be the cleanest man there with the shiniest shoes. If his clothes were shabby, they were as clean and presentable as he could make them, and he was handsome, which went a long ways toward making up for any deficiency in station. By then he was a young man, grown tall, with a bronze cast to his skin, not as dark as most, and that was as good as a smile, he reckoned, for he did not look so alien to the white faces who did the picking and choosing. He was a townsman, put to work on the docks for one of the ship's chandlers at the harbor. He liked being close to the sea, and his labors had made him strong and lean, but the work was hard, and it led nowhere. The house folk in the fine homes fared the best. You could tell them just by looking, with their cast-off finery and their noses in the air, knowing their station—higher than most folks.

The fetching little cook noticed him—he took care that this should be so, but he was patient in his courting of her, for he had more on his mind than a tumble on a corn shuck mattress. For many weeks he was as gentlemanly as a prince in a fairy story, taking no more liberties than pressing her hand in farewell as they left the church service. Finally when the look in her eyes told him that she thought he'd hung the moon, he talked marriage. He could not live without her, he said. He wanted no more of freedom than the right to grow old at her side.

Presently the determined Rachel ushered

him into the presence of her mistress, the old
woman who kept her servants as pets, and he
set out to charm her with all the assurance of
golden youth, condescending to old age. The
gambit would not work forever, but this time
it did, and he received the mistress's blessing
to wed the pretty young cook. The mistress
would buy him, she said, and he could join
the household, as butler and coachman—or
whatever could be done by an assiduous
young man with strength and wit.

The joining took place in a proper white
frame church, presided over by a stately cler-
gyman as dignified and elegant as any white
minister in Charleston. No broom jumping
for the likes of them. And the mistress herself even came to the wedding, sat there in
the pew with two of her lady friends and
wept happy tears into a lace handkerchief.

Then the newlyweds went back to their
room behind the kitchen that would be
their home for the next dozen years. Being
a town servant was easy, not like dock work.
The spinster lady didn't really need a coachman and butler, not more than a few hours
a week, so she let him hire out to the inn to
work as a porter there, and she even let him
keep half of what he earned there. He could
have saved up the coins, should have perhaps. One of the cooks there at the inn had

been salting away his pay to purchase his freedom, but he didn't see much point in that. As it was, he and Rachel lived in a fine house, ate the same good food as the old lady, and never had to worry about food or clothes or medicine. The free folks might give themselves airs, but they lived in shacks and worked harder than anybody, and he couldn't see the sense of that. Maybe someday they'd think about a change, but no use to deprive himself of fine clothes and a drink or two against that day, for after all, the old missus might free them in her will, and then all those years of scrimping would have been for naught.

All this was *before the train ride . . .*

Dr. George Newton — 1852

Just as Lewis Ford and I were setting out from the college on Telfair Street, one of the local students, young Mr. Thomas, happened along in his buggy and insisted upon driving us over the river to the depot at Hamburg so that we could catch the train to Charleston. When Thomas heard our destination, he began to wax poetic about the beauties of that elegant city, but I cut short his rhapsody. "We are only going on business, Dr. Ford and I," I told him. "We shall acquire a servant for the college and come straight back tomorrow."

The young man left us off the depot, wishing us godspeed, but I could see by his expression that he was puzzled, and that only his good manners prevented his questioning us further. *Going to Charleston for a slave?* he was thinking. *Whatever for? Why not just walk down to sale at the Lower Market on Broad Street here in Augusta?*

Well, we could hardly do that, but I was not at liberty to explain the nature of our journey to a disinterested party. We told people that we had gone to secure a porter to perform custodial services for the medical college, and so we were, but we wanted no one with any ties to the local community. Charleston was just about far enough away, we decided.

For all that the railroad has been here twenty years, Lewis claims he will never become accustomed to jolting along at more than thirty miles per hour, but he allows that it does make light of a journey that would have taken more than a day by carriage. I brought a book along, though Lewis professes astonishment that I am able to read at such a speed. He contented himself with watching the pine trees give way to cow pastures and cotton fields and back again.

After an hour he spoke up. "I suppose this expense is necessary, Newton."

"Yes, I think so," I said, still gazing out the window. "We have all discussed it, and agreed that it must be done."

"Yes, I suppose it must. Clegg charges too much for his services, and he really is a most unsatisfactory person. He has taken to drink, you know."

"Can you wonder at it?"

"No. I only hope he manages to chase away the horrors with it. Still, we cannot do business with him any longer, and we have to teach the fellows somehow."

"Exactly. We have no choice."

He cleared his throat. "Charleston. I quite understand the need for acquiring a man with no ties to Augusta, but Charleston is a singular place. They have had their troubles there, you know."

I nodded. Thirty years ago the French Caribbean slave Denmark Vesey led an uprising in Charleston, for which they hanged him. All had been quiet there since, but Dr. Ford is one of nature's worriers. "You may interview the men before the auction if it will ease your mind. You will be one-seventh owner," I reminded him. We had all agreed on that point: All faculty members to own a share in the servant, to be bought out should said faculty member leave the employ of the college.

He nodded. "I shall leave the choosing to you, though, Newton, since you are the dean."

"Very well," I said. Dr. Ford had been my predecessor—the first dean of the medical college—but after all it was he who had engaged the services of the unsatisfactory Clegg, so I thought it best to rely upon my judgment this time.

"Seven hundred dollars, then," said Ford. "One hundred from each man. That sum should be sufficient, don't you think?"

"For a porter, certainly," I said. "But since this fellow will also be replacing Clegg, thus saving us the money we were paying out to him, the price will be a bargain."

"It will be if the new man has diligence and ingenuity. And if he can master the task, of which we are by no means certain," said Ford.

"He will have to. Only a slave can perform the task with impunity."

We said little else for the duration of the journey, but I was hoping for a good dinner in Charleston. After my undergraduate days at the University of Pennsylvania, I went abroad to study medicine in Paris. There I acquired a taste for the fine food and wines that Charleston offers in abundance. It is the French influence—all those refugees from the French Caribbean improved the cuisine immeasurably.

When we had disembarked and made our way to the inn to wash off the dust of the journey, there were yet a few hours of daylight before dinner, and after I noted down the costs of our train fares and lodging for the college expense record, I decided that it would be prudent to visit the market in preparation for the next day's sale. Slaves who are to be auctioned are housed overnight in quarters near the market, and one may go and view them, so as to be better prepared to bid when the time came.

It was a warm afternoon, and I was mindful of the mix of city smells and sea air as I made my way toward the old market. I presented myself at the building quartering those who were to be sold the next day, and a scowling young man ushered me inside. No doubt the keeping of this establishment made for unpleasant work, for some of its inhabitants were loudly lamenting their fate, while others called out for water or a clean slop bucket, and above it all were the wails of various infants and snatches of song from those who had ceased to struggle against their lot.

It was a human zoo with but one species exhibited, but there was variation enough among them, save for their present unhappiness. I wanted to tell them that this was the worst of it—at least I hoped it was.

I made my way into the dimly lit barracks, determined to do my duty despite the discomfort I felt. *Slave* . . . We never use that word. *My servant,* we say, or *my cook,* or *the folks down on my farm . . . my people . . . Why, he's part of the family,* we say . . . We call the elderly family retainers by the courtesy title of Uncle or Aunt . . . Later, when we have come to know and trust them and to presume that they are happy in our care, it is all too easy to forget by what means they are obtained. From such a place as this.

In truth, though, it hardly matters that I am venturing into slave quarters, for I am not much at ease anywhere in the company of my fellow creatures. Even at the orphan asylum supported by my uncle, my palms sweat and I shrink into my clothes whenever I must visit there, feeling the children's eyes upon me with every step I take. I find myself supposing that every whisper is a mockery of me, and that all eyes upon me are judging me and finding me wanting. It is a childish fear, I suppose, and I would view it as such in anyone other than myself, but logic will not lay the specter of ridicule that dogs my steps, and so I tread carefully, hearing sniggers and seeing scorn whether there be any or not.

Perhaps that is why I never married, and why, after obtaining my medical degree, I chose the role of college administrator to that of practicing physician—I hope to slip through life unnoticed. But I hope I do my duty, despite my personal predilections, and that evening my duty was to enter this fetid human stable and to find a suitable man for the college. I steeled myself to the sullen stares of the captives and to the cries of their frightened children. The foul smell did not oppress me, for the laboratories of the college are much the same, and the odor permeates the halls and even my very office. No, it was the eyes I minded. The cold gaze of those who fear had turned to rage. I forced myself to walk slowly, and to look into the face of each one, nodding coolly, so that they would not know how I shrank from them.

"Good evening, sir." The voice was deep and calm, as if its owner were an acquaintance, encountering me upon some boulevard and offering a greeting in passing.

I turned, expecting to see a watchman, but instead I met with a coffee-colored face, gently smiling: an aquiline nose, pointed beard, and sharp brown eyes that took in everything and gave out nothing. The man looked only a few years younger than myself—perhaps thirty-five—and he wore the elegant clothes of a dandy, so that he stood out from the rest like a peacock among crows.

The smile was so guileless and open that I abandoned my resolve of solemnity and smiled back. "How do you do?" I said. "Dreadful place, this. Are you here upon the same errand as I?" Charleston has a goodly number of half castes, a tropical mixture of Martinique slaves and their French masters. They even have schools here to educate them, which I think a good thing, although it is illegal to do so in Georgia. There are a good many freedmen in every city who have prospered and have taken it in turn to own slaves themselves, and I supposed that this light-colored gentleman must be such a free man in need of a workman.

There was a moment's hesitation and then the smile shone forth again. "Almost the same," he said. "Are you here in search of a servant? I am in need of a new situation."

In momentary confusion I stared at his polished shoes, and the white shirt that shone in the dimness. "Are you—"

He nodded, and spoke more softly as he explained his position. For most of his adult life he had been the principal manservant of a spinster lady in Charleston, and he had also been permitted in his free time to hire out to a hotel in the city, hence his mannered speech and the clothes of a dandy.

"But—you are to be sold?"

He nodded. "The mistress is ailing, don't you know. Doesn't need as much help as before, and needs cash money more. The bank was after her. So I had to go. Made me no never mind. I'll fetch a lot. I just hope for a good place, that's all. I'm no field hand."

I nodded, noting how carefully he pronounced his words, and how severely clean and well-groomed his person. Here was a man whose life's course would be decided in seconds tomorrow, and he had done all he could to see that it went well.

"And the mistress, you know, she cried and carried on to see me go. And she swore that she would never part with my wife."

I nodded. It is regrettable that such things happen. Money is the tyrant that rules us all. I said, "I am the dean of a medical college in Augusta. In Georgia. Do you know where that is?"

"A good ways off, sir."

"Half a day's journey south by train. Over the Savannah River and into the state of Georgia."

"A college. That sounds like a fine situation indeed, sir. What kind of place is it?"

"We teach young men to be doctors and surgeons."

"No, sir," He smiled again. "The *place*. The position you've come here wanting to fill."

"Oh, that." I hesitated. "Well—Porter, I suppose you'd say. General factotum about the college. And *something else*, for which, if the man were able to do it, we should *pay*." I did not elaborate, but I thought he could read expressions much better than I, for he looked thoughtful for a few moments, and then he nodded.

"You'd pay . . . Enough for train fare?"

"If the work is satisfactory. Perhaps enough, if carefully saved, to make a larger purchase than that. But the extra duty . . . it is not pleasant work."

He smiled. "If it was pleasant, you wouldn't pay."

And so it was done. It was not the sordid business of buying a life, I told myself, but more of a bargain struck between two men of the world. True, he would have to leave his wife behind in Charleston, but at least we were saving him from worse possible fates. From cane fields farther south, or from someone who might mistreat him. He could do worse, I told myself. And at least I saved him from one ordeal—that of standing upon the block not knowing what would become of him. I thought the man bright enough and sufficiently ambitious for the requirements of our institution. It may seem odd that I consulted him beforehand as if he had a choice in his fate, but for our purposes we needed a willing worker, not a captive. We needed someone dependable, and I felt that if this man believed it worth his while to join us, we would be able to trust him.

They must have thought him wonderfully brave the next day. On the block, before upturned white faces like frog spawn, peering up at him, he stood there smiling like a missionary with four aces. It was over in the space of a minute, only a stepping stone from one life to the next, crossed in the blink of an eye.

Seven hundred dollars bid and accepted in the span of ten heartbeats, and then the auctioneer moved on to the next lot, and we went out. As we counted out the gold pieces for the cashier, and signed the account

book, Lewis Ford was looking a little
askance at the whole procedure.

"So you're certain of this fellow, Newton?"

"Well, as much as one can be, I suppose,"
I said. "I talked at length with him last evening. Of course I did not explain the partic-
ulars of the work to him. That would have
been most imprudent."

Lewis Ford grunted. "Well, he has the
back for it, I grant you that. And, as you say,
perhaps the temperament as well. But has
he the stomach for it? After our experience
with Clegg, that's what I wonder."

"Well, *I* would, Dr. Ford. If my choice in
life was the work we have in store for this fellow or a short, hard life in the cane fields
further south, by God, I would have the
stomach for it."

"Indeed. Well, I defer to your judgment. I
don't suppose what we're asking of him is
much worse than what we do for a living, after all."

"We'll be serving the same master, anyhow," I said. "The college, you know, and
the greater good of medicine."

"What is the fellow's name, do you know?"

I nodded. "He told me. It is Grandison.
Grandison Harris."

"Odd name. I mean they *have* odd names,

of course. Xerxes and Thessalonians, and all that sort of thing. People will give slaves and horses the most absurd appellations, but I wouldn't have taken Grandison for a slave name, would you?"

I shrugged. "Called after the family name of his original owner, I should think. And judging by the lightness of his skin, there's some might say he's entitled to it."

Grandison Harris had never been on a train before, and his interest in this new experience seemed to diminish what regrets he might have about leaving his home in Charleston. When the train pulled out of the depot, he leaned out the window of the car and half stood until he could see between the houses and over the people all the way to the bay—a stand of water as big as all creation, it looked from here. Water that flowed into the sky itself where the other shore ought to be. The glare of the afternoon sun on the water was fierce, but he kept on twisting his head and looking at the diminishing city and the expanse of blue.

"You'll hurt your eyes staring out at the sun like that," I said.

He half turned and smiled. "Well, sir, Doctor," he said, "I mean to set this place in my memory like dye in new-wove cloth. My eyes may water a little, but I reckon that's all right, for dyes are sot in salt. Tears will fix the memories to my mind to where they'll never come out."

After that we were each left alone with our thoughts for many miles, to watch the unfamiliar landscapes slide past the railway carriage, or to doze in relief that, although the future might be terrible, at least this day was over.

Instead of the sea, the town of Augusta had the big Savannah River running along beside it, garlanded in willows, dividing South Carolina from the state of Georgia. From the depot in Hamburg they took a carriage over the river into town, but it was dark by then, and he couldn't see much of the new place except for the twinkling lights in the buildings. Wasn't as big as Charleston, though. They boarded him for the night with a freed woman who took in lodgers, saying that they would come to fetch him in the morning for work.

For a moment in the lamplight of the parlor, he had taken her for a white woman, this haughty lady with hair the brown of new leather and green eyes that met everybody's gaze without a speck of deference. Dr. Newton took off his hat to her when they went in, and he shook her hand and made a little bow when he took his leave.

When he was alone with this strange land-lady, he stared at her in the lamplight and said, "Madame, you are a red bone, not?"

She shrugged. "I am a free person of color. Mostly white, but not all. They've told you my name is Alethea Taylor. I'll thank you to call me Miz Taylor."

"You sure look white," he said. *Act it, too,* he thought.

She nodded. "My mama was half-caste and my daddy was white. So was my hus-band, whose name I ought to have. But it was Butts, so maybe I don't mind so much."

She smiled at that and he smiled back.

"We married up in Carolina where I was born. It's legal up there. I was given school-ing as well. So don't think this house is any low class place, because it isn't. We have standards."

The new lodger looked around at the tidy little parlor with its worn but elegant ma-hogany settee and a faded turkey carpet. A book shelf stood beside the fireplace, with a big leather Bible on top in pride of place. "Your white husband lives here, too?" he asked.

"Of course not." Her face told him that the question was foolish. "He was rich enough to buy up this whole town, Mr. Butts was. But he's dead now. Set me and our children free, though, when he passed. Seven young'uns we had. So now I do fine sewing for the town ladies, and my boys work to keep us fed. Taking in a lodger helps us along, too. Though I'm particular about who I'll accept. Took you as a favor to Dr. George Newton. Would you tell me your name again?"

"Grandison Harris," he said. "I guess the doctors told you: I'm the porter at the college."

She gave him a scornful look. "'Course you are. Dr. Newton's uncle Tuttle is my guardian, so I know all about the college."

"Guardian?"

"Here in Georgia, freed folk have to have white guardians."

"What for?"

She shrugged. "To protect us from other white men, I suppose. But Mr. Isaac Tuttle is a good man. I can trust him."

He watched her face for some sign that this Tuttle was more to her than a disinterested legal guardian, but she seemed to mean no more than what she said. It made no difference to him, though. Who she shared her bed with was none of his business, and never would be. She had made her opinion of him plain. He was a slave, and she was a free woman, his landlady, and a friend of his owners. You couldn't cross that gulf on a steamboat.

"It's late," she said, "But I expect you are hungry as well as tired. I can get you a plate of beans if you'd care to eat."

"No, ma'am, I'm good 'til morning. Long day."

She nodded, and her expression softened. "Well, it's over now. You've landed on your feet."

"The college—It's a good place, then?" he asked.

"Hard work," she said. She paused as if she wanted to say more, but then she shook her head. "Better than the big farms, anyhow. Dr. George is a good man. Lives more in his books than in the world, but he means well. Those doctors are all right. They treat sick black folks, same as white. You will be all right with them if you do your job. They won't beat you to show they're better than you." She smiled. "Doctors think they are better than most everybody else, anyhow, so they don't feel the need to go proving it with a bull whip."

"That's good to hear."

"Well, just you mind how *you* treat *them*," she said. "You look like you wouldn't be

above a little sharp practice, and those doctors can be downright simple. Oh, they
know a lot about doctoring and a lot about
books, but they're not very smart about people. They don't expect to be lied to. So you
take care to be straight with them so that
you can keep this good place."

He followed her meekly to a clean but spar-
tan room. A red rag quilt covered the bed,
and a chipped white pitcher and basin stood
on a small pine table next to a cane-seat chair.
Compared to the faded splendor of Miz Taylor's parlor, the room was almost a prison
cell, but he was glad enough to have it. Better
here with a family than in some makeshift
room at the medical college. He wasn't sure
whether the doctors kept sick people around
the place, but he didn't like the thought of
sleeping there all the same. In a place of
death. The best thing about this small bare
room was what it did *not* contain: no shackles,
no lock on the door or barred window. He
was a boarder in a freedman's house.

He turned to the woman, who stood on
the threshold holding the lamp.

"Aren't they afraid I'll run off?" he asked.

She sighed. "I told you. They don't have
good sense about people. I reckon they figure you'd be worse off running than staying
here. You know what happens to runaways."

He nodded. He had seen things in Charleston, heard stories about brandings and toes lopped off. And of course the story of Denmark Vesey, whose rebellion had consisted mostly of talk, was never far from the surface of any talk about running or disobedience.

She set the lamp beside the basin. "I'll tell you what's the truth, Mr. Harris. If you give satisfaction at the college—do your work and don't steal, or leastways don't get caught at it—those doctors won't care about what you do the rest of the time. They won't remember to. They don't want to have to take care of a servant as if he were a pet dog. All they want is a job done with as few ructions as possible, and the less trouble you give them, the happier they'll be. You do your job well, you'll become invisible. Come and go as you please. You'll be a freedman in all but name. That's what I think. And I know the doctors, you see?"

"I won't give them no trouble," he said.

"See you don't. Can you read, Mr. Harris?"

He shook his head. There had been no call for it, and the old miss in Charleston wasn't averse to her folks getting book learning, but she had needed him to work.

"Well," she said, "I school my young'uns every evening. If you would like to join us, one of my girls can start by teaching you your letters."

"I thank you."

She nodded and turned to leave. "Reading is a good skill," she said as she closed the door. "You can write out your own passes."

He had seen fine buildings in Charleston, but even so, the Medical College on Telfair Street was a sight to behold. A white temple, it was, with four stone columns holding up the portico and a round dome atop the roof, grand as a cathedral, it was. You stepped inside to an open space that stretched all the way up to the dome, with staircases curving up the sides that led to the upper floor rooms. The wonder of it wore off before long, but it was grand while it lasted. Soon enough the architectural splendor failed to register, and all he saw were floors that needed mopping and refuse bins that stank.

For the first couple of days he chopped firewood, and fetched pails of water when they needed them.

"Just until you are settled in," Dr. Newton had said. "Then we will have a talk about why you are here."

He didn't see much of the doctors during

the couple of days they gave him to get acquainted with his new surroundings. Perhaps they were busy with more pressing matters, and, remembering Alethea Taylor's advice about giving no trouble, he got on with his work and bothered no one. At last, though, clad in one of the doctors' clean cast-off suits, he was summoned into the presence, a little shy before the all-powerful strangers, but not much afraid, for they had paid too much good money for him to waste it by harming him.

For a night or two he had woken up in the dark, having dreamed that the doctors were going to cut him open alive, but this notion was so patently foolish that he did not even mention it to his landlady, whose scorn would have been withering.

George Newton was sitting behind his big desk, tapping his fingers together, looking as if his collar were too tight. "Now Grandison," he began, "you have settled in well? Good. You seem to be a good worker, which is gratifying. So now I think we can discuss that other task that your duties entail."

He paused, perhaps to wait for a question, but he saw only respectful interest in the man's face. "Well, then . . . This is a place where men are taught to be doctors. And also to be surgeons. A grim task, that: the cutting open of living beings. Regrettably necessary. A generation ago there was an English surgeon who would vomit before every operation he performed. Do you know why?"

The listener shook his head.

"Because the patient is awake for the operation, and because the pain is so terrible that many die of it. We lose half the people on whom we operate, even if we do everything right. They die of shock, of heart failure, perhaps, from the pain. But despite these losses, we are learning. We *must* learn. We must help more people, and lessen the torture of doing so. This brings me to your function here at the college." He paused and tapped his pen, waiting in case the new servant ventured a question, but the silence stretched on. At last he said, "It was another English surgeon who said, *we must mutilate the dead in order not to mutilate the living.*" Another pause. "What he meant was that we physicians must learn our way around the human body, and we must practice our surgical skills. It is better to practice those skills upon a dead body rather than a living one. Do you see the sense of that?"

He swallowed hard, but finally managed to nod. "Yes, sir."

George Newton smiled. "Well, if you *do* understand that, Grandison, then I wish you were the governor of Georgia, because *he* doesn't. The practice is against the law in this state—indeed, in all states—to use cadavers for medical study. People don't want us defiling the dead, they say—so, instead, out of ignorance, we defile the living. And that cannot be permitted. We must make use of the dead to help the living."

"Yes, sir," he said. The doctor still seemed lost in thought, so he added encouragingly, "It's all right with me, sir."

Again the smile. "Well, thank you, Grandison. I'm glad to have your permission, anyhow. But I'm afraid we will need more than that. Tell me, do you believe that the spirits of the dead linger in the graveyard? Object to being disturbed? That they'd try to harm anyone working on their remains?"

He tried to picture dead people loitering around the halls of the college, waiting for their bodies to be returned. This was a place of death. He didn't know whether to smile or weep. Best not to think of it at all, he decided. "They are gone, ain't they?" he said at last. "Dead. Gone to glory. They're not sitting around waiting for Judgment Day in the grave, are they?"

Another doctor sighed. "Well, Grandison, to tell you the truth, I don't know where the souls of the dead are. That is something we don't teach in medical college. However, I don't believe they're sitting out there in the graveyard, tied to their decaying remains. I think we can be sure of that."

"And you need the dead folks to learn doctoring on?"

Dr. Ford nodded. "Each medical student should have a cadaver to work on, so that he can learn his trade without killing anyone in the learning process. That seems a sufficiently noble reason to rob graves, doesn't it?"

He considered it, more to forestall the rest of the conversation than anything else. "You could ask folks before they dies," he said. "Tell them how it is, and get them to sign a paper for the judge."

"But since the use of cadavers is against the law, no judge would honor such a paper, even if people could be persuaded to sign it, which most would not. I wish there were easy answers, but there aren't. You know what we must ask of you."

"You want me to bring you dead folks? Out the graveyard?"

"Yes. There is a cemetery on Watkins Street, not half a mile from here, so the journey would not be long. You must go at night, of course."

He stood quite still for some time before

he spoke. It was always best to let white folks think you took everything calmly and agreed with them on every particular. To object that such a deed would frighten or disgust him would make no difference. The doctor would dismiss his qualms as fear or superstition. The doctors had explained the matter to him, when they could have simply given him an order. That was something, anyhow. At last he nodded. The matter was settled, and the only considerations now were practical ones. "If I get caught, what then?"

"I don't suppose you will *get caught*, as you put it, if you are the least bit clever about it, but even if you should, remember that slaves are not prosecuted for any crime. They are considered property and therefore not subject to prosecution. The authorities simply hand them back over to their masters." Newton smiled. "And you don't suppose that *we* would punish you for it, do you?"

The others nodded in agreement, and the matter was settled.

He was given a lantern and a shovel, and a horse-drawn cart. Dr. Newton had written out a pass, saying that the bearer, Grandison Harris, servant of the medical college, was allowed to be abroad that night to pick up supplies for the doctors. "I doubt very much that the city's watchmen can read," Newton had told him. "Just keep this pass until it wears out, and then one of us will write you a new one."

He kept the pass in his jacket pocket, ready to produce if anyone challenged him, but he had met no one on his journey from Telfair Street to the burying ground. It was well after midnight, and the sliver of moon had been swallowed by clouds, so he made his way in darkness. Augusta was a smaller place than Charleston. He had walked around its few streets until he knew it by day and by night, and he had been especially careful of the route to Cedar Grove, where the town buried its slaves and freedmen. Now he could navigate the streets without the help of the lantern. Only the horse's footfalls broke the silence. Nearer to the town center, perhaps, people might still be out drinking and wagering at cards, but no sounds of merriment reached him here on the outskirts of town. He would have been glad of the sound of laughter and music, but the silence blanketed everything, and he did not dare to whistle to take his mind off his errand.

Do you want me to dig up just any old grave? he had asked the doctor.

No. There were rules. A body rots quick. Well, he knew that. Look at a dead cat in the road, rippling with maggots. After two, three days, you'd hardly know what it was. *Three days buried and no more,* the doctor told him. *After that, there's no point in bringing the corpse back up; it's too far gone to teach us anything. Look for a newly-dug grave,* Newton told him. Flowers still fresh on a mound of newly-spaded earth. *Soon,* he said, *you will get to know people about the town, and you will hear about deaths as they happen. Then you can be ready. This time, though, just do the best you can.*

He knew where he was going. He had walked in the graveyard that afternoon, and found just such a burial plot a few paces west of the gate: a mound of brown dirt, encircled by clam shells, and strewn across it a scattering of black-eyed susans and magnolia flowers, wilting in the Georgia sun, but newly placed there.

He wondered whose grave it was. No mourners were there when he found it. Had there been, he would have hesitated to inquire, for fear of being remembered if the theft were ever discovered. There was no marker to tell him, either, even if he had been able to read. The final resting place of a slave—no carved stone. Here and there, crude wooden crosses tilted in the grass, but they told him nothing.

He reached the cemetery gate. Before he began to retrace his steps to the new grave, he lit the lantern. No one would venture near a burying ground so late at night, he thought, and although he had paced off the steps to the grave, he would need the light for the task ahead.

Thirty paces with his back to the gates, then ten paces right. He saw the white shape of shells outlining the mound of earth, and smelled the musk of decaying magnolia. He stood there a long time staring down at the flower-strewn grave, a colorless shape in the dimness. All through the long afternoon he had thought it out, while he mopped the classroom floors and emptied the waste bins, and waited for nightfall. His safety lay in concealment: No one must suspect that a grave had been disturbed. No one would look for a grave robber if they found no trace of the theft. The doctor had told him over and over that slaves were not jailed for committing a crime, but he did not trust laws. Public outrage over this act might send him to the end of a rope before anyone from the college could intervene. Best not to get caught.

He would memorize the look of the burial plot: the position of the shells encircling the mound, and how the flowers were placed, so that when he had finished his work he could replace it all exactly as it had been before.

Only when he was sure that he remembered the pattern of the grave did he thrust his shovel into the soft earth. He flinched when he heard the rasp of metal against soil, and felt the blade connect with the freshly-spaded dirt. The silence came flowing back. What had he expected? A scream of outrage from beneath the mound? When he had first contemplated the task before him, he had thought he could endure it by thinking only of the physical nature of the work: It is like digging a trench, he would tell himself. Like spading a garden. It is just another senseless task thought up by the white people to keep you occupied. But here in the faint lantern light of a burying ground, he saw that such pretenses would not work. The removing of dirt from a newly-filled hole was the least of it. He must violate consecrated ground, touch a corpse, and carry it away in darkness to be mutilated. He could not pretend otherwise.

All right, then. If the spirits of the dead hovered outside the lantern light, watching him work, so be it. Let them see. Let them hear his side of it, and judge him by that.

"Don't you be looking all squinty-eyed at me," he said to the darkness as he worked. "Wasn't my doing. You all know the white folks sent me out here. Say they need to study some more on your innards."

The shovel swished in the soft earth, and for a moment a curve of moon shimmered from behind a cloud, and then it was gone. He was glad of that. He fancied that he could make out human shapes in the shadows beneath the trees. Darkness was better. "You all long dead ones don't have no quarrel with me," he said, more loudly now. "Doctors don't want you if you gone ripe. You all like fish—after three days, you ain't good for nothing except fertilizer."

He worked on in the stillness, making a rhythm of entrenchment. The silence seemed to take a step back, giving him breathing room as he worked. Perhaps two hours now before cock crow.

He struck wood sooner than he had expected to. Six feet under, people always said. But it wasn't. Three feet, more like. Just enough to cover the box and then some for top soil. Deep enough, he supposed, since the pine boards would rot and the worms would take care of the rest.

He didn't need to bring up the coffin itself. That would disturb too much earth, and the doctors had no use for the coffin, anyhow. Dr. Newton told him that. It might be stealing to take a coffin, he had said. Wooden boxes have a monetary value. Dead bodies, none.

He stepped into the hole, and pushed the dirt away from the top of the box. The smell of wet soil made him dizzy, and he willed himself not to feel for worms in the clods of earth. He did not know whose grave this was. They had not told him, or perhaps they didn't know.

"You didn't want to be down there anyhow," he said to the box. "Salted away in the wet ground. You didn't want to end up shut away in the dark. I came to bring you back. If the angels have got you first, then you won't care, and if they didn't, then at least you won't be alone in the dark any more."

He took the point of the shovel and stove in the box lid, pulling back when he heard the wood splinter, so that he would not smash what lay beneath it. On the ground beside the grave, he had placed a white sack, big enough to carry away the contents of the box. He pulled it down into the hole, and cleared away splinters of wood from the broken box, revealing a face, inches from his own.

Its eyes were closed. Perhaps—this first time—if they had been open and staring up at him, he would have dropped the shovel and run from the graveyard. Let them sell him south rather than to return to such terrors. But the eyes were shut. And the face in repose was an old woman, scrawny and grizzled, lying with her hands crossed over her breast, and an expression of weary resignation toward whatever came next.

He pulled the body out through the hole in the coffin lid, trying to touch the shroud rather than the flesh of the dead woman. She was heavier than he had expected from the look of her frail body, and the dead weight proved awkward to move, but his nerves made him hurry, and to finish the thing without stopping for breath: only get her into the sack and be done with it.

He wondered if the spirit of the old woman knew what was happening to her remains, and if she cared. He was careful not to look too long at the shadows and pools of darkness around trees and gravestones, for fear that they would coalesce into human shapes with burning eyes.

"Bet you ain't even surprised," he said to

the shrouded form, as he drew the string tight across the mouth of the sack. "Bet you didn't believe in that business about eternal rest, no more'n the pigs would. Gonna get the last drop of use out you, same as pigs. But never mind. At least it ain't alone in the dark."

She lay there silent in the white sack while he spent precious long minutes refilling the hole, smoothing the mound, and placing the shells and flowers back exactly as he had found them.

He never found out who the old woman was, never asked. He had trundled the body back to the porter's entrance of the medical college, and steeped her in the alcohol they'd given him the money to buy as a preservative. Presently, when the body was cured and the class was ready, the old woman was carried upstairs to perform her last act of servitude. He never saw her again—at least not to recognize. He supposed that he had seen remnants of her, discarded in bits and pieces as the cutting and the probing progressed. That which remained, he put in jars of whiskey for further study or scattered in the cellar of the building, dusting it over with quicklime to contain the smell. What came out of the classes was scarcely recognizable as human, and he never tried to work out whose remains he was disposing of in a resting place less consecrated than the place from which he had taken them.

"Well, I suppose the first one is always the worst," said Dr. Newton the next day when he had reported his success in securing a body for the anatomy class. He had nodded in agreement, and pocketed the coins that the doctor gave him, mustering up a feeble smile in response to the pat on the back and the hearty congratulations on a job well done.

The doctor had been wrong, though. The first one was not the worst. There were terrors in the unfamiliar graveyard, that was true, and the strange feel of dead flesh in his hands had sent him reeling into the bushes to be sick, so that even he had believed that the first time was as bad as it could get, but later he came to realize that there were other horrors to take the place of the first ones. That first body was just a lump of flesh, nothing to him but an unpleasant chore to be got over with as quick as he could. And he would have liked for them all to be that way, but he had a quota to fill, and to do that he had to mingle with the folks in Augusta, so that he could hear talk about who was ailing and who wasn't likely to get well.

He joined the Springfield Baptist Church, went to services, learned folks' names, and passed the time of day with them if he happened to be out and about. Augusta wasn't such a big town that a few months wouldn't make you acquainted with almost the whole of it. He told people that he was the porter up to the medical college, which was true enough as far as it went, and no one seemed to think anything more about him. Field hands would have been surprised by how much freedom you could have if you were a town servant in a good place. There were dances and picnics, camp meetings and weddings. He began to enjoy this new society so much that he nearly forgot that they would see him as the fox in the henhouse if they had known why he was set among them.

Fanny, Miz Taylor's eldest girl, made sport of him because of his interest in the community. "I declare, Mister Harris," she would say, laughing, "You are worse than two old ladies for wanting to know all the goings-on, aren't you?"

"I take an interest," he said.

She shook her head. "Who's sick? Who's

in the family way? Who's about to pass?—
Gossip! I'd rather talk about books!" Miss
Fanny, with her peach-gold cheeks and clus-
ters of chestnut curls, was a pretty twelve-
year-old. She and her young sister Nannie
were soon to be sent back to South Carolina
for schooling, so she had no time for the
troubles of the old folks in dull old Augusta.

When she thought he was out of earshot,
Fanny's mother reproved her for her teasing. "Mary Frances," she said. "You should
not poke fun at our lodger for taking an interest in the doings of the town. Do you not
think he might be lonely, with no family
here, and his wife back in Charleston? It is
our Christian duty to be kind to him."

"Oh, *duty*, mama!"

"And, Fanny, remember that a lady is always kind."

But he had not minded Miss Fanny's teasing. To be thought a nosey "old lady" was
better than to be suspected of what he really
was. But in the few months before she left
for school, Miss Fanny had made an effort
to treat him with courtesy. She was well on
her way to being a lady, with her mother's
beauty and her father's white skin. He wondered what would become of her.

He was in the graveyard again, this time in the cold drizzle of a February night. He barely needed a lantern anymore to find his way to a grave, so accustomed had he become to the terrain of that hallowed field. And this time he would try to proceed without the light, not from fear of discovery but because he would rather not see the face of the corpse. Cheney Youngblood, a soft-spoken young woman whose sweet serenity made her beautiful, had gone to death with quiet resignation on Saturday night. It had been her first child, and when the birthing went wrong, the midwife took to drink and wouldn't do more than cry and say it weren't her fault. At last Miz Taylor was sent for, and she had dispatched young Jimmie to fetch Dr. Newton. He had come readily enough, but by then the girl had been so weak that nothing could have saved her. "I'd have to cut her open, Alethea," Dr. Newton had said. "And she'd never live through that, and I think the baby is dead already. Why give her more pain when there's nothing to be gained from it?"

At dawn the next morning he had just been going out the door to light the fires at the college when Alethea Taylor came home, red-eyed and disheveled from her long night's vigil. "It's over," she told him, and went inside without another word.

The funeral had been held the next afternoon. Cheney Youngblood in her best dress had been laid to rest in a plain pine box, her baby still unborn. He had stood there before the flower-strewn grave with the rest of the mourners, and he'd joined in the singing and in the prayers for her salvation. And when the minister said, *Rest in peace,* he had said "Amen" with the rest of them. But he knew better.

Three-quarters of an hour in silence, while the spadefuls of earth fell rhythmically beside the path. He would not sing. He could not pray. And he tried not to look at the shadows that seemed to grow from the branches of the nearby azaleas. At last he felt the unyielding wood against his spade, and with hardly a pause for thought, he smashed the lid, and knelt to remove the contents of the box. There had been no shroud for Cheney Youngblood, but the night was too dark for him to see her upturned face, and he was glad.

"Now, Cheney, I'm sorry about this," he whispered, as he readied the sack. "You must be in everlasting sorry now that you ever let a man touch you, and here I am seeing that you will get more of the same. I just hope you can teach these fool doctors something about babies, Cheney. So's maybe if they see what went wrong, they can help the next one down the road."

He stood at the head of the coffin, gripping her by the shoulders, and pulled until the flaccid body emerged from the box. Fix his grip beneath her dangling arms, and it would be the act of a moment to hoist the body onto the earth beside the grave, and then into the sack. He did so, and she was free of the coffin, but not free.

Attached by a cord.

He stood there unmoving in the stillness, listening. Nothing.

He lit the lamp, and held it up so that he could see inside the box.

The child lay there, its eyes closed, fists curled, still attached to its mother's body by the cord.

His hand was shaking as he set down the lantern on the edge of the grave, and reached down for the child. After so much death, could he possibly restore to life . . . He took out his knife, but when he lifted the cord, it was withered and cold—like a pumpkin vine in winter.

Dr. Newton sat before the fire in his study, clad in a dressing gown and slippers. First light was a good hour away, but he had made no complaint about being awakened by the trembling man who had pounded on his door in the dead of night, and, when the doctor answered, had held out a sad little bundle.

He was sitting now in a chair near the fire, still shaking, still silent.

Dr. Newton sighed, poured out another glass of whiskey, and held it out to his visitor. "You could not have saved it, Grandison," he said again. "It did not live."

The resurrection man shook his head. "I went to the burying, Doctor. I was there. I saw. Cheney died trying to birth that baby, but she never did. She was big with child when they put her in the ground."

"And you think the baby birthed itself there in the coffin and died in the night?"

He took a gulp of whiskey, and shuddered. "Yes."

"No." Newton was silent for a moment, choosing his words carefully. "I saw a man hanged once. I was in medical school in those days, and we were given the body for study. When we undressed the poor fellow in the dissecting room, we found that he had soiled himself in his death agonies. The professor explained to us that when the body dies, all its muscles relax. The bowels are voided . . . And, I think, the muscles that govern the birth process must also relax, and the gases build up as the body decays, so that an infant in the birth canal is released in death."

"And it died."

"No. It never lived. It never drew breath. It died when its mother did, not later in the coffin when it was expelled. But it does you credit that you tried to save it."

"I thought the baby had got buried alive." The doctor shook his head, and Grandison said, "But people do get buried alive sometimes, don't they?"

Newton hesitated, choosing his words carefully. "It has happened," he said at last. "I have never seen it, mind you. But one of my medical professors in Paris told the tale of a learned man in medieval times who was being considered for sainthood. When the church fathers dug him up, to see if his body was in that uncorrupted state that denotes sanctity, they found the poor soul lying in the coffin on his back, splinters under his fingernails and a grimace of agony frozen on his withered features." He sighed. "To add insult to injury, they denied the fellow sainthood on the grounds that he seemed to be in no hurry to meet his Maker."

They looked at each other and smiled. It was a grim story, but not so terrible as the sight of a dead child wrapped in its mother's winding sheet. Besides, first light had just begun to gray the trees and the lawn outside. That night was over.

Cheney Youngblood had been early on, though. And he was sorry for her, because she was young and kindly, and he had thought her child had lived, however briefly. A year or so after that—it was hard to remember after so long a time, with no records kept—a steaming summer brought yellow fever into Augusta, and many died, burning in their delirium and crying for water. Day after day wagons stacked with coffins trundled down Telfair Street, bound for the two cemeteries, black and white. The old people and the babies died first, and here and there someone already sick or weakened by other ailments succumbed as well. New graves sprouted like skunk cabbage across the green expanse of the burying field.

Now he could dig and hoist with barely a thought to spare for the human remains that passed through his hands. By now there had been too many dark nights, and too many still forms to move him to fear or pity. His shovel bit into the earth, and his shoulders heaved as he tossed aside the covering soil, but his mind these days ranged elsewhere.

"I want to go home," he told George Newton one night, after he had asked for the supplies he needed.

The doctor looked up, surprised and then thoughtful. "Home, Grandison?"

His answer was roundabout. "I do good work, do I not, doctor? Bring you good subjects for the classes, without causing you any trouble. Don't get drunk. Don't get caught."

"Yes. I grant you all that, but where is home, Grandison?"

"I have a wife back in Charleston."

Dr. Newton considered it. "You are lonely? I know that sometimes when people are separated by circumstance, they find other mates. I wonder if you have given any thought to that—or perhaps she—"

"We were married legal," he said. "I do good work here. Y'all trust me."

"Yes. Yes, we do. And you want to go back to Charleston to see your wife?"

He nodded. No use in arguing about it until the doctor thought it out.

At last Newton said, "Well, I suppose it

might be managed. We could buy you a train ticket. Twelve dollars is not such a great sum, divided by the seven of us who are faculty members." He tapped his fingers together as he worked it out. "Yes, considered that way, the cost seems little enough, to ensure the diligence of a skilled and steady worker. I think I can get the other doctors to go along. You would have to carry a pass, stating that you have permission to make the journey alone, but that is easily managed."

"Yes. I'd like to go soon, please." He was good at his job for just this reason, so that it would be easier to keep him happy than to replace him.

Not everyone could do his job. The free man who was his predecessor had subsided into a rum-soaked heap; even now he could be seen shambling along Bay Street, trying to beg or gamble up enough money to drown the nightmares.

Grandison Harris had no dreams.

"Excuse me, Dr. Newton, but it's time for my train trip again, and Dr. Eve said it was your turn to pay."

"Hmm . . . what? Already?"

"Been four weeks." He paused for a moment, taking in the rumpled figure elbow-deep in papers at his desk. "I know you've had other things on your mind, sir. I'm sorry to hear about your uncle's passing."

"Oh, yes, thank you, Grandison." George Newton ran a hand through his hair, and sighed. "Well, it wasn't a shock, you know. He was a dear old fellow, but getting up in years, you know. No, it isn't so much that. It's the chaos he's left me."

"Chaos?"

"The mess. In his will my uncle left instructions that his house be converted to use as an orphanage, which is very commendable, I'm sure, but he had a houseful of family retainers, you know. And with the dismantling of his household on Walker Street, they have all moved in with me on Greene Street. I can't walk for people. Eleven of them! Women. Children. Noise. Someone tugging at my sleeve every time I turn around. And the Tuttle family heirlooms, besides. It's bedlam. And Henry, my valet, is at his wit's end. He's getting on in years, you know, and accustomed to having only me to look after. I would not dream of turning them out, of course, but . . ."

Grandison nodded. Poor white folks often thought that servants solved all the problems rich people could ever have, but he could see how they could be problems as well. They had to be fed, clothed, looked after when they got sick. It would be one thing if Dr. George had a wife and a busy household already going—then maybe a few extra folks wouldn't make much difference, but for a bachelor of forty-five used to nobody's company but his own, this sudden crowd of dependents might prove a maddening distraction. It would never occur to George Newton to sell his uncle's slaves, either. That was to his credit. Grandison thought that things ought to be made easier for them so he wouldn't be tempted to sell those folks to get some peace. He considered the situation, trying to think of a way to lighten the load. He said, "Have you thought about asking Miz Alethea if she can help you sort it out, Doctor?"

"Alethea Taylor? Well, I am her guardian now, I know." Newton smiled. "Is she also to be mine?"

"You know she does have seven young'uns. She's used to a house full. Maybe she could set things in order for you."

George Newton turned the idea over in his mind. Women were better at managing a household and seeing to people's needs. He had more pressing matters to contend with here at the medical school. He reached into his pocket and pulled out a roll of greenbacks. "Well, we must get you to Charleston," he said. "Twelve dollars for train fare, isn't it? And, thanks. I believe I will take your advice and ask Alethea to help me."

George Newton's problems went out of his head as soon as the door shut behind him. He went off to the depot to wait for the train, and he wanted no thought of Augusta to dampen his visit to Rachel.

Three days later he walked into Alethea Taylor's parlor near suppertime, and found that one of the family was missing. "Where's Miss Mary Frances?" he asked as they settled around the big table.

Young Joseph waved a drumstick and said, "Oh, Mama sent her over to Dr. George's house. You know how he's been since Mr. Tuttle passed. People just running all over him, asking for things right and left. And Mr. George he can't say no to anybody, and he has about as much common sense as a day-old chick. He asked Mama to come help him, but she's too busy with her sewing work. So we sent Fanny instead."

Jane, who was ten, said, "Mama figured Fanny would put a stop to that nonsense. She'll sort them all out, that's certain. Ever since she got back from that school in South Carolina she's been bossing all of us something fierce, so I'm glad she's gone over there. It'll give us a rest."

"But she's what—seventeen?"

Joseph laughed. "Sixteen going-on-thirty," he said. "Those folks at Newton's will think a hurricane hit 'em. Fanny's got enough sand to take on the lot of them, and what's more she won't need a pass to go there, either."

Harris nodded. No, she wouldn't need a pass. Fanny Taylor was a gray-eyed beauty, whiter than some of the French Creole belles he'd seen in Charleston. With her light skin, her education and her poise, she could go anywhere unchallenged, and she had the same fire and steel as Miss Alethea, so he didn't think she'd be getting any back talk from the Newton household.

"She's living over there now?"

Jim laughed. "No-oo, sir! Mama wouldn't sit still for that." He glanced at his mother to see if it was safe to say more, but her expression was not encouraging.

"She'll be home directly," said Anna. "She goes first thing in the morning and she comes home after dinner time."

Miss Alethea spoke up then. "Children, where are your manners? Pass Mr. Harris those fresh biscuits and some gravy, and let him talk for once. Hand round the chicken, Jim. Mr. Harris, how was your journey?"

"The day was fine for a train ride," he said, careful to swallow the last bit of chicken before he spoke. The Taylors were sticklers for table manners. "Though we did have to stop once for some cows had got out and would not leave the track."

Miss Alethea was not interested in cows. "And your wife, Mr. Harris? I hope you found her well?"

"She's well enough." He hesitated. "She is with child."

Miss Alethea glanced at her own brood, and managed to smile. "Why, don't say that news with such a heavy heart, Mr. Harris. This will be your first born, won't it! You should be joyful!"

He knew it was his child. The old miss would never permit any goings-on in her house. Not that he thought Rachel would have countenanced it anyhow. But a child was one more millstone of Charleston to burden him. He couldn't be with his child, couldn't protect it. And the old missus professed to be delighted at this new addition to the household, but he was afraid that a baby on the premises would be more annoying to her than she anticipated. He thought of Dr. George's fractious household. Might the old missus part with Rachel and the infant to restore her house to its former peacefulness? Was it any wonder that he was worried?

Miss Alethea gave her children a look, and one by one they left the table, as if a command had been spoken aloud. When the two of them were alone, she said, "It's not right to separate a husband from his wife. I don't know what Dr. George was thinking when he brought you here to begin with."

"No, I asked him to. It seemed for the best. And my Rachel wasn't to be sold, so there wasn't any question of bringing her, too."

"Be that as it may, you have been here now, what? Three years? It is high time that Medical College did something about your situation. And a baby on the way as well. Yes, they must see about that."

"I suppose the doctors thought—"

"I know what they thought. They thought what all you men think—that you'd replace your wife and be glad of the chance. Folks said that about Mr. Butts, too, but they were wrong. Seven children we had, and he stayed with me until the day he died. Those doctors must see by now that you have not deserted your wife. You going so faithful on the train to see her every chance you get. Well, it's early days still. The baby not born yet, and many a slip, as they say. Let us wait and see if all goes well, and if it does, one day we will speak to Dr. George about it."

The anatomy classes did not often want babies. He was glad of that. He thought he might take to drink as old Clegg had done if he'd had to lift shrouded infants out of the ground during the months that he waited for his own child to be born in Charleston.

Women died in childbirth. No one knew better than he. The men he pulled from their shrouds in Cedar Grove were either old husks of humanity, worn out by work and weariness at a great age, or else young fools who lost a fight, or died of carelessness, their own or someone else's. But the women . . . It was indeed the curse of Eve. Sometimes the women died old, too, of course. Miss Alethea herself had borne seven babies, and would live to make old bones. She came of sturdy stock. But he saw many a young woman put into the clay before her time, with her killer wrapped in swaddling cloths and placed in her arms.

And the doctors did want those young mothers. Their musculature was better for study than the stringy sinews of old folks, Dr. Newton had told him. "A pregnant woman will make a good subject," he said, examining the body Grandison had brought in just before dawn. "Midwives see to all the normal births, of course, but when something goes wrong, they'll call in a doctor. When we attend a birth, it's always a bad sign. We need to know all we can."

"But why does birthing kill them?" Grandison had asked. It was when he'd first learned about Rachel, and he wondered if the doctors here had some new sliver of knowledge that might save her, if it came to that. Surely this long procession of corpses had amounted to something.

George Newton thought the matter over carefully while he examined the swollen form of the young woman on the table before them. In the emptiness of death she looked too young to have borne a child. Well, she did not bear it. It remained inside her, a last secret to take away with her. Grandison stared at her, trying to remember her

as a living being. He must have seen her
among the crowds at the city market, perhaps, or laughing among the women on the
lawn outside the church. But he could not
place her. Whoever she had been was gone,
and he was glad that he could summon no
memory to call her back. It was easier to
think of the bodies as so much cordwood to
be gathered for the medical school. Had it
not been for her swollen belly, he would not
have given her a thought.

At last Dr. Newton said, "Why do they die?
Now that's a question for the good Reverend Wilson over at the Presbyterian
church across the street. He would tell you
that their dying was the will of God, and the
fulfillment of the curse on Eve for eating the
apple, or some such nonsense as that. But I
think . . ." He paused for a moment, staring
at the flame of his match as if he'd forgotten
the question.

"Yes, doctor? Why do you think they die?"

"Well, Grandison, I spent my boyhood
watching the barn cats give birth and the
hounds drop litters of ten at a time, and the
hogs farrow a slew of piglets. And you know,
those mothers never seemed to feel any
pain in those birthings. But women are different. It kills some and half kills the rest.
And I asked myself why, same as you have,

and I wondered if we could find something other than God to blame for it."

"Did you? Find something to blame besides God?"

Dr. Newton smiled. "Ourselves, I guess. The problem in childbirth is the baby's head. The rest of that little body slides through pretty well, but it's the head that gets caught and causes the problems. I suppose we need those big heads because our brains are bigger than a dog's or a pig's, but perhaps over the eons our heads have outgrown our bodies."

He thought it over. "But there's nothing I can do about that." he said. "I can't help Rachel."

The doctor nodded. "I know," he said. "Perhaps in this case Reverend Wilson would be more help to you than we doctors are. He would prescribe prayer, and I have nothing better to offer."

Newton turned to go, but another thought occurred to him. "Grandison, why don't you come in to class today?" He nodded toward the girl's swollen body. "She will be our subject today. Perhaps you'll feel better if you understood the process."

Grandison almost smiled. It would never occur to the studious bachelor that a man with a pregnant wife might be appalled by

such a sight. Dr. George considered learning
a cure in itself. Grandison did not think that
was the case, but since learning was often useful for its own sake, he would not refuse the
offer. And he would take care not to show disgust or fear, because that might prevent other
offers to learn from coming his way. Doctoring would be a good skill to know. He had
seen enough of death to want to fight back.

He had watched while the doctors cut open
the blank-faced woman, and now he knew
that the womb looked like a jellyfish from
the Charleston docks, and that the birth
canal made him think of a snake swallow-
ing a baby rabbit, but the knowledge did
nothing to allay his fears about Rachel's
confinement. It was all right, though, in
the end. Whether the prayers accomplished their object or whether his wife's
sturdy body and rude good health had
been her salvation, the child was safely delivered, and mother and baby thrived. He
called that first son "George," in honor of
Dr. Newton, hoping the gesture would
make the old bachelor feel benevolent toward Rachel and the boy.

After that he got into the habit of sitting

in on the medical classes when he could spare the time from his other duties. Apart from the big words the doctors used, the learning didn't seem too difficult. Once you learned what the organs looked like and how to find them in the body, the rest followed logically. They were surprised to learn that he could read—his lessons with the Taylor children had served him well. After a while, no one took any notice of him at all in the anatomy classes, and presently the doctors grew accustomed to calling on him to assist them in the demonstrations. He was quiet and competent, and they noticed his helpfulness, rather than the fact that he, too, was learning medicine.

He had been in Augusta four years. By now he was as accustomed to the rhythm of the academic year as he had once been attuned to the seasonal cadence of the farm. He had taken Alethea Taylor's advice and made himself quietly indispensable, so that at work the doctors scarcely had to give him a thought, except to hand over money for whatever supplies he needed for the task at hand or for his personal use. No one ever questioned his demands for money these days. They simply handed over whatever he asked for, and went back to what they had been doing before he had interrupted.

Sixteen bodies per term for the anatomy class. He could read well now, thanks to the Taylor daughters, although they would be shocked if they knew that he found this skill most useful in reading the death notices in the *Chronicle*. When there were not enough bodies available in the county to meet this need, Grandison was authorized to purchase what he needed. A ten-dollar gold piece for each subject. Two hundred gallons of whiskey purchases each year for the preservation of whole corpses or of whatever organs of interest the doctors wished to keep for further study, and if he bought a bit more spirits than that amount, no one seemed to notice. It never went to waste.

He tapped on the door of George Newton's office. "Morning, Dr. George. It's train time again."

The doctor looked up as if he had forgotten where he was. "Train time?—Oh, yes, of course. Your family. Sit down, Grandison. Perhaps we should talk."

He forced himself to keep smiling, because it didn't do any good to argue with a man who could break your life in two. He wasn't often asked to sit down when he talked to the doctors, and he made no move toward the chair. He assumed an expression of anxious concern. "Is there anything I can help you with, Dr. George?" he said.

The doctor tapped his pen against the ledger. "It's just that I've been thinking, you know. Twelve dollars a month for train fare, for you to go and see your wife."

"And child," said Grandison, keeping his voice steady.

"Yes, of course. Well, I was thinking about it, and I'll have to talk it over with the rest of the faculty—"

I could take a second job, he was thinking. *Maybe earn the money for train fare myself . . .*

But Dr. George said, "I shall persuade them to purchase your family."

It took him a moment to sort out the words, so contrary were they to the ones he had anticipated. He had to bite back the protests that had risen in his throat. "Buy Rachel and George?"

The doctor smiled. "Oh, yes. I shall explain that we could save enough money in train fare to justify the purchase price within a few years. It does make fiscal sense. Besides, I have lately come to realize how much you must miss them."

Grandison turned these words over in his mind. If one of the cadavers had got up from the dissecting table and walked away, he could not have been more surprised. He never mentioned his wife and son except to respond with a vague pleasantry on the rare occasion that someone asked after them. Why had the doctor suddenly taken this charitable notion? Why not when the baby was first born? Dr. George was a kind man, in an absent-minded sort of way, but he hardly noticed his own feelings, let alone anybody else's. Grandison stood with his back to the door, the smile still frozen to his lips, wondering what had come over the man.

George Newton rubbed his forehead and sighed. He started to speak, and then shook his head. He began again, "It may be a few months before we can find the money, mind you. It should take about thirteen hundred dollars to buy both your wife and son. That should do it, surely. I'll write to your wife's mistress in Charleston to negotiate the purchase."

Grandison nodded. "Thank you," he whispered. The joy would come later, when the news had sunk in. Just now he was still wondering what had come over Dr. George.

"I'm going to be moving out one of these days," he told Alethea Taylor that night after supper.

She sat in her straight-backed chair closest to the lamp, embroidering a baby dress. "You'll be needing to find a place for your family to live," she said, still intent upon her work.

He laughed. "The world can't keep nothing from you, Miz Taylor. Dr. George told you?"

"Fanny told me." She set the baby dress down on the lamp table, and wiped her eyes. "She's been after George to bring them here, and he promised he would see to it."

"I wondered what put it into his head. Saying he was going to buy them, right out of the blue, without me saying a word about it. I can't make out what's come over him."

She made no reply, but her frown deepened as she went on with her sewing.

"I don't suppose you know what this is all about?"

She wiped her eyes on the hem of the cloth. "Yes. I know. I may as well tell you. Dr. George and Fanny are—well, man and wife, I would say, though the state of Georgia won't countenance it. Fanny has a baby coming soon."

He was silent for a bit, thinking out what to say. Dr. George was in his forties, and looked every minute of it. Fanny was a slender and beautiful sixteen. He knew how it would sound to a stranger, but he had known Dr. George five years now, and for all the physician's wealth and prominence, he couldn't help seeing him as a gray-haired mole, peering out at the world from his book-lined burrow, while the graceful Fanny seemed equal to anything. He knew—he *knew*—of light-skinned women forced to become their owners' mistresses, but Fanny was free, and besides he couldn't see her mother allowing such a thing to happen. Miss Alethea did not have all the rights of a white woman, though you'd take her for one to look at her, but still, there were some laws to protect free people of color. Through her dress-making business, Miss Alethea had enough friends among her lady clientele that if she'd asked, some lady's lawyer husband would have intervened. The white ladies hated the idea of their menfolk taking colored mistresses, and they'd jump at the chance to put a stop to it. Someone would have been outraged by such a tale, and they would have been eager to save Miss Alethea's young daughter from a wicked seducer. But . . . *Dr. George?* He couldn't see it.

Why, for all his coolness in cutting up the dead, when it came to dealing with live folks, Dr. George wouldn't say boo to a goose.

"He didn't . . . force her?" he asked, looking away as he said it. But when he looked back and saw Miss Alethea's expression, his lips twitched, and then they both began to laugh in spite of it all.

Miss Alethea shook her head. "*Force? Dr. George?* Oh, my. I can't even think it was his idea, Mr. Harris. You know how he is."

"Well, is Miss Fanny happy?" he said at last.

"Humph. Sixteen years old and a rich white doctor thinks she hung the moon. What do you think?" She sighed. "When a man falls in love for the first time when he's past forty, it hits him hard. Seems like he's taken leave of his senses."

"Oh. Well," he cast about for some word of comfort, and settled on, "I won't tell anybody."

She stabbed her needle at the cloth. "Shout it from the rooftops if you feel like it, Mr. Harris. It's not as if *they're* keeping it a secret. He wants to marry her."

He smiled. "Anybody would, Miss Alethea. Mary Frances is a beautiful girl."

"You misunderstand, Mr. Harris. I'm saying that he *means* to marry her."

"And stay here? And let folks know about it?"

She nodded. "I'm saying. Live as man and wife, right there on Greene Street."

Now he realized why George Newton had suddenly understood the pain of his separation from Rachel, but he felt that the doctor's newfound wisdom had come at the price of folly. St. Paul's seeing the light on the road to Damascus might have been a blessed miracle, but Dr. George's light was more likely to be a thunderbolt. "He can't do that," he said. "Set her up as his wife."

"Not without losing his position he can't." The needle stabbed again. "Don't you think I've told them that?"

"And what did he say?"

"He's going to resign from the medical school, that's what. Says he has money enough. Going to continue his work in a laboratory at home. Huh!" She shook her head at the folly of it.

He thought about it. Perhaps in Charleston such a thing might work. Down in the islands, certainly. Martinique. Everybody knew that the French . . . But *here?*

"I even asked him, Mr. Harris, I said

straight out, *Do you remember Richard Mentor Johnson?*" His expression told her that he did not remember, either. But she did. "Richard Mentor Johnson of Kentucky. He was the vice president of the United States, back when I was a girl. Under President Van Buren. Folks said that he had killed the Indian chief Tecumseh, which they thought made him a hero. But then he had also married a woman of color, and when word of that got out, they tried to run him out of office on account of it. When his first term was over, he gave up and went home to Kentucky. And, do you know, Mr. Johnson's wife wasn't even alive by that time. She had died before he ever went to Washington to be vice president. Just the memory of her was enough to ruin him. Now, how well does Dr. George think he will fare in Georgia with a *live* colored wife in his house?"

"But Miss Fanny—to look at her—"

"I know. She's whiter to look at than some of the doctors' wives, but that makes no difference. This is a small town, Mr. Harris. Everybody knows everybody. Fanny can't pass in Augusta, and they both say they've no mind to go elsewhere."

He thought he had made all the proper expressions of sympathy and commiseration, but he was thinking just as much about the effect that Dr. George's folly would have on him. Would this change of heart mean no more robbing Cedar Grove? Or in his madness would the doctor insist on obtaining an equal number of bodies from the white burying ground? Equality was a fine thing, but not if it got him hanged by a white lynch mob.

He swept the upstairs hall four times that morning, waiting for Dr. George to be alone in his office. Finally the last visitor left, and he tapped on the door quickly before anyone else could turn up. "Excuse me, Dr. George. We're getting low on supplies for the anatomy classes," he said.

He always said "supplies" instead of "bodies" even when they were alone, just in case anyone happened to overhear.

Dr. George gave him a puzzled frown. "Supplies? Oh—oh, I see. Not filled our quota yet? Well, are there any fresh ones to be had?"

"A burying today," he said. "Little boy fell off a barn roof. I just wondered if you wanted me to take him."

"Yes, I suppose so. He's needed. Though we could use a yellow fever victim if you hear of one. Must teach the Southern diseases, you know. Medical schools up north don't know a thing about them." Dr. George looked up. "Why did you ask about this boy in particular? Do you know him?"

That didn't matter. He had known them all for years now. Some he minded about more than others, but all of them had long ceased to be merely lumps of clay in his hands. "It's all right," he said. "I don't mind bringing him in. I just wondered what you wanted me to do, and if there's to be a new dean—"

The doctor leaned back in his chair and sighed. "Yes, I see, Grandison. You have heard."

"Yes."

"It's true that I am resigning the post of dean. I felt that it was better for the college if I did so." He picked up a sheaf of papers from his desk and held it out with a bemused smile. "But it seems that I shall be staying on as Emeritus Professor of Anatomy, after all. This is a petition, signed by all of the students and faculty, asking that I stay. And the Board of Trustees has acceded to their request."

"Do they know?"

"About Fanny? They do. They profess not to care. I suppose when one is a doctor, one sees how little difference there really is between the races. Just a thin layer of skin, that's all, and then it's all the same underneath. Whatever the reason, they insist that I stay on in some capacity, and I shall."

"So nothing will change? For me, I mean?"

George Newton shook his head. "We still must have bodies, and the only safe place to obtain them is from Cedar Grove. That has not changed. And I fancy that I shall still have enough influence to bring your family to Augusta. I do not intend to shirk my duty, so you may go and see to yours."

Madison Newton was born on the last day of February, red-faced, fair-haired, and hazel-eyed, looking like a squashed cabbage leaf, but a white one, after all.

"It's a fine baby," he had said to Fanny, when she brought the baby to her mother's house on a mild day in March.

Fanny switched the blanket back into place, so that only the infant's nose peeped out. "People only want to look at him to see what color he is," she said. "What do they expect? He had sixteen great-great grandparents, same as everybody, and only one of them was colored. All the rest of him from then on down is white. Of course, that doesn't change what he is to most folks' way of thinking."

He had kept smiling and said the plain truth: that the infant was a fortunate child, but he had been angry, and his annoyance had not left him. That night in Cedar Grove in a fine mist of rain, he dug as if he could inflict an injury upon the earth itself. "I reckon Miss Fanny is whiter in her head than she is on her face," he said to the darkness, thrusting the shovel deep into the ground. "Feeling sorry for a light-eyed baby born free, his daddy a rich white doctor. I guess pretty Miss Fanny wants the moon, even when it's raining."

He spared hardly a thought for the man in the box below. Some drunken laborer from the docks, hit too hard over the head in a brawl. He had even forgotten the name. An easy task tonight. No shells or flowers decorated this grave site. The dead man had been shunted into the ground without grief or ceremony. Just as well take him to the doctors, where he could do some good for once. His thoughts returned to his grievance. Spoiled Miss Fanny had never given a thought to his baby when she was complaining about her own son's lot in life. How would she have liked to be Rachel—separated from her husband, and left to raise a child without him, knowing that at any time old missus might take a notion to sell that child, and nothing could be done to stop it.

He brushed the dirt from the pine box, and stove in the lid with his shovel point. Miss Fanny Taylor didn't know what trouble was, complaining about—

A sound.

Something like a moan, coming from inside the smashed coffin. He forgot about Fanny and her baby, as he knelt in the loose dirt of the open grave, pressing his ear close to the lid of the box. He held his breath, straining to hear a repetition of the sound. In the stillness, with all his thoughts focused on the dark opening before him, he realized that something else was wrong with the grave site. The smell was wrong. The sickly sweet smell of newly decaying flesh should have been coming from the box, but it wasn't. Neither was the stench of voided bowels, the last letting-go of the dead. All he smelled was rotgut whiskey.

He gripped the corpse under the armpits and pulled it out of the grave, but instead of sacking it up, he laid the body out on the damp grass. It groaned.

He had heard such sounds from a corpse before. The first time it happened, he had been unloading a sack from the wagon into the store room at the medical college. He had dropped the sack and gone running to Dr. George, shouting that the deader from the burying ground had come back to life.

George Newton had smiled for an instant, but without a word of argument, he'd followed the porter back to the store room and examined the sacked-up body. He had felt the wrist and neck for a pulse, and even leaned into the dead face to check for breath, but Grandison could tell from his calm and deliberate movements that he knew what he would find. "The subject is dead," he said, standing up, and brushing traces of dirt from his trousers.

"It just died then. I heard it moan."

Dr. George smiled gently. "Yes, I believe you did, Grandison, but it was dead all the same."

"A ghost then?"

"No. Merely a natural process. When the body dies, there is still air trapped within the lungs. Sometimes when that air leaves the lungs it makes a moaning sound. Terrifying, I know. I heard it once myself in my student days, but it is only a remnant of life, not life itself. This poor soul has been dead at least a day."

He never forgot that sound, though in all the bodies that had passed through his hands on the way to the dissecting table, he had never heard it since.

The sound coming now from the man stretched out on the grass was different. And it changed—low and rumbling at first, and then louder. He knelt beside the groaning man and shook his shoulder.

"Hey!" he said. "Hey, now—" His voice was hoarse and unnaturally loud in the still darkness of Cedar Grove. *What can you say to a dead man?*

The groan changed to a cough, and then the man rolled over and vomited into the mound of spaded earth.

He sighed, and edged away a few feet. He had seen worse. Smelled worse. But finding a live body in the graveyard complicated matters. He sat quietly, turning the possibilities over in his mind, until the retching turned to sobbing.

"You're all right," he said, without turning around.

"This is the graveyard. Badger Benson done killed me?"

"I guess he tried. But you woke up. Who are you, anyhow?"

"I was fixing to ask you that. How did you come to find me down in the ground? You don't look like no angel."

He smiled. "Might be yours, though. You slave or free, boy?"

"Belong to Mr. Johnson. Work on his boat."

"Thought so. Well, you want to go back to Mr. Johnson, do you?"

The man stretched and kicked his legs, stiff from his interment. "I dunno," he said. "Why you ask me that?"

"'Cause you were dead, boy, as far as anybody knows. They buried you this morning. Now if you was to go back to your master, there'd be people asking me questions about how I come to find you, and they'd take you back to Johnson's, and you'd still be a slave, and like as not I'd be in trouble for digging you up. But if you just lit out of here and never came back, why nobody would ever even know you were gone and that this grave was empty. You're dead. You don't let 'em find out any different, and they'll never even know to hunt for you."

The man rubbed the bruise on the back of his head. "Now how did you come to find me?"

Grandison stood up and retrieved the shovel. "This is where the medical school gets the bodies to cut up for the surgery classes. The doctors at the college were fixing to rip you open. And they still can, I reckon, unless you light out of here. Now, you tell me, boy, do you want to be dead again?"

The young man raised a hand as if to ward off a blow. "No. No!—I understand you right enough. I got to get gone."

"And you don't go back for nothing. You don't tell nobody good-bye. You are dead, and you leave it at that."

The young man stood up and took a few tentative steps on still unsteady legs. "Where do I go then?"

Grandison shrugged. "If it was me, I would go west. Over the mountains into Indian country. You go far enough, there's places that don't hold with slavery. I'd go there."

The man turned to look at him. "Well, why don't you then?" he said. "Why don't *you* go?"

"Don't worry about me. I'm not the one who's dead. Now are you leaving or not?"

"Yeah. Leaving."

"You've got three hours before sunup." He handed the shovel to the resurrected man. "Help me fill in your grave, then."

———

DR. GEORGE NEWTON — DECEMBER 1859

It is just as well that I stepped down as dean of the medical college. I haven't much time to wind up my affairs, and the fact that Ignatius Garvin is ably discharging my former duties leaves me with one less thing to worry about. If I can leave my dear Fanny and the babies safely provided for, I may leave this world without much regret. I wish I could have seen my boy grow up ... wish I could have grown old with my dearest wife ... And I wish that God had seen fit to send me an easier death.

No one knows yet that I am dying, and it may yet be weeks before the disease carries me off, but I do not relish the thought of the time before me, for I know enough of this illness to tremble at the thought of what will come. I must not do away with myself, though. I must be brave, so as not to cause Fanny any more pain than she will feel at losing me so soon.

So many papers to sift through. Investments, deeds, instructions for the trustees— my life never felt so complicated. Soon the pain will begin, and it may render me incapable of making wise decisions to safeguard my little family. At least I have safeguarded the family of our faithful college servant, Grandison Harris. Thank God I was able to do that in time, for I had long promised him that I would bring his Rachel and her boy to Augusta, so I did a few months back. I am not yet fifty, sound in body and mind, and newly married. I thought I had many years to do good works and to continue my medical research. I suppose that even a physician must think that he will never face death. Perhaps we would go mad if we tried to live thinking otherwise.

I wonder how it happened. People will say it was the buggy accident just before Christmas, and perhaps it was. That gelding is a nervous horse, not at all to be depended upon in busy streets of barking dogs and milling crowds. I must remember to tell Henry to sell the animal, for I would not like to think of Fanny coming to harm if the beast became spooked again. I was shaken and bruised when he dumped me out of the carriage and into the mud, but did I sustain any cuts during the fall? I do not remember any blood.

Dr. Eve came to look me over, and he pronounced me fit enough, with no bones broken, and no internal injuries. He was right as far as it went. My fellow physicians all stopped by to wish us good cheer at Christ-

mas, and to pay their respects to their injured
friend. They did not bring their wives, of
course. No respectable white woman accepts
the hospitality of this house, for it is supposed that Fanny's presence taints the household. We are not, after all, legally married in
the eyes of the law here. Fanny professes not
to care. *Dull old biddies*, anyhow, she declares.
But she has certainly charmed the gentle-
men, who consider me a lucky man. And so I
was, until this tragedy struck—though none
of those learned doctors suspected it.

I wish that I had not. I wish that I could go
innocently into the throes of this final illness, as would a child who had stepped on a
rusty nail, not knowing what horrors lay before me. But I am a trained physician. I do
know. And the very word clutches at my
throat with cold fingers.

Tetanus.

Oh, I know too much, indeed. Too
much—and not enough. I have seen people
die of this. The muscles stretch and spasm,
in the control of the ailment rather than the
patient, an agonizing distension such as prisoners must have felt upon the rack in olden
days. The body is tortured by pain beyond
imagining, but beyond these physical tor-
ments, the patient's mind remains clear and
unaffected. I doubt that the clarity is a bless-

ing. Delirium or madness might prove a release from the agony, yet even that is denied to the sufferer. And there is no cure. Nothing can stop the progression of this disease, and nothing can reverse its effects. I have, perhaps, a week before the end, and I am sure that by then I will not dread death, but rather welcome it as a blessed deliverance.

Best not to dwell on it. It will engulf me soon enough. I must send for James Hope. I can trust him. As the owner of the cotton mill, he will be an eminently respectable guardian for my wife's business interests, and since James is a Scotsman by birth, and not bound by the old Southern traditions of race and caste, he will see Fanny as the gentlewoman that she is. He treats her with all the courtly gentility he would show to a duchess, and that endears him to both of us. Yes, I must tell James what has happened, and how soon he must pick up where I am forced to leave off.

My poor Fanny! To be left a widow with two babies, and she is not yet twenty. I worry more over her fate than I do my own. At least mine will be quick, but Fanny has another forty years to suffer if the world is unkind to her. I wish that the magnitude of my suffering could be charged against any sorrow God had intended for her. I must speak to James Hope. How aptly named he is! I must entrust my little family to him.

It was nearly Christmas, and Rachel had made a pound cake for the Newtons. He was to take it around to Greene Street that afternoon, when he could manage to get away from his duties. Grandison looked at the cake, and thought that Dr. George might prefer a specimen from the medical school supply for his home laboratory, but he supposed that such a gesture would not be proper for the season. Rachel would know best what people expected on social occasions. She talked to people, and visited with her new friends at church, while he hung back, dreading the prospect of talking to people that he might be seeing again some day.

He took the cake to the Newton house, and tapped on the back door, half expecting it to open before his hand touched the wood. He waited a minute, and then another, but no one came. He knocked again, harder this time, wondering at the delay. As many servants as the Newtons had, that door ought to open as soon as his foot hit the porch. What was keeping them so busy?

Finally, after the third and loudest spate of

knocking, Fanny herself opened the door. He smiled and held out his paper-wrapped Christmas offering, but the sight of her made him take a step backward. His words of greeting stuck in his throat. She was big-bellied with child again, he knew that. She looked as if it could come at any moment, but what shocked him was how ill she looked, as if she had not eaten or slept for a week. She stared out at him, hollow-eyed and trembling, her face blank with weariness. For a moment he wondered if she recognized him.

"My Rachel made y'all a pound cake. For Christmas," he said.

She nodded, and stepped back from the door to admit him to the kitchen. "Put it on the table," she said.

He set down the cake. The house was unnaturally quiet. He listened for sounds of baby Madison playing, or the bustle of the servants, who should have been making the house ready for the holiday, but all was still. He looked back at Fanny, who was staring down at the parcel as if she had never seen one before, as if she had forgotten how it got there, perhaps.

"Are you all right?" he asked. "Shall I fetch Miss Alethea for you?"

Fanny shook her head. "She's been already. She took Madison so that I can stay with George," she whispered. "And I've sent most of the others around there, too. Henry stayed here, of course. He won't leave George."

Something was the matter with Dr. George, then. It must be bad. Fanny looked half dead herself. "Shall I go for Dr. Eve?" he asked.

"He was here this morning. So was Dr. Garvin. Wasn't a bit of use. George told me that from the beginning, but I wouldn't have it. I thought with all those highfalutin doctors somebody would be able to help him, but they can't. They can't."

"Is he took bad?"

"He's dying. It's the lockjaw. You know what that is?"

He nodded. Tetanus. Oh, yes. They had covered it in one of the medical classes, but not to consider a course of treatment. Only to review the terrible symptoms and to hope they never saw them. He shivered. "Are they sure?"

"George is sure. Diagnosed himself. And the others concur. I was the only one who wouldn't believe it. I do now, though. I sit with him as long as I can. Hour after hour. Watch him fighting the pain. Fighting the urge to scream. And then I go and throw up, and I sit with him some more."

"I could spell you a while."

"No!" She said it so harshly that he took a step back in surprise. She took a deep breath, and seemed to swallow her anger. "No, thank you very kindly, Mr. Harris, but I will not let you see him."

"But if Dr. George is dying—"

"That's exactly why. Don't you think I know what you do over there at the medical college? Porter, they call you. *Porter.* I know what your real duties are, Mr. Harris. Known for a long time. And that's fine. I know doctors have to learn somehow, and that nothing about doctoring is pretty or easy. But you are not going to practice your trade in this house. You are not going to take my husband's body, do you hear?"

He said softly, "I only wanted to help you out, and maybe to tell him good-bye."

"So you say. But he is weak now. Half out of his mind with the pain, and he'd promise anything. He might even suggest it himself, out of some crazy sense of duty to the medical college, but I won't have it. My husband is going to have a proper burial, Mr. Harris. He has suffered enough!"

It doesn't hurt, he wanted to tell her. *You don't feel it if you're dead.* He did not bother to speak the words. He knew whose pain Fanny was thinking of, and that whatever Dr.

George's wishes might be, it was the living who mattered, not the dead. Best to soothe her quickly and with as little argument as possible. He did not think that the other doctors would accept George Newton's body anyhow. That would be bringing death too close into the fold, and he was glad that he would not be required to carry out that task. Let the doctor lie in consecrated ground: There were bodies enough to be had in Augusta.

"I'll go now, Miss Fanny," he said, putting on his best white folks manners, if it would give her any comfort. "But I think one of the doctors should come back and take a look at you." He nodded toward her distended belly. "And we will pray for the both of you, my Rachel and I. Pray that he gets through this." It was a lie. He never prayed, but if he did, it would be for Dr. George's death to come swiftly—the only kindness that could be hoped for in a case of tetanus.

Dr. George died after the new year in 1860. The illness had lasted only two weeks, but the progress of the disease was so terrible that it had begun to seem like months to those who could do nothing but wait for his release from the pain. Grandison joined the crowd at the doctor's funeral, though he took care to keep clear of Fanny, for fear of upsetting her again. In her grief she might shout out things that should not be said aloud in Augusta's polite society. The doctors knew his business, of course, but not the rest of the town. He reckoned that most of Augusta would have been at the funeral if it weren't for the fact of the doctor's awkward marriage arrangements. As it was, though, his fellow physicians, the students, and most of the town's businessmen came to pay their respects, while their wives and daughters stayed home, professing themselves too delicate to endure the sight of the doctor's redbone widow. Not that you could see an inch of her skin, whatever its color, for she was swathed from head to foot in black widow's weeds and veils, leaning on the arm of Mr. James Hope, as if he were the spar of her sinking ship.

"Left a widow at eighteen," said Miss Alethea, regal in her black dress, her eyes red from tears of her own. "I had hoped for better for my girl."

He nodded. "She will be all right," he said. "Dr. George would have seen to that."

Miss Alethea gave him the look usually reserved for one of her children talking foolishness. "She's back home again, you know.

Dr. George was too clouded at the last to do justice to a will, and Mr. James Hope had to sell the house on Greene Street. He vows to see her settled in a new place, though, over on Ellis, just a block from Broad Street. Having it built. There's all Dr. George's people to be thought of, you know, and the Tuttle folks, as well. Fanny has to have a house of her own, but I'm glad to have her by me for now, for the new baby is due any day—if it lives through her grief. We must pray for her, Mr. Harris."

Grandison looked past her at the tall, fair-haired Scotsman, who was still hovering protectively beside the pregnant young widow, and wondered if the prayer had already been answered.

The cellar was paved with bones now. Each term when the anatomy class had finished with its solemn duties of dissection, the residue was brought to him to be disposed of. He could hardly rebury the remains in any public place or discard them where they might be recognized for what they were. The only alternative was to layer them in quicklime in the basement on Telfair Street. How many hundred had it been now? He had lost count. Mercifully the faces and the memories of the subjects' resurrection were fading with the familiarity of the task, but sometimes he wondered if the basement resounded with cries he could not hear, and if that was why the building's cat refused to set foot down there. The quicklime finished taking away the flesh and masked the smell, but he wondered what part of the owners remained, and if that *great getting up in the morning* that the preacher spoke of was really going to come to pass on Judgment Day. And who would have to answer for the monstrous confusion and scramble of bones that must follow? Himself? Dr. George? The students who carved up the cadavers? Sometimes as he scattered the quicklime over a new batch of discarded bones, he mused on Dr. George peering over the wrought iron fence of white folks' heaven at an angry crowd of colored angels shaking their fists at him.

"Better the dead than the living, though," he would tell himself.

Sometimes on an afternoon walk to Cedar Grove, he would go across to the white burying ground to pay his respects to Dr. George, lying there undisturbed in his grave, and sometimes he would pass the

time of day with the grassy mound, as if the
doctor could still hear him. "Miss Mary
Frances finally birthed that baby," he said
one winter day, picking the brown stems of
dead flowers off the grave. "Had a little girl
the other day. Named her Georgia Frances,
but everybody calls her Cissie, and I think
that's the name that's going to stick. She's a
likely little thing, pale as a Georgia peach.
And Mr. James Hope is building her that
house on Ellis like he promised, and she's
talking about having her sister Nannie and
young Jimmie move in along with her. I
thought maybe Mr. James Hope would be
moving in, too, the way he dotes on her, but
he's talking about selling the factory here
and going back to New York where his family is, so I don't think you need to linger on
here if you are, sir. I think everything is going to be all right."

Dr. George hadn't been gone hardly more
than two years when the war came, and that
changed everything. Didn't look like it
would at first, though. For the rest of the
country, the war began in April in
Charleston, when Fort Sumpter fell, but
Georgia had seceded in January, leaving Augusta worried about the arsenal on the hill,

occupied by federal troops. Governor Joe Brown himself came to town to demand the surrender of the arsenal, and the town was treated to a fine show of military parades in the drizzling rain. Governor Brown himself stood on the porch of the Planters Hotel to watch the festivities, but Captain Elzey, who was in command of the eighty-two men at the arsenal, declined to surrender it. He changed his mind a day or so later when eight hundred soldiers and two brigadier generals turned up in the rain to show the arsenal they meant business. Then Captain Elzey sent for the governor to talk things over, and by noon the arsenal and its contents had been handed over to the sovereign State of Georgia, without a shot fired. That, and a lot of worrying, was pretty much all that happened to Augusta for the duration of the war.

When the shooting actually started in Charleston, he was glad that Rachel and the boy were safe in Augusta, instead of being caught in the middle of a war, though personally he would have liked to see the battle for the novelty of it. Everybody said the war was only going to last a few weeks, and he hated to have missed getting a glimpse of it.

Folks were optimistic, but they were making preparations anyhow. Two weeks after

Fort Sumpter, Augusta organized a local company of home guards, the Silver Grays, composed mostly of men too old to fight in the regular army. Mr. James Hope came back from New York City to stand with the Confederacy and got himself chosen second member of the company, after Rev. Joseph Wilson, who was the first. Rev. Wilson's boy Tommy and little Madison Newton were the same age, and they sometimes played together on the lawn of the Presbyterian church, across the road from the college. Sometimes the two of them would come over and pepper him with questions about bodies and sick folks, and he often thought that you'd have to know which boy was which to tell which one wasn't the white child. Fanny kept young Madison as clean and well-dressed as any quality child in Augusta.

The months went by, and the war showed no signs of letting up. One by one the medical students drifted away to enlist in regiments back home.

"I don't suppose you'll have to worry about procuring any more cadavers for classes, Grandison," Dr. Garvin told him.

"No, sir," he said. "I've heard a lot of the students are fixing to quit and join up."

Dr. Garvin scowled. "I expect they will, but even if the school stays open, this war will produce enough cadavers to supply a thousand medical schools before it's over."

There wasn't any fighting in Augusta, but they saw their share of casualties anyhow. A year into the war, the wounded began arriving by train from distant battlefields, and the medical school suspended operation in favor of setting up hospitals to treat the wounded. The City Hotel and the Academy of Richmond County were turned into hospitals in '62 to accommodate the tide of injured soldiers flowing into the city from far off places with unfamiliar names, like Manassas and Shiloh. Many of the faculty members had gone off to serve in the war as well. Dr. Campbell was in Virginia with the Georgia Hospital Association, seeing to the state's wounded up there; Dr. Miller and Dr. Ford were serving with the Confederate forces at different places up in Virginia, and Dr. Jones was somewhere on the Georgia coast contributing his medical skills to the war effort.

Grandison worked in one of the hospitals, assisting the doctors at first, but as the number of casualties strained their ability to treat them, he took on more and more duties to fill the gap.

"I don't see why you are working so hard to patch those Rebels up," one of the porters said to him one day, when he went looking for a roll of clean bandages. "The Federals say they are going to end slavery, and here you are helping the enemy."

He shrugged. "I don't see any Federals in Augusta, do you? I don't see any army coming here to hand me my freedom. So meanwhile I do what I'm supposed to do, and we'll see what transpires when the war is over." Besides, he thought, it was one thing to wish the Confederacy to perdition, and quite another to ignore the suffering of a single boy soldier who couldn't even grow a proper beard yet.

Sometimes he wondered what had happened to the man he "resurrected" who wasn't dead—whether the fellow had made it to some free state beyond the mountains, and whether that had made any difference.

He didn't know if freedom was coming, or what it would feel like, but for the here and now there was enough work for ten of him. So he stitched, and bandaged, and dressed wounds. *I've handled dead people*, he told himself. *This isn't any worse than that.*

But of course it was.

———

The boy was a South Carolina soldier, eighteen or so, with copper-colored hair and a sunny nature that not even a gaping leg wound could dampen. The pet of the ward, he was, and he seemed to be healing up nicely what with all the rest and the mothering from Augusta's lady hospital visitors. The nurses were already talking about the preparations to send him home.

Grandison was walking down the hall that morning, when one of the other patients came hobbling out into the hall and clutched at his coat sleeve. "You got to come now!" the man said. "Little Will just started bleeding a gusher."

He hurried into the ward past the crippled soldier and pushed his way through the patients clustered around the young man's cot. A blood-soaked sheet was pulled back revealing a skinny white leg with a spike of bone protruding through the skin. Jets of dark blood erupted from the bone splinter's puncture. Without a word Grandison sat down beside the boy and closed his fingers over the ruptured skin.

"I just tried to walk to the piss pot," the boy said. He sounded close to passing out. "I got so tired of having to be helped all the time. I felt fine. I just wanted to walk as far as the wall."

He nodded. The mending thigh bone had snapped under the boy's weight, severing a leg artery as the splintered bone slid out of place. The men crowded around the bed murmured among themselves, but no one spoke to the boy.

"Shall I fetch the surgeon?" one of the patients asked Grandison.

He shook his head. "Surgeon's amputating this morning. Wouldn't do no good to call him anyhow."

The boy looked up at him. "Can you stop it, sir?"

He looked away, knowing that the *sir* was for his medical skills and not for himself, but touched by it all the same. The red-haired boy had a good heart. He was a great favorite with his older and sadder comrades.

"Get a needle?" somebody said. "Sew it back in?"

He kept his fingers clamped tight over the wound, but he couldn't stay there forever. He wanted to say: *Y'all ever see a calf killed? Butcher takes a sharp knife and slits that cord in his throat, and he bleeds out in—what? A minute? Two?* It was the same here. The severed artery was not in the neck, no, but the outcome would be the same—and it was just as inevitable.

"But I feel all right," said the boy. "No pain."

He ignored the crowd around the bed and looked straight into the brown eyes of the red-haired boy. "Your artery's cut in two," he said. "Can't nothing remedy that."

"Can you stop the bleeding?"

He nodded toward his fingers pressed against the pale white skin. The warmth of the flesh made him want to pull away. He took a deep breath. "I have stopped it," he said, nodding toward his hand stanching the wound. "But all the time you've got is until I let go."

The boy stared at him for a moment while the words sunk in. Then he nodded. "I see," he said. "Can you hold on a couple minutes? Let me say a prayer."

Somebody said, "I got paper here, Will. You ought to tell your folks good-bye. I'll write it down."

The boy looked the question at Grandison, who glanced down at his hand. "Go ahead," he said. "I can hold it."

In a faltering voice the boy spoke the words of farewell to his parents. He sounded calm, but puzzled, as if it were happening to someone else. That was just as well. Fear wouldn't change anything, and it was contagious. They didn't need a panic in the ward. The room was silent as the boy's voice rose and fell. Grandison turned away from the tear-stained faces to stare at a fly speck on the wall, wishing that he could be elsewhere while this lull before dying dragged on. These last minutes of life should not be witnessed by strangers.

The letter ended, and a few minutes after that the prayers, ending with a whispered amen as the last words of the Lord's Prayer trailed off into sobs.

He looked at the boy's sallow face, and saw in it a serenity shared by no one else in the room. "All right?" he said.

The boy nodded, and Grandison took his hand away.

A minute later the boy was dead. Around the bedstead the soldiers wept, and Grandison covered the still form with the sheet and went back to his duties. He had intended to go to the death room later to talk to the boy, to tell him that death was a release from worse horrors and to wish him peace, but there were so many wounded, and so much to be done that he never went.

The war came to Augusta on stretchers and in the form of food shortages and lack of mercantile goods—but never on horseback with flags flying and the sound of bugles. Augusta thought it would, of course. When Sherman marched to the sea by way of Savannah, troops crowded into the city to defend it, and the city fathers piled up bales of cotton, ready to torch them and the rest of the town with it to keep the powder works and the arsenal out of Union hands, but Sherman ignored them and pushed on north into South Carolina.

Three months later the war ended, and federal troops did come to occupy the city.

"I am a throne, Grandison!" Tommy Wilson announced one May morning. "And Madison here, he's only a dominion."

"That's fine," he said without a glance at the two boys. He was cleaning out the little work room at the college on Telfair Street. It had been his headquarters and his storage room for thirteen years now, but the war was over and he was free. It was time to be his own master now somewhere else. He thought he might cross the river to Hamburg. Folks said that the Yankees over there were putting freedmen into jobs to replace the white men. He would have to see.

Tommy Wilson's words suddenly took shape in his mind. "A throne?" he said. "I thought a throne was a king's chair."

"Well, a throne can be that," said Tommy, with the air of one who is determined to be scrupulously fair. "But it's also a rank of angels. We're playing angels, me and Madison. We're going to go out and convert the heathens."

"Well, that's a fine thing, boys. You go and—*what* heathens?"

"The soldiers," said Madison.

Tommy nodded. "They misbehave something awful, you know. They drink and fight and take the Lord's name in vain."

"And by God we're gonna fix 'em," said Madison.

"Does your father know where you are?"

Tommy nodded. "He said I could play outside."

Madison Newton shrugged. "Mr. Hope don't care where I go. He's living up at my house now, but he's not my daddy. He says he's gonna take Momma and their new babies up north with him, but me and Cissie can't go."

Grandison nodded. Fanny Newton was now called Fanny Hope, and she had two more babies with magnolia skin and light eyes. He wondered what would become of Dr. George's two children.

"Don't you go bothering the soldiers now," he told the boys. "They might shoot the both of you."

Tommy Wilson grinned happily. "Then we shall be angels for real."

"Do we call you *judge* now, Mr. Harris?" Either the war or the worry of family had turned Miss Alethea into an old woman. Her hair was nearly white now, and she peered up at him now through the thick lenses of rimless spectacles.

He had taken his family to live across the river in South Carolina, but he still came back to Augusta on the occasional errand. That morning he had met Miss Alethea as she hobbled along Broad Street, shopping basket on her arm, bound for the market. He smiled and gave her a courtly bow. "Why, you may call me judge if it pleases you, ma'am," he said. "But I don't expect I'll be seeing you in court, Miss Alethea. I'll be happy to carry your shopping basket in exchange for news of your fine family. How have you been?"

"Oh, tolerable," she said with a sigh. "My eyes aren't what they used to be—fine sewing in a bad light, you know. The boys are doing all right these days, grown and gone you know. But I do have young Madison and Cissie staying with me now. Mr. James Hope has taken their mother off to New York with him. Their little girls, too. You know they named the youngest after me? Little Alethea." She sighed. "I do miss them. But tell me about you, Mr. Harris. A judge now, under the new Reconstruction government! What's that like?"

He shrugged. "I don't do big law. Just little matters. Fighting drunks. Disturbing the peace. Stealing trifling things—chickens, not horses." They both smiled. "But when I come into the court, they all have to stand up and show me respect. I do like that. I expect Fanny—er, Mrs. Hope—knows what I mean, being up there in New York and all."

The old woman sighed. "She hates it up there—would you credit it? Poor James Hope is beside himself with worry. Thought he was handing her heaven on a plate, I reckon. Come north where there's been no slaves for fifty years, and maybe where nobody knows that Fanny is a woman of color anyhow. Be really free." She shook her head. "Don't you suppose he expected her to thank God for her deliverance and never want to come back."

"I did suppose it," he said.

"So did the Hopes. But she's homesick and will not be swayed. Why, what do you suppose Mr. James Hope did? He took Fanny to meet with Frederick Douglass. The great man himself! As if Mr. Douglass didn't have better things to do than to try to talk

sense into a little Georgia girl. He did his
best, though, to convince her to stay. She'll
have none of it."

"Do you hear from her, Miz Alethea?"

She nodded. "Regular as clockwork. In
every letter she sounds heartbroken. She
misses me and her brothers and sisters.
Misses Madison and Cissie something fierce.
She says she hates northern food. Hates the
cold weather and that ugly city full of more
poor folks and wickedness than there is in
all of Georgia. Fanny has her heart set on
coming home."

"But if she stays up there, she could live
white, and her children could be white
folks."

Alethea Taylor stared. "Why would she
want to do that, Mr. Harris?"

She already knew the answer to that, of
course, but stating the truth out loud would
only incur her wrath, so he held his peace,
and wished them all well.

A year later, James and Fanny Hope did
return to take up residence in Augusta, and
perhaps it was best that they had, for Miz
Alethea died before another year was out.
At least she got to be reunited with her family again, and he was glad of that.

He did not go to the burying. They laid
her to rest in Cedar Grove, and he forced

himself to go for the sake of their long acquaintance. At least she would rest in peace.
He alone was sure of that.

He wished that she had lived to see her
new grandson, who was born exactly a year after his parents returned from the North. The
Hopes named the boy John, and he was as
blond and blue-eyed as any little Scotsman.

Privately Grandison had thought Fanny
had been crazy to come back south when
she could have passed in New York and dis-
solved her children's heritage in the tide of
immigrants. But before the end of the decade, he knew he had come round to her
way of thinking, for he quit his post of judge
in South Carolina, and went back over the
river to work at the medical school. Perhaps
there were people talking behind his back
then, calling him a graven fool, as he had
once thought Fanny Hope, but now he had
learned the hard way. For all the promises of
the Reconstruction men, he got no respect
as a judge. The job was a sham whose purpose was not to honor him or his people,
but to shame the defeated Rebels. He grew
tired of being stared at by strangers whose
hatred burned through their feigned respect, and as the days went by, he found
himself remembering the medical school
with fondness.

He had been good at his job, and the doctors had respected his skills. Sometimes he even thought they forgot about his color. Dr. George had said something once about the difference being a thin layer of skin, and then underneath it was all the same. Many of the faculty had left during the war, but one by one they were coming back now to take up their old jobs at the medical college, and he knew that he was wishing he could join them as well.

He was wearing his white linen suit, a string tie, and his good black shoes. He stood in front of the desk of Dr. Louis Dugas, hat in hand, waiting for an answer.

Dugas, a sleek, clean-shaven man who looked every inch a French aristocrat, had taken over as dean of the college during the war years. In his youth he had studied in Paris, as Dr. George had, and it was Dugas who had traveled to Europe to purchase books for Augusta's medical library. It was said that he had dined with Lafayette himself. Now he looked puzzled. Fixing his glittering black eyes on Harris's face in a long-nosed stare, he said, "Just let me see if I understand you, my good man. You wish to leave a judiciary position across the river and come back here to work as a porter."

Grandison inclined his head. "I do, sir."

"Well, I don't wish to disparage the virtues of manual labor, as I am sure that the occupation of porter is an honorable and certainly a necessary one, but could you just tell me why it is that you wish to abandon your exalted legal position for such a job?"

He had been ready for this logical question, and he knew better than to tell the whole truth. The law had taught him that, at least. Best not to speak of the growing anger of defeated white men suddenly demoted to second-class citizens by contemptuous strangers. He'd heard tales of a secret society that was planning to fight back at the conquerors and whoever was allied with them. But as much as the rage of the locals made him uneasy, the patronizing scorn of his federal overseers kindled his own anger. They treated him like a simpleton, and he came to realize that he was merely a pawn in a game between the white men, valued by neither side. It would be one thing to have received a university education and then to have won the job because one was qualified to do it. Surely they could have found such a qualified man of color in the North, and if not, why not? But to be handed the job only as a calculated insult to others—that made a mockery of his intelligence and skills. At least the doctors had respected him for his work and valued what he did. Fifteen years he'd spent with them.

Best not to speak of personal advantage—of the times in the past when he had prevailed upon one or another of the doctors to treat some ailing neighbor or an injured child who might otherwise have died. The community needed a conduit to the people in power—he could do more good there than sentencing his folks to chain gangs across the river.

Best not to say that he had come to understand the practice of medicine and that, even as he approached his fiftieth year, he wanted to know more.

At last he said simply, "I reckon I miss y'all, Dr. Dugas."

Louis Dugas gave him a cold smile that said that he himself would never put sentiment before other considerations, but loyalty to oneself is a hard fault to criticize in a supplicant. "Even with the procuring of the bodies for the dissection table? You are willing to perform that task again as before?"

We must mutilate the dead so that we do not

mutilate the living. He must believe that above all.

He nodded. "Yes, sir."

"Very well then. Of course we must pay you now. The rate is eight dollars per month, I believe. Give your notice to the South Carolina court and you may resume your post here."

And it was done. What he had entered into by compulsion as a slave so many years before, he now came to of his own volition as a free man. He would return to the cart and the lantern and the shovel and begin again.

Well, all that was a long time ago. It is a new century now, and much has changed, not all of it for the better.

He steps out into the night air. The queasy medical student has tottered away to his rooms, and now the building can be locked again for the night. He still has his key, and he will do it himself, although his son George is the official porter now at the medical college—not as good as he himself once was, but what of that? Wasn't the faculty now packed with pale shadows—the nephews and grandsons of the original doc-

tors? A new century, not a patch on the old
one for all its motorcars and newfangled
gadgets.

He will walk home down Ellis Street, past
the house where James and Fanny Hope
had raised their brood of youngsters. One
of the Hope daughters lived there now, but
that was a rarity these days. There was a colored quarter in Augusta now, not like the
old days when people lived all mixed together and had thought nothing about it.

James and Fanny Hope had enjoyed eight
years in that house on Ellis Street, before a
stroke carried him off in 1876. They had let
his white kinfolk take him back to New York
for burying. Better to have him far away,
Fanny Hope had said, than separated from
us by a cemetery wall here in Augusta.

Fanny raised her brood of eight alone,
and they did her credit. She had lived three
years into the twentieth century, long
enough to see her offspring graduate from
colleges and go on to fine careers. Little
blue-eyed John Hope was the best of them,
folks said. He had attended Brown University up north, and now he was president of a
college in Atlanta. So was little Tommy Wilson, the white preacher's son, who now
went by his middle name of Woodrow, and
was a "throne" at Princeton College up

north. You never could tell about a child, how it would turn out.

Though he never told anyone, Grandison had hoped that Dr. George's son Madison might be the outstanding one of Fanny's children, but he had been content to work at low wage jobs in Augusta and to care for his aging mother. He and Dr. George had that in common—neither of the sons had surpassed them.

Funny to think that he had outlived the beautiful Fanny Hope. In his mind she is still a poised and gentle young girl, and sometimes he regrets that he did not go to her burying in Cedar Grove. The dead rested in peace there now, for the state had legalized the procuring of cadavers by the medical schools some twenty years back, but around that time, rumors had surfaced in the community about grave robbing. Where had the doctors got the bodies all those years for their dissecting classes? Cedar Grove, of course. There was talk of a riot. Augusta had an undertaker now for people of color. The elegant Mr. Dent, with his fancy black oak hearse with the glass panels, and the plumed horses to draw it along in style. Had John or Julia Dent started those rumors to persuade people to be embalmed so the doctors wouldn't get you? There had been sharp looks and angry mutterings at the time, for everyone knew who had been porter at the medical college for all these years, but he was an old man by then, a wiry pillar of dignity in his white suit, and so they let him alone, but he did not go to buryings anymore.

The night air is cool, and he takes a deep breath, savoring the smell of flowers borne on the wind. He hears no voices in the wind, and dreams no dreams of dead folks reproaching him for what he has done. In a little while, a few months or years at most, for he is nearly ninety, he too will be laid to rest in Cedar Grove among the empty grave sites, secret monuments to his work. He is done with this world, with its new machines and the new gulf between the races. Sometimes he wonders if there are two heavens, so that Fanny Hope will be forever separated from her husbands by some celestial fence, but he rather hopes that there is no hereafter at all. It would be simpler so. And in all his dissecting he has never found a soul.

He smiles on the dark street, remembering a young minister who had once tried to persuade him to attend a funeral. "Come now, Mr. Harris," the earnest preacher had said. "There is nothing to fear in a cemetery. Surely those bodies are simply the discarded

husks of our departed spirits. Surely the
dead are no longer there."

BIBLIOGRAPHY

Allen, Lane. "Grandison Harris, Sr.: Slave, Resurrectionist and Judge." Athens, GA: *Bulletin of the Georgia Academy of Science,* 34:192–199.

Ball, James M. *The Body Snatchers.* New York: Dorset Press, 1989.

Blakely, Robert L., and Judith M. Harrington. *Bones in the Basement: Post Mortem Racism in Nineteenth Century Medical Training.* Washington, DC: Smithsonian Institution, 1997.

Burr, Virginia Ingraham, ed. *The Secret Eye: The Journal of Ella Gertrude Clanton Thomas, 1848–1889.* Chapel Hill, NC: University of North Carolina Press, 1990.

Cashin, Edward J. *Old Springfield: Race and Religion in Augusta, Georgia.* Augusta, GA: The Springfield Village Park Assoc. 1995.

Corley, Florence Fleming. *Confederate City: Augusta, Georgia 1860–1865.* Columbia, SC: University of South Carolina Press; Rpt. Spartanburg, SC: The Reprint Company, 1995.

Davis, Robert S. *Georgia Black Book: Morbid Macabre and Disgusting Records of Genealogical Value.* Greenville, SC: Southern Historical Press, 1982.

Fido, Martin. *Body Snatchers: A History of the Resurrectionists.* London: Weidenfeld & Nicolson, 1988.

Fisher, John Michael. Fisher & Watkins Funeral Home, Danville, VA. Personal Interview, March 2003.

Kirby, Bill. *The Place We Call Home: A Collection of Articles About Local History from the Augusta Chronicle.* Augusta, GA: *The Augusta Chronicle,* 1995.

Lee, Joseph M. III. *Images of America: Augusta and Summerville.* Charleston, SC: Arcadia Publishing, 2000.

Spalding, Phinizy. *The History of the Medical College of Georgia.* Athens, GA: University of Georgia Press, 1997.

Torrence, Ridgely. *The Story of John Hope.* New York: Macmillan, 1948.

United States Census Records: Richmond County, GA: 1850; 1860; 1870; 1880; 1990.